THE SECOND WAVE

What Reviewers Say About
Jean Copeland's GCLS Award Winner
The Revelation of Beatrice Darby

"Debut author Jean Copeland has come out with a novel that is abnormally superb."—*Curve Magazine*

"...filled with emotion and the understanding of what it feels like for a girl to discover that she likes girls and what it will do to her life."—*The Lesbian Review*

"...Uplifting and an amazing first novel for Jean Copeland"—*Inked Rainbow Reads*

Visit us at www.boldstrokesbooks.com

By the Author

The Revelation of Beatrice Darby

The Second Wave

THE SECOND WAVE

To Debra —
Thanks so much for
support! All my best!

by

Jean Copeland

2016

THE SECOND WAVE

© 2016 By Jean Copeland. All Rights Reserved.

ISBN 13: 978-1-62639-830-6

This Trade Paperback Original Is Published By
Bold Strokes Books, Inc.
P.O. Box 249
Valley Falls, NY 12185

First Edition: October 2016

CREDITS
EDITOR: SHELLEY THRASHER
PRODUCTION DESIGN: SUSAN RAMUNDO
COVER DESIGN BY SHERI (GRAPHICARTIST2020@HOTMAIL.COM)

Acknowledgments

Writing may be a solitary endeavor, but the process of getting a book to print is anything but. I'd first like to thank Radclyffe and Sandy Lowe of Bold Strokes Books for their faith in my stories. Writing at times feels easy, but publishing always seems hard, so I'm grateful to have a quality publishing company like BSB behind me. Thank you also to my trusty editor, Shelley Thrasher, for her keen eye and great advice. I also want to thank Anne Santello for her speedy, first-draft editorial skills and Denise Spallone for her photography and part-time marketing services. Who knew when we met as kids you'd both offer such important literary assistance. Also, a shout-out to nurses Michelle Murolo and Cindy Woods and OT Jamie Coyle for patiently replying to my text inquiries about strokes. Lastly, I couldn't keep bringing my imaginary world to life without the unwavering support of family, friends, and the readers who purchase my novels. Many thanks to you all!

Dedication

To all the women who've had the courage
to make heart-wrenching choices and
the strength to live with them.

CHAPTER ONE

Alice rushed down the hall of Intensive Care toward Leslie's room. Her nose twitched at the pungent aroma of disinfectant as she counted off room numbers while negotiating her way around portable patient-information computers, linen hampers, and gurneys. The Facebook message from Leslie's daughter, Rebecca, was startling enough, but when she'd read that Leslie had a stroke the day before, it shoved her off the fragile foundation she'd finally rebuilt after losing Maureen. After all these years, just reading Leslie's name was enough to send her heart scattering in all the wrong directions.

Nearing the room, she rounded the corner, trembling at what she might encounter. Who would be there? How would she handle seeing Leslie after all this time in a hospital bed, hooked up to all kinds of wires and tubes? An hour after responding to Rebecca's message, she was packed and off on the two-hour drive from Boston to New Haven without having considered if it was the right thing for either of them. But since her daughter had gone to the trouble of locating her, it had to be serious. Not too serious, she'd hoped. God, please, not too serious.

When she found the room, she poked her head in. "Rebecca?" she said softly.

"Alice?" Rebecca got up from the chair parked by her mother's bed and smoothed down the tailored blazer that contoured her athletic build. She bypassed Alice's extended hand and went right in for an embrace. "Thank you for coming."

"Thanks for contacting me," Alice said, staring over at a Leslie she didn't recognize.

"She can use all the prayers and good vibes she can get right now. From what I recall, you two were pretty close friends at one time."

Alice smiled, her eyes still fixed on Leslie. "It's been a long time since I've seen my old friend." She sat in the chair beside Leslie's bed and gently held her hand, taped and purpled from an IV needle. "Hey, Bella," she said. "It's me, Betty." She smiled when she felt what she thought was movement in Leslie's fingers.

"What happened?" Rebecca asked, hopeful. "Did she just squeeze your hand?"

"I don't think so. I mean I think I felt her fingers move slightly." Alice surveyed Leslie's face. It was thin and pale, but even a condition like this couldn't entirely eclipse her perennial beauty.

Rebecca smiled at Alice. "Whatever it was, I think I had the right idea messaging you."

"Boy, this is something of a time warp," Alice said. "You were so little the last time I saw you." She turned to Leslie. "You did all right with this one, Bella. She seems like a real smart cookie."

"Too smart for my own good, she always told me." The light of Rebecca's smile dimmed. "I'm scared," she whispered.

Alice twisted her body to face her. "I'm sure you are. I remember how close you and your mom were back then, both you and your brother."

"He'll be coming by later when he gets off work. I wish the doctors could tell us something definite."

"What do you know so far?"

"They're calling it a mild stroke. She was in and out for a bit yesterday, but today she's just been out."

Alice tried to stay focused on what Rebecca was saying, but her eyes kept drifting back to Leslie. She kept Leslie's hand safely tucked into her own.

"So what's up with the nicknames?" Rebecca asked.

Alice smiled. "It was a little joke we had. Betty Friedan and Bella Abzug from the feminist movement."

"That's right. You had that crochet thing in the seventies. She really loved that group. In fact, I can still recall an argument it caused between my parents."

"Argument? Why?" Alice's palms were suddenly sweaty.

"My dad's an old-fashioned, working-class guy. He didn't get feminism. I was young at the time, but I remember him saying something like it was the first step in making men obsolete. I got panicked thinking someone was gonna come and take my dad away."

Alice chuckled. "That was the toughest part of being a feminist, trying to convince everyone it wasn't at all about undermining men."

"He wasn't having any of it. I think he kind of shamed my mom into abandoning the philosophy."

"I'm surprised. She seemed quite taken with it when she first started coming to the meetings." Alice grinned at the recollection. "But your mom must've watched too many *Leave it to Beaver* reruns as a kid—the good wife and mother above all else."

"Which is why it was such a shock to my brother and me when they divorced a year after I left for college."

"They did?" After the initial shock, Alice avoided Rebecca's eyes.

"It was the weirdest thing. Out of nowhere she said she wasn't happy anymore and asked for a divorce. I was furious with my dad for finding a girlfriend less than a year later, but it sort of explained their split. They'd just grown apart."

"Do they still talk?"

"They're cool with each other," Rebecca said. "My mom says he's a great guy, and she'd never want my brother and me to feel uncomfortable around them."

"That's always been your mother. She'd do anything for you kids."

"You didn't know any of this?" Before Alice could contrive a response, Rebecca said, "Oh, I think you'd moved away by then."

Alice was quiet, still reeling from the information.

"How come you didn't stay in contact?"

"We did, sort of," she said, mustering her wits. "We would talk on the phone from time to time after I moved to Boston."

"You guys always seemed to have so much fun together."

Alice shifted uncomfortably in the chair.

"I'm sorry if I'm asking too many questions."

"No, no, that's okay," Alice said. "It's just been a long time since I've thought about that part of my life."

"She seemed happiest during those times when she had your friendship. I couldn't figure out why you didn't remain close. I asked her once, but she was her usual evasive self when it came to my probing."

"What did she say?"

"You know, how people get so busy in their lives with jobs and family that time slips away. When I was younger, I thought it was a lame excuse until I started to experience it with my college friends."

"Especially if one of you moves out of state."

"That does complicate matters," Rebecca said. "Do you want to take a walk to the cafeteria with me?"

"Sure."

"Mom, we'll be back in a few minutes, okay?" Rebecca gave Leslie's foot a tender pinch.

Alice smiled at the way Leslie's daughter loved her. Then again, Leslie gave everyone reasons to love her.

❖

As Alice sipped her coffee, she stared at Rebecca, who was chewing a tuna sandwich. Despite her short, gelled hair and forearm tattoo sneaking out from her blazer sleeve, she was unmistakably her mother's daughter—identical dimpled right cheek and heavenly blue eyes beneath symmetrical, Rita Hayworth eyebrows.

"Do you mind if I take a turn questioning you?"

Rebecca smiled as she took another bite of her sandwich. "I think I know where this is headed. Let me help you out. Yes, I'm a lesbian, in case you weren't entirely convinced."

Alice frowned. "I'm sorry for being so transparent. But actually, what I wanted to ask is when did you know?"

Rebecca wiped her mouth with her napkin and leaned back in her chair. "I think I always knew. I didn't come out until my senior year in college, though. I did the normal-chick routine. You know, boyfriends in high school and mixers in college, but I never connected with any of them."

"What do you mean, 'connected'?" Alice asked.

"Well, now I know that subconsciously, I always felt something was missing when I was dating guys, but it was when I fell for a woman that I realized what it was. It's amazing how all it took was one kiss from a pretty girl to make everything crystal clear."

Alice nodded enthusiastically and then caught herself. "Did you have sex with men?" she asked in a barely audible whisper.

Rebecca smirked. "I don't know if this conversation is totally awkward or I find you incredibly cool."

"I'm so sorry for prying," Alice said, her cheeks hot with embarrassment. "Forget I even asked that."

"Yes, I had sex with men, three of them, one in high school and two in college. I found it to be…" She looked up toward the fluorescent lights for help. "Kind of enjoyable but a galaxy away from being with a woman."

Lost in the familiarity of Rebecca's words, she nodded again. She then remembered herself and reached for a casual reply. "It must've been quite a confusing time for you."

Rebecca slurped the last of her Diet Coke through a straw and scanned the cafeteria. "Alice, I want to ask you something."

Alice's neck prickled with the heat of accusation as she fingered her coffee's plastic lid. "Umm, sure."

"It's pretty personal."

"Go ahead. It's only fair," Alice said, bracing herself.

Rebecca hesitated, clearly negotiating her words. "Did you and my mother have something more than friendship?"

Alice's face felt like it was about to combust. "What would make you ask that?"

"Just wondering." Rebecca shrugged and piled scrunched-up napkins on her empty plate. "Are you a lesbian?"

Alice's time-honored reticence at a straightforward answer to that question prevailed even while she maintained eye contact with Rebecca.

"I'm sorry," Rebecca said. "I hope I didn't offend you. It wasn't supposed to be an offensive question."

"No, no, it's not," Alice said, pausing for a breath. "In fact, I am."

"Is my mother?"

Alice attempted to laugh the question off. "Rebecca, well, how should I…I mean that's a question you ought to ask her, don't you think?"

"She's not real talkative right now."

"I mean when she's better."

"If she gets better. They don't know the full extent of the damage yet."

"You have to believe she will," Alice said, remembering Leslie's face when it was alive with youth and the promise of dreams.

"I thought she was going to be all right when she whispered your name Saturday night."

Alice's heart plummeted. "She said my name?"

"I could swear I heard 'Alice,' twice. That's why I thought to look you up. It's the only thing she's said since I found her yesterday afternoon. Not my name, not my brother's, or her grandkids'. Yours."

A fire spread up Alice's neck and across her face. Could that be true? Could she actually have said her name? "She's going to be okay, you know."

Rebecca's eyes watered. "I want things to be different between us when she is."

"What do you mean? She doesn't have a problem that you're a lesbian?"

"Not at all. She's been great from the moment I came out to her. She loves my partner, Sage, and our son. It's my father who's had the problem."

Alice averted her eyes. "Then what do you want to be different?"

"I want her to talk to me. We used to be so close when I was a kid. I don't think she's been happy for a long time, but I can never get her to open up."

"You think it was the divorce?"

"I think it's something else," Rebecca said. "She's fine with my father and his wife. They've been known to get together for dinner once in a while."

"Has she dated much?"

"At first she did, but she never seemed to click with anyone. Then a few years ago she started saying she's fine alone, that she's too old to fall for anyone again, and that all the men her age are only looking for caretakers. I called 'bullshit' on that excuse and suggested she try dating a woman, but she just gave me an 'Oh, Rebecca' and walked away."

Alice sipped her coffee to wash down the jealousy creeping up from the thought of Leslie dating.

"Hey, you two should hang out again. You could revive the old feminist crocheting club." The suggestion brightened Rebecca's face.

Alice entertained a momentary glimmer of hope, too. "That's a lovely idea, but I'm afraid we're both too old to be driving two hours back and forth every other Friday."

"Ever think of moving back to the area?"

"I have, especially since my wife passed last year."

"I'm sorry." Rebecca placed a hand on Alice's. "I didn't even think to ask about you."

"Understandable, given the circumstances. Her name was Maureen, and she was an exceptional person. We had twenty-eight wonderful years together."

"Listen to me. I don't even know you, and I'm trying to convince you to move back to Connecticut like you and my mom can relive the past or something." Rebecca's eyes watered. "I'd do anything to make her young and healthy again."

Alice smiled. "It's a lovely wish. Those were good times."

"Not for me," Rebecca said. "I had to wear those awful crocheted vests and scarves she made me."

Alice laughed. "Those were all the rage in the seventies."

"I'll stick with tattoos and Birkenstocks, thanks," Rebecca said with a thumbs-up.

"Should we go back and see how she's doing?"

"So you never answered my question before," Rebecca said as they carried their trays to the trash receptacles.

"What question?"

"Were you and my mother ever more than friends?"

"Rebecca," a voice suddenly called out. Bill, Rebecca's father, walked into the cafeteria and approached them.

"Thanks for coming, Dad. I wouldn't have texted you if I'd known you were away." She kissed him on the cheek.

"That's okay, honey. I'd be mad if you hadn't," Bill said as he eyed Alice. While age had thinned his hair and stooped his shoulders a bit, he was still handsome.

"Hello, Bill," Alice said, extending her hand. "Alice Burton, Leslie's old friend."

"I remember." His tone was less than affable, his handshake flaccid. "How's it going?" Without waiting for her reply, he turned to Rebecca. "How is she?"

"Not better but not worse either. Stable."

Alice shrunk from the eerily familiar feeling of being the outsider during poignant Burton family moments. "I've got to get going, Rebecca."

Rebecca stopped her father to address Alice. "Are you heading back to Boston?"

"No. I'm staying with my sister in Branford for a few days."

"Will you message me before you go?"

"Sure." Alice gave Rebecca a cordial kiss on the cheek and the obligatory courtesy nod to Bill before leaving.

Driving back to her sister's house in Branford, Alice missed the exit off the interstate as memories of Leslie hijacked her attention. She turned onto Route One and headed back toward her sister's house in the Stony Creek section of town. When Abba's song "S.O.S." came on the oldies station she'd barely been listening to, she cranked up the volume. When she heard the line about how hard it is to go on when someone you've loved is gone, her eyes clouded with tears. Leslie had to wake up.

CHAPTER TWO

T he next morning Alice surprised herself with an impetuous decision to hop into her car and head to Yale-New Haven hospital. She couldn't bear the thought of Leslie lying there alone in that bed; it had taunted her in her dreams. As attentive and devoted a daughter as Rebecca was, she couldn't be there every moment of the day.

Sitting by her bed, she caressed Leslie's forearm, careful to avoid the IV lines taped to her wrist. She'd been in a similar situation at Mass General only a year earlier when her wife, Maureen, was dying from complications of MS. Too familiar, too soon.

"I never imagined this is how we'd meet again," Alice whispered. She wiped away a tear with the back of her hand. No more tears. She'd cried enough last night. "I can't believe it's been almost forty years since we met. First American Insurance doesn't even exist anymore." Alice settled into a chair beside Leslie's bed as she reminisced.

"I'll never forget your first day at work. I felt so bad for you. You were such a nervous wreck."

September 1976

Leslie O'Mara had returned to the workforce on the same day her youngest child, Rebecca, started first grade. Walking into the office after her employee orientation session, she'd had a look on her face similar to what her daughter's must've been while climbing onto a school bus with her older brother, Billy, for the first time.

With ten years under her belt, Alice was considerably more laid-back that morning. As the typing-pool supervisor at First American Insurance in New Haven, she was in charge of training all the new girls.

She wheeled a chair next to Leslie's desk. "So how does it feel to be back in the old salt mines?"

"Scary."

"I'll bet, but you'll get back in the swing in no time."

"Let me apologize in advance for all the mistakes I'm going to make today," Leslie said with a timid smile. "It's been so long since I've worked in an office."

"Don't be silly," Alice said. "Everyone makes mistakes, especially the way some of these dudes mumble into the Dictaphones. They sound like squirrels storing acorns in their cheeks."

Leslie smiled and relaxed her shoulders. "Thanks. I'll do my best to correctly interpret the chittering."

"That's the spirit," Alice said with a friendly tap on her shoulder. "So here's the list of insurance agents we work for with their phone extensions, territories, and such. Later I'll give you a list of the lechers you shouldn't bend over in front of."

Leslie's eyes bulged. "What?"

"I'm just kidding." Alice tilted her head in consideration. "Well, not really. But just make it clear right off the bat that they can't pull that crap with you, and you'll be fine."

"I'm safe anyway. Nobody's going to get fresh with a married mother of two. I'm thirty years old, after all."

"You think that matters to some of these cats? The married ones will go gaga over you. You're quite pretty and, even better, not in the market for a husband."

"Nope. Have one of those."

"Would you look at that," Alice said. "It's time for morning break. C'mon. Let's get a cup of America's famous Eight O'Clock Coffee that tastes like it was brewed at eight o'clock last night."

Leslie grinned. "I can't wait."

As they headed down the hall toward the cafeteria, Alice said, "Gee, it's refreshing to see that they actually will hire a woman over twenty-one here once in a while. It'll be nice to have lunch with someone I can relate to."

"Aren't the girls here nice?"

"Sure they are, super nice. But aside from Myrna, who was probably transcribing onto stone tablets when her career began, most of the secretarial pool is made up of young girls hunting for husbands. And all the horny, highly paid executives here keep the cat-and-mouse games constant."

"Wow," Leslie said. "I've missed quite a bit raising my kids over the last nine years."

"It's rather amusing to watch, but I'm glad I'm past that stage." Alice stirred Cremora into her coffee. "Look! You're about to observe Julie, a young huntress, stalking her prey." She pointed to a twenty-two-year-old blonde smiling seductively at a handsome young man with thick sideburns and wavy brown hair parted low. "That's Steve Briller, an accountant. Tells the worst jokes ever, but he's very available. Watch. He's setting up the punch line right now."

Leslie giggled. "You're pretty amusing, too, Alice."

"Shhh. Here it comes."

Steve became animated, and suddenly, Julie flipped back a mane of golden curls as she shrieked with laughter.

Alice smiled with satisfaction.

"That was amazing," Leslie said.

Alice shrugged. "Not really. Stick around for the next showing at lunchtime."

Leslie laughed and sipped her coffee. "I'm glad I'm over that stage, too. Bill may not be an executive with an expensive sports car, but I did all right with him. He's a good man."

"What does he do?"

"He's in the carpenters' union. Do you have a husband or children?"

"Neither. Tony and I divorced three years ago, partly because of children. He wanted them, and I couldn't have them."

"I'm so sorry."

No matter how often the topic arose, Alice couldn't help cringing at the outpouring of pity from fertile women when they learned she couldn't bear children, like she was a raincoat that couldn't repel water or something.

"Had you discussed adoption?" Leslie asked.

Apparently, this childless-woman thing was more of a problem than she'd realized.

"The Giovanni family doesn't know from adoption," Alice said. "Italian, hairy, and masculine, they don't adopt babies. They just get a new wife who's capable of harvesting their seed."

"Oh." Leslie was quiet for a moment.

"Hey, it's no big deal. I've made peace with it. Not every woman is meant to have children. Surely, some of us can find another purpose in life, right?"

"Of course," Leslie said but looked like she couldn't possibly imagine what that purpose could be.

"We better get back to the office now," Alice said, suddenly feeling awkward.

As they left the break room, they were both quiet. Alice tried to imagine what Leslie must think of her. Obviously, she must've considered her a failure, divorced and childless at thirty-two years old.

"You know something?" Leslie said as they arrived at their neighboring desks.

"What's that?"

"You were obviously meant to be a career woman. Someone has to be in charge of us hapless moms stumbling back into the workforce."

Alice smiled with gratitude. "I'm gonna like working with you, Leslie O'Mara."

"Likewise, Alice Burton," Leslie replied with the most adorable half-dimpled smile.

❖

Early in the afternoon, Alice was summoned out of her reminiscence when Rebecca walked in with a bag of takeout from a nearby sushi place.

"Alice," Rebecca said. "I didn't know you'd be here."

"I hope you don't mind. I was thinking of your mom all night and wanted to talk to her."

"Did she answer?" Rebecca smiled ironically as she pulled up a chair and tore into her lunch.

Alice shook her head.

"And I don't mind at all. I'm glad she wasn't alone while I was at work. We're just too swamped for me to take full days off right now. I think my brother was here for a bit first thing this morning. Of course, if she were conscious and needed me, that would be a different story. Sushi?"

"No, thanks."

"So what were you talking to her about?"

"Reminiscing about when we first met at work." Alice kept glancing at Leslie as though any moment she might wake up ready to jump in the story with her version of it. "It's nice for me. I'm remembering some really good times."

"I'd love to hear about some good times."

Alice smiled. So many fond recollections flooded her heart and mind. Some things she simply couldn't share, not with Leslie's daughter, anyway.

"Let's see," she said, relaxing into her chair. "Your mother's first night at our feminist crocheting klatch is definitely worthy of mention." Alice laughed out loud. "She had no idea what she was stepping into."

November 1976

Two months working together in the secretarial pool at First American had fostered a genuine connection between Alice and Leslie. They grew to be friends as well as coworkers, sharing everything from wicked office gossip to all the mundane details of their lives. Alice, for one, loved how her lunch hour had upgraded from thumbing through old Star *magazines and eavesdropping on the conversations of semi-interesting coworkers to chats with a new friend and confidante.*

One day, Leslie seemed adrift in thought as she nibbled her turkey sandwich.

"Is everything okay?" Alice asked.

"Next week is the Thanksgiving pageant at Rebecca's school, and I'm going to miss it. I guess I didn't think about all the little things I wouldn't get to do if I went back to work."

Poor Leslie looked so sad, a style that didn't suit her usually effervescent, wildly-enthusiastic-about-life countenance.

"What time are they having it?"

"Around eleven a.m."

"Why don't you take your lunch hour early and run over to the school?"

Leslie's eyes sparkled like a spinning disco ball. "I could do that?"

"I don't see why not," Alice said, elated by her role in returning the light to Leslie's eyes. "I'll run it by Mr. Engle, but I'm sure he'll be fine with it."

"That would be wonderful." Leslie beamed. "You're the best coworker I've ever had." She squeezed Alice's hand and took a hearty bite of her sandwich.

"You should be able to go. One of the edicts of the women's lib movement says that a woman shouldn't have to choose between having a career and a family."

"It does? I thought they were against marriage?"

Alice arched an eyebrow. "That's what you've heard about women's lib?"

Leslie shrank in her chair. "Well, I, um, I guess because I'm married with children, I never paid too much attention to what's going on with it."

"Every woman should, married or not. It's about equality, fair pay, and economic independence," Alice said, banging off the tenets with her fist on the table. "What would you do if Bill suddenly decided to split on you?"

Leslie's eyes widened. "He would never do that."

"A lot of women on welfare thought that, too. It's a real issue for married women with children who are financially dependent on men."

"But Bill loves being a husband and father."

"What if he was a bum? What if you wanted to dump him because he was beating you or the kids?"

Leslie scoffed. "He's never laid a hand on me or the kids."

"It's just a for-instance, Leslie. What would you do? Could you support yourself and your kids?"

Two male coworkers walked by with their lunch trays. "Look out, everybody. Alice is firing off shots from her soapbox again."

"Sit on it, Freddie," Alice said and returned her attention to Leslie without missing a beat. "Do you like to crochet?"

Leslie appeared confused at the quick shift in the conversation. "I tried it once but wasn't very good at it. I'd like to learn. I've seen some really lovely vests in Ladies' Home Journal.*"*

"Excellent. I'm certain you'll find our little crocheting klatch very enlightening. Think you could get away for a few hours on Friday night?"

As they cleared their lunch trash and headed to the garbage can, Leslie smiled as though unsure what to make of Alice. "Sure. I think I can manage that."

"Fantastic," Alice said, pleased with her new recruit.

Friday finally arrived, and when Alice got home from work in the early evening, an inexplicable day-long anxiety was at its peak. She'd been assembling bi-monthly with her girlfriends for over a year now and felt she'd known Leslie long enough to feel comfortable around her socially. So why was she so keyed up? She sipped a glass of Cold Duck to settle her nerves as she brushed her hair and retouched her makeup before leaving for Leslie's.

On the ride to Cynthia's house in Middletown, Alice's angst faded as she and Leslie listened to AM radio. They laughed after a particularly loud, off-key sing-along to "Turn the Beat Around."

"I love disco," Alice said. "I can tell this music is here to stay."

"For sure," Leslie said.

"Well, here we are." Alice pulled up along the curb at Cynthia's house.

"Gee, I hope your friends don't think I'm a big nerd."

"Nonsense. They're gonna love you. You represent everything we've been talking about."

"I do?"

"Absolutely—a woman tired of the drudgery of housework and child-rearing reclaims her individual identity by forging ahead with a new career."

"Actually, Bill and I just wanted some extra money to start a vacation club."

"They don't have to know that," Alice said out of the corner of her mouth.

She knocked on the door, excited to introduce Leslie to her friends.

"Betty, baby," Cynthia said upon opening the door. She pushed her large Gloria Steinem-esque eyeglasses back up her nose and received Alice in a hug.

"Gloria, baby," Alice replied, nearly choking in Cynthia's grip. "Cynthia, this is my friend, Leslie, I was telling you about."

Cynthia nearly crushed Leslie's hand in a firm handshake. "Leslie, my sister, welcome."

She indicated the pile of shoes on the floor by the door. "Make yourself comfortable."

"Thank you so much." Leslie seemed a bit rigid as she handed Cynthia a bottle of wine.

"Ah, the fruit of the goddesses," Cynthia said with a smile. "Right on."

Alice removed her shoes and motioned for Leslie to follow her lead. They trailed Cynthia into the living room adorned with vibrant wall tapestries and a bubbly blue lava lamp.

"Ladies, we have a new member to our organization," Cynthia announced to Kathy and Dolores, both seated Indian-style, almost knee-high in a red shag carpet.

"Welcome to the Second Wave," Kathy said, and she and Dolores raised their crochet hooks in unison.

Alice jerked her head at Leslie to follow her and take a spot on the floor within the circle. Leslie followed her so closely that she bumped into Alice from behind when she stopped.

"What's the Second Wave?" she whispered to Alice.

"You'll see," Alice said, enjoying tantalizing her with anticipation.

"We finally have our fifth member," Dolores said. "She can be Bella."

"Bella?" Leslie said, furrowing her brow.

"Bella Abzug, the congresswoman from New York," Cynthia chimed in. "We've all taken on honorary nicknames of our fore-mothers. You're the last one, so now our coalition is complete."

Leslie smiled. "I'm sorry, foremothers of what? Crocheting?"

The room plunged into dead silence. Alice patted Leslie's hand in solidarity.

"No, feminism," Cynthia said. "We have a little group. We call ourselves the Second Wave. It's what they're calling the women's lib movement."

Poor Leslie appeared clueless.

"The suffragists?" Cynthia said. "Surely, you've heard of them. They were the first wave."

"Of course," Leslie said. "Susan B. Anthony and women's right to vote."

"Right-on," Kathy said, and the others cheered.

"So is crocheting just a cover?" Leslie asked.

The women tried not to snigger.

"Relax," Cynthia said. "We don't need a cover. We're not commies."

"We actually do crochet," Alice said. "Look at that far-out afghan over there on the chair."

"We're also strong, politically minded women," Dolores added.

"Speak, Lucretia, speak," Cynthia said like a Baptist preacher.

"Lucretia Mott," Alice whispered. "She goes back to the first wave in the 1800s."

"Anyways," Dolores said, "we talk about feminism, what we want from our government, and what's going on with the ERA. Stuff like that. You know, stuff we can't talk about with our husbands."

Cynthia leaned across the center of the circle piled with pillows, patterns, yarn, and hooks, and handed Alice and Leslie glasses of red wine. "So, Leslie," she said, "since you're new, why don't you start us off on a discussion topic?"

Leslie looked around like a sheep surrounded by wolves. "Gee, I'm not really sure. I barely know how to crochet."

"Look at what I'm doing," Alice said as she wound the yarn around her hook and pulled it through a loop. "You just need some practice, that's all."

"Are you politically active at all?" Kathy asked in a kindly way.

Leslie seemed to shrink into herself. "It's not that I have anything against it..."

"Let's go easy on her for her first meeting," Alice said like a protective older sister. "She was home knee-deep in raising her kids for the last nine years."

A variety of gasps and eye-rolls emanated from the group.

"Come on, ladies," Alice said. "It's still a job."

"A thankless one you don't get paid for," Dolores said. "I should know. I raised four kids, three of whom are actually productive members of society."

The ladies laughed with Dolores.

"Okay, so she's not politically active," Kathy said to the group, then turned to Leslie. "You still have a voice, honey. What's on your mind?"

"My mind?"

"Yeah." Kathy gave her an encouraging nod.

"Right now?"

"Mmm-hmm," she said patiently.

Alice gave Leslie a nudge of support on the arm.

"Well, I like that new detective show, Charlie's Angels. It's good."

A groan came from the group. "I wouldn't know," Cynthia said. "Whenever I've turned it on, I was blinded by big teeth and even bigger tits."

"Not to mention all that Wella Balsam hair," Dolores added.

"Sure, they're attractive," Leslie said, "but they're also smart and strong. I like that the characters are more than just someone's wife. Haven't we had enough of that?"

A reverent silence descended over the room. Kathy sparked up a joint, nodded as she took a hit, and passed it to her left.

"She's got a real point there," Cynthia said.

Kathy finally exhaled. "Yes, we've certainly had enough of women only ever playing wives, prostitutes, and victims on television, but look around the room. Real women don't look like those actresses playing those detectives. They're sex objects. The show is written for men, and it creates unrealistic expectations about what women should look like."

"You're just trying to justify not shaving your armpits," Alice said with a smirk.

The ladies cackled as Kathy flung a handful of popcorn in Alice's direction.

"So evidently, this is our discussion topic: the objectification of women through hyper-sexualized characters and the unrealistic depiction of women in television. Far-out. Thank you for this, Leslie."

Leslie smiled as Alice nudged her with pride before offering her the joint. Leslie looked at it like it was a live hand grenade and raised the "no thanks" hand.

"I have an assignment idea," Dolores said. "Let's each write letters to the three television networks complaining about how they're misrepresenting women."

"A written protest campaign," Cynthia said, her eyes gleaming almost demonically. "Wild."

"I'll call Information for their addresses," Dolores said.

"All right, ladies," Cynthia said. "When we meet in two weeks, have drafts of all three of your letters ready. We'll review them and mail them in together."

"This is exciting," Leslie said, innocence crowning her like a halo. "What should we say?"

Kathy took this one. "We'll say that while we appreciate them letting women have careers like in Charlie's Angels, we don't appreciate them all looking like fashion models flashing their tits and asses in every episode."

Alice sipped her wine and then took another hit. Still half holding in the puff, she said, "All the networks are run by men. How do you propose we convince them that tits and asses are a bad thing?"

"A boycott," Dolores said excitedly. "We threaten to boycott the products they're advertising during these shows."

"Exactly," Cynthia said. "We won't buy their shitty dishwashing liquid. We won't buy our husbands and boyfriends the lousy aftershave Joe Namath claims he wears."

"Husbands, hell." Kathy scoffed. "I won't buy their aftershave for myself."

The ladies all looked at Leslie, anticipating her reaction, but Kathy's insinuation didn't seem to register.

"Um, Stayfree maxi pads are advertised during that show," Alice said. "I suggest we let them slide."

They all muttered in agreement.

"Now that that's settled, can we get down to the other important business of this meeting?" Dolores said.

"Of course." Cynthia jumped up. "I'll get another bottle of wine."

"I made a spinach quiche," Dolores said, trailing her to the kitchen.

"My Jell-O mold is in the fridge," Kathy announced. "With peaches and marshmallows," she said, following the others.

Alice and Leslie exchanged smiles.

Around ten thirty, as they walked down Cynthia's mum-lined sidewalk under a harvest moon, Alice's cheeks hurt from their evening of bona fide sisterhood.

"So what do you think of our little club?" she said.

"It was wonderful," Leslie said. "I didn't get very far on my scarf, but I can't wait for the next meeting. I hope I didn't make a fool of myself. I'm kind of ashamed I know so little about women's liberation."

"Don't worry. Hang out with these ladies, and you'll be a radical in no time."

"I look forward to it," Leslie said with a smile.

"Sorry about the weed. Hope it didn't bother you."

"I didn't mind," Leslie said. "Who knows? Maybe I'll give that a try sometime."

Alice expressed her approval with a double thumbs-up like the Fonz over the roof of her car.

CHAPTER THREE

After the nurse finished checking Leslie's vitals and changing an IV line, she informed them that the doctor would be in soon for an update and pushed her portable computer out into the hall. Alice and Rebecca moved back into their positions in the chair and on the foot of the bed, respectively.

"Please tell me my mother tried it," Rebecca said. "She caught me smoking once when I was in high school, and man, she tore me a new one."

Alice smiled. "You and your questions. What kind of friend would I be if I revealed all her secrets?"

"I'm not writing a tell-all about her. I'm her daughter. I feel like I only know this one side of her, this Stepford-like Mother-of-the-Year persona. Evidently, you can show me a brand-new side of her."

Alice quietly considered that one for a moment. "I have to say, if there was such an award, she'd win it hands down. But yes, even though she loved being a mother more than any other part of her identity, she definitely had more going on, which I discovered as our friendship grew."

"I want to know that woman," Rebecca said with a pensive sigh.

"Wouldn't that discovery have more meaning if it came in a conversation with her?"

Rebecca bit her lip as it began to quiver. "What if I don't ever get the chance?"

Alice patted Rebecca's knee. "Honey, if I've learned one thing on my journey thus far, it's that nobody wins in the 'what if' game. You have to stay positive until you're given a solid reason not to."

Rebecca looked at her mother. "Isn't this solid enough?"

"I don't believe so, but then I'm sure it's easier for me to be optimistic. It's not my mother lying there."

"I can't believe it's mine." Rebecca covered her eyes with her hand.

Alice fought with all of her being to temper her emotions. This stoic, stiff-upper-lip bullshit wasn't any easier decades later. But looking at Rebecca and seeing her as the little girl she'd remembered Leslie doting over, she'd slipped into a sort of protective mode.

"Yes, she tried it," she blurted.

Rebecca looked up and sniffled. "What?"

"She tried pot."

Rebecca laughed as she dried her face with the side of her hand. "Finally, some evidence of a wild side."

Alice cleared her throat at the allusion and shifted her gaze to the nurses' bulletin board on the opposite wall.

"Was it at one of your feminist-manifesto meetings?"

"No, Christmas, actually. Your parents' straggler party."

"I remember those," Rebecca said with a chuckle. "They would send us to bed, but Billy and I would hide at the top of the stairs listening to everyone getting drunk and dancing to disco records."

"I'm glad that's all you heard."

"Really? Well, happy birthday, Jesus."

December 1976

"Hey, look, it's starting to snow." Leslie called out from her picture window framed with white garland and twinkling Christmas lights.

"Sleepover," Bob shouted from the opposite corner of the living room, and everyone roared with approval. He adjusted the belt on his rust-colored pantsuit and gave his wife, Candie, a thin brunette with feathered hair and a very low-cut top for December in Connecticut, a look that Alice found suspicious.

The couple had kept her a verbal hostage for the better part of an hour by the roaring fireplace, and Alice was starting to feel damp under her armpits. "I could use more punch," she said, fanning herself, hoping that excuse would facilitate a clean getaway.

"I've got it. You keep Candie company," Bob insisted, and dashed off to the bar.

"Gee, I'm kind of hoping we all get snowed in tonight," Candie said. She locked eyes with Alice. "It would be fun, wouldn't it?"

"Not really," Alice said. "I don't have a toothbrush or pajamas."

"Who needs pajamas? Bob and I sleep in the nude. Our therapist says it helps maintain intimacy."

Alice stared at them, not sure which was making her more uncomfortable, the conversation topic or the way Candie seemed to be sizing her up as she spoke.

"Ever tried it?" Candie asked.

"What? Sleeping in the nude?" C'mon, Bob. Get back here with those drinks.

"Right on. We've found it to be some righteous advice."

"Unless someone's offering to pay my winter oil bill along with that advice, I'm sticking with peejays."

"You're so funny, Alice." Candie addressed Bob as he returned with their drinks. "Isn't she so funny, babe?"

"Funny and gorgeous," Bob said.

Alice noticed the zipper on his pantsuit had been lowered, revealing a mat of chest hair in which the male circle-and-arrow symbol dangled from a gold chain.

"So, are you open to new experiences, Alice?" Bob said, wrapping his arm around Candie's waist.

"That depends," she said, her curiosity getting the better of her.

He moved in closer. "Have you ever had a couple?"

"A couple of what?"

Candie tossed her head back and gave her shoulder a gentle shove. "I just love your sense of humor."

Bob sent his wife an eye signal as he took a healthy swig of punch.

"*Have you ever made love with a couple?*" *Candie said in a whisper.*

As they leered at her, Bob licked his top lip hiding under a bristly mustache.

"*Uh, I should go check and see if Leslie needs any help,*" *Alice said.*

"*Hey, that's cool. Do your thing,*" *Bob said.*

Candie took Alice's arm as she tried to make a break for it. "*Think about it. It's a mind-blowing, sensual experience.*"

"*We've never had any complaints,*" *Bob added.*

"*Quite the opposite,*" *Candie said, resting her head on Bob's shoulder.*

"*Well, you've certainly got the sales pitch down.*" *Alice placed her glass on the mantel and spotted Leslie across the room bringing out a tray of mini quiches.*

"*Well, hi,*" *Leslie said as Alice approached.* "*I see you've hit it off with our neighbors, Bob and Candie. Aren't they great?*"

Alice peered over her shoulder to be certain she hadn't been followed. "*How close are you with them?*"

"*They just moved in a few months ago, but they've been so friendly to everyone.*"

Alice smirked. "*I'll bet they have.*"

"*Why? What's the matter?*"

"*Nothing. I'd just think twice before accepting any slumber-party invitations from them.*"

Leslie chuckled. "*Why on earth would they invite us over for a slumber party?*"

Alice leaned into her ear. "*They're swingers.*"

"*Swingers? What's that?*" *Leslie said out loud.*

Alice shushed her. "*They swap—you know, orgies?*"

"*Oh, swingers,*" *Leslie said, the lightbulb of recognition blazing over her head.*

"*Will you keep your voice down? They're going to hear you and come over here.*"

"*Where'd they go?*" *Leslie searched the crowd of guests.*

"*I don't know, but I smell weed. C'mon, let's follow the scent.*"

"They must be in the family room," Leslie said. "Let me go get Bill. He's either going to kick them out or join them."

"I hope he doesn't kick them out. Their shit smells good."

They collided into each other in a fit of laughter.

❖

"Mr. and Mrs. Shaw were swingers? Gross." Rebecca snickered. "If my mother's pot experience led to my parents swinging with the Shaws, I'm definitely done asking you questions."

Alice covered her mouth to muffle her laughter. "No, no. Back then, everyone had an 'anything goes' attitude, but none of us went in for that sort of thing."

"So did everyone end up getting wasted that night?"

Alice grinned.

"No way," Rebecca said, her eyebrows reaching her forehead. "Why don't I remember any of this?"

"Your grandparents had you and Billy that night. Your parents would never smoke while you kids were in the house."

"Amazing. My parents were seventies hipsters, and I had no idea. Tell me more."

December 1976

With most of the guests gone as it neared one a.m., Alice and Leslie sat rapping with the Shaws on the sectional as Bill snored in his well-worn easy chair.

"Thanks for clueing us in on Bill's disposition," Bob said as he filled a glass bong with smoke and inhaled. "We're not about killing anyone's vibe."

"No way," Candie said as she took a hit and bobbed her head to "I Wanna Kiss You All Over" playing softly on the hi-fi.

"Well, we believe in live and let live," Leslie said as she swiped a potato chip in a glass dish of clam dip.

Alice smiled as she held in her bong hit and then offered the gadget to Leslie. Leslie looked at the Shaws and then back to Alice, as if seeking someone's permission. She glanced over at Bill, still sound asleep.

"You don't have to." Alice exhaled.

"Wait," Leslie said as Alice was about to pass it to Bob. She took the glass holder in her hand and fumbled to position it so her index finger covered the hole at the end. Then she sucked at the glass until it filled with smoke and inhaled.

Alice and the Shaws hooted their approval until Leslie started coughing her lungs out. Leslie rubbed smoke from her eye as she sipped from a can of Tab.

"Are you okay?" Alice tried her best to suppress a smile.

After another sip of Tab, Leslie said, "C'mon, pass it back here."

"Aww sooky, sooky," Candie said.

The room erupted with whoops and hollers of approval, but Bill only twitched in his chair.

As it neared two o'clock, Alice's head was spinning. The combination of too much wine and too much weed was starting to play tricks on her.

Leslie was laughing so vigorously, she kept falling against Candie, and each time, Bob would find some excuse to touch her hair, or face, or arm. He seemed to know how far he could go with her husband asleep ten feet away. That was Alice's first encounter with an unexpected wave of jealousy. She was surprised at herself, suddenly so angry with Bob, and even Candie, for egging on Leslie's silliness. They should've known better. It was Leslie's first time getting high, and they were baiting her to smoke more.

"Leslie, I think that's enough. You're going to get sick."

"Easy does it, Alice," Bob said through his stupid mustache. "No one gets sick from weed."

"Let's not make Leslie the first case." Alice stood up and helped her up off the couch.

"I'm starving," Leslie said and wandered off toward the kitchen.

"You folks can head home," Alice said, keeping one eye in Leslie's direction. "I'll make sure she and Bill get off to bed."

"It's after midnight and Cinderella turns into a narc," Bob said, staying put.

"It's two a.m. I think we've already overstayed our welcome." Alice appealed to Candie with a pointed glare.

"C'mon, Bob. It's late." Candie used his arm to hoist herself from the couch. "It was nice meeting you, Alice." She lowered her voice. "Think about our offer." She gave Alice a sensual peck on the lips.

As they gathered their coats and left the room, Alice stood momentarily frozen in place. Her lips stunned and tingling from Candie's, she wondered why she wasn't appalled by what Candie had just done. Maybe it was time to cut down on the bud. She walked into the kitchen and grinned at Leslie leaning against the counter savaging a cold fried-chicken leg.

"Alice," she said dramatically. "I can't believe how delicious this is, and it's two days old. Here, try some."

Alice deflected Leslie's hand as the stripped chicken leg came perilously close to her nose. "No, thanks. I'm stuffed. Why don't you finish that and get ready for bed. I have to get going now."

"You do?" Leslie pouted and threw her arms around Alice's neck, burying her face in her shoulder. "But we're having so much fun."

"Don't worry. We can do this again sometime." Alice closed her eyes for a moment and delighted in a deep whiff of Leslie's hair, smoky with traces of freshness from her Prell shampoo.

"Okay," Leslie said, finally releasing her. "I'm so tired."

Alice smiled at this new side of Leslie. "Then go get your husband and go to sleep."

"Unless you have a stick of dynamite in your purse, he's there for the night."

"Okay." She led Leslie to the foot of the staircase in the living room. "See you Monday."

As Alice descended their front steps dusted with the snow that had fallen earlier in the evening, she felt strangely forlorn. Monday morning seemed so far away.

❖

She awoke the next morning with the strange and vivid events of the party and Leslie rumbling through her mind. She looked out at the gray December day and hid under her pillow. Other than Bill and Leslie's Christmas gathering, she'd had no plans for the rest of the weekend. Since her divorce from Tony a year ago, her social circle had consisted of the crochet klatch; her single cousin, Phyllis; or the least-appealing option, being the third wheel with her sister, Mary Ellen, or her other married girlfriends. When she remembered how Leslie had mentioned that she sometimes took the kids to the indoor ice-skating rink on Saturday afternoons, she popped her head out from her flannel hideaway and jumped out of bed.

Sitting on the bleachers at the rink later that day, Alice stared at Leslie's profile as Leslie called out to Billy to hold Rebecca's hand when they skated by. Billy's arms flailed as he zoomed unsteadily past them without acknowledging his mother.

"He knows he's supposed to watch out for her," Leslie said with a sigh.

"From where I'm sitting, it looks like he'd benefit more from holding her hand," Alice said. "She's got a nice, steady pace going."

Leslie smiled. "She's my little tomboy. So athletically coordinated."

"I'd rather see a young woman balance herself on skates than stiletto heels any day."

"I'm glad you called this morning. This is so much nicer than sitting here alone waiting for one of them to fall and crack their head open."

"I was just calling to see if you were okay. That was some party last night."

"It was," Leslie said. "I had such cotton-mouth this morning. When Bill brought the kids home," she said, overtaken with silliness, "Billy asked why it smelled like a skunk died on the sofa in the family room."

"Was it the weed or Bob's aftershave?"

"Maybe that was it." Leslie leaned into Alice and continued laughing.

Alice watched her mouth to see if it was cold enough in the rink to see her breath. It certainly felt like it. She then recalled the odd feeling of jealousy she'd experienced the night before when Bob was leering at Leslie. Was it so odd, really, to admire a woman like her? She had the silkiest, creamy-white skin, warmest personality, and the most charming family life. What woman wouldn't have been a little jealous of her?

"Your neighbors are an interesting couple," Alice said.

"Good God, I had no idea. I'm sorry I exposed you to that."

"I'm a big girl. I can handle myself against the lascivious intentions of harmless perverts."

Leslie shook her head in amusement. "Better than I can. I can't believe I smoked marijuana with them."

"You were fine. Bill was right there in the chair, albeit unconscious, but he was there." Alice suddenly got serious. "And I wouldn't have let anything happen to you."

Leslie grabbed her hand. "You're such a good friend, always there when I need you."

Alice made the universal empowerment fist with her free hand. "Hey, we ladies of the Second Wave feminist crocheting movement have to stick together—right, Bella?"

Leslie smiled and raised their clenched hands as though they were activists at a rally. "Right-on, Betty."

❖

Rebecca sprang up from her prone position lying across her mother's feet. "You were crushing on my mother."

Alice blushed. "What? No, I wasn't. I wasn't even gay then."

"Yes, you were," Rebecca said. "You just didn't know it yet."

Alice's shoulders tensed as her trip down Memory Lane veered too far off the safe, well-traveled path.

"You were totally crushing on her," Rebecca said. "I can't blame you. She was quite a hottie back then."

"Shhh," Alice said as though Leslie might overhear them.

As Dr. Winston walked in, Rebecca was still teasing Alice. "This is good," he said with a handsome smile. "You're maintaining a positive atmosphere."

Alice stood along with Rebecca, her heart beating wildly in anticipation of the doctor's report. "Should I step outside?"

"No." Rebecca touched Alice's back. "Doctor, this is Alice, a very good friend of my mother."

He shook her hand and addressed them both. "Your mom's latest scans are looking better. From what I can tell right now, there doesn't seem to be any serious damage to the brain, but we'll know for sure once she regains consciousness."

"So she's gonna be okay?" Rebecca said. "When will she wake up?"

"I can't say for sure, but she's holding her own, so she could wake any time. The best thing to do is keep talking to her."

"Will she be able to talk when she wakes?" The question slipped out before Alice could stop it.

"Again, it doesn't look like there's any permanent damage, but we won't know the specific effects of the stroke until she wakes." His face turned softer. "She's improving. That's what counts. I'm scheduling another MRI for her for tomorrow if she doesn't wake before then."

"Thank you, Doctor." Rebecca shook his hand effusively. "I have to text Billy."

After the doctor left, Alice needed a moment to catch her breath. "That's some good news, right?"

Rebecca looked up from her cell phone and smiled. "She's getting better."

"Looks like you'll be able to have that conversation you've wanted to have with her after all."

"So will you." Rebecca winked and returned to her phone.

CHAPTER FOUR

At the hospital the next morning, Alice had the chair parked next to Leslie's bed by eight-thirty a.m. In the rare moment of privacy she studied Leslie's face, the fine lines around her eyes, the few dark spots on her forehead, all the natural changes she hadn't been around to notice as they'd occurred. Growing old with someone was a precious gift only some got to enjoy, a harsh reality that had cuffed Alice last year when she'd made Maureen's funeral arrangements. Although she was a seventy-one-year-old widow, at least she'd had many good years with Maureen. What did Leslie have?

She gently rubbed some hand lotion on Leslie's forearms, willing her to open her eyes.

"So what do you think about last month's Supreme Court ruling?" she asked. "Full marriage equality." She leaned back in her chair and folded her hands behind her head. "Boy, times sure have changed, huh? With lightning speed, it seems. Imagine if we'd met now? How different things would've been—I think. Who knows?"

"Good morning," a nurse said, pushing her computer cart into the room.

"Good morning." Alice got up to make room for her.

"You're fine, hon," the nurse said. She consulted the screen displaying Leslie's vitals. "Oxygen and heart rates look good, Mrs. O'Mara. Let's check that temperature." She looked at Alice. "Are you two related?"

"No, just very good friends." *And since you asked, passionate lovers for a freckle of a moment in time about a thousand years ago.* She smiled at her private cheekiness and couldn't help wondering how Leslie would've answered that question.

The nurse smiled. "I knew there was some special connection. You're here as often as her kids."

"Beats Mah-Jongg at the senior center."

As the nurse was leaving, Rebecca came around the corner with a tray of Dunkin Donuts coffees and a sleepy ten-year-old boy lagging behind, chewing a straw in a bottle of chocolate milk.

"Hey, Alice. Black, one sugar," Rebecca said, handing off one of the coffees.

"Thanks so much." Alice directed the cup right to her mouth. "How did you know I'd be here?"

"Just a hunch." She winked and guided her son to a chair against the wall. "Sit here and have your egg, Jake. Did you say hi to Alice?"

He offered a quiet "hi" and kept his big blue eyes fixed on Alice as he nibbled his breakfast sandwich.

"Those eyes of his eliminate all the guesswork as to who carried him," Alice said, recalling when Leslie's were that brilliant.

Rebecca smiled as she attempted to tame his blond bedhead with her fingers. "If you saw my partner, you'd know instantly. She's half Indian, half Italian."

"Interesting combination. When will I meet her?"

"Uh, that's tough to say. She's in California right now on business."

"It must be difficult handling this on your own, emotionally, I mean."

Rebecca's mouth twisted as she looked away.

"I'm sorry," Alice said. "That sounded rather judgmental."

"I told her not to rush home—in light of recent events with us."

"I see. Now I'm sorry for even bringing it up."

"That's okay. You didn't know." She handed her phone to Jake. "Here, baby. Want to listen to your music?"

His face lit up as he laid his sandwich aside and seized the phone. Once he attached the headphones, Rebecca sat at the foot of Leslie's bed.

"We've been separated for about a month now. She's staying with a friend."

"I'm so sorry. Are you in counseling?"

"We're going to start when Mom gets better. I hope it isn't too late. We kind of let our problems fester for a while—a long while."

"It's never too late to try," Alice said. Although it had been decades, she could still recall the anguish of losing Leslie, pain that had uprooted her like a sapling in a hurricane.

"Yes, I suppose," Rebecca said. "That's partly why I was asking you so many questions about my mother the other day."

"You think there's a connection?"

Rebecca considered it. "Maybe. My mother's the most remarkably positive person in the world, but I don't know. It's always seemed like real happiness has stayed one step ahead of her. Maybe that's a thing, and it's hereditary."

"I highly doubt you and your mother have the same issue."

Rebecca cocked her head to the side. "Does that mean you know what my mother's issue was?"

"No." Alice took a long sip of her coffee, miffed at herself for almost being outsmarted. "Rebecca, whether your mother has something she does or doesn't want you to know, that's her business. It's certainly not my place to say."

"Then you do know something. She had an affair, didn't she?"

Alice shifted in the chair, her leg numb from sitting cross-legged. "I don't know. And what does it matter now?"

"She had an affair, and they couldn't be together," Rebecca said dreamily. "I bet the jerk seduced her, promised her the world, and then took off."

Alice nearly choked sipping her coffee. "I'm sure you have a very active imagination," she said, fighting the compulsion to defend herself.

"It would explain why she was never able to find anyone after the divorce. She dated a lot of different guys before finally giving up. She must've still been hooked on with this mystery person."

Alice's heart ached at the fact and fiction mixed up in Rebecca's speculation. Fearing it would show on her face, she turned to the Purell dispenser and rubbed her hands until she caught her breath.

She turned around when Leslie's son, Billy, his wife, and their twin teenage daughters came trooping around the corner. After Rebecca greeted them with hugs and introduced Alice, the room became claustrophobic. She suddenly remembered some place she didn't need to be and excused herself.

Still lost in nostalgia, she'd stopped at a McDonald's drive-through, ordered another black coffee, and allowed her car to steer itself down to Branford Point. Visiting so many ghosts from her past had left her melancholy. As the afternoon sun lowered in the sky, she pulled into a spot overlooking Branford Harbor and began to feel rather guilty. Being back in Connecticut, holding what amounted to a bedside vigil for Leslie had made her forget Maureen—not entirely, of course, but enough that Maureen's memory wasn't constantly occupying her thoughts as it had been since her passing a year ago. Sadly, she couldn't do anything for Maureen, but Leslie was a different story.

She turned off the ignition and cracked her window, letting in the smell of salty air and decaying sea life. Her mind began to wander freely, without having to temper its recollections while in Rebecca's presence. She recalled the first time she and Leslie had parked here before going home after an evening with the crochet klatch.

March 1977

"I hope Bill doesn't make me quit," Leslie said.

"It was just an argument, Leslie. I'm sure it'll blow over."

"He's mentioned it to me a few times before. Last night was the first time it actually became an argument. He doesn't seem to want to drop it."

"Why doesn't he want you to work?"

"I'm not there for the kids. I don't get home from work until five thirty."

"They stay at your mother-in-law's after school, don't they?"

"Yes, but baseball season starts soon for Billy, and Brownies for Rebecca. She'd have to take them to practice and troop meetings, and she's not really comfortable driving."

Alice's throat became parched at the thought of Leslie quitting. What would she do on breaks and lunch hour without her? And for what? So she could be the kids' afternoon chauffeur?

"How do you feel about it?"

Leslie sulked. "I don't want to. I like my job."

Alice drummed her fingers on the steering wheel, staring out at the cone-shaped light the moon cast over the water. "Can't you tell Bill you don't want to?"

"I could, and I don't think he would keep fighting me on it, but it would create a lot of tension between us. Besides, I would feel awful not being there for my kids."

Alice clenched her jaw in desperation. "What if I ask Engle if you could cut your hours? Maybe work until three instead of five?"

"Really? That would be perfect." Leslie's eyes twinkled in the moonlight bouncing off the water. "Do you think he'd go for it?"

"It won't hurt to ask. I always tell him what an efficient worker you are. I'm sure he wouldn't want to lose you."

"Thank you, Alice." Leslie reached over from the passenger seat and gripped Alice like Killer Kowalski from the side.

"It's nothing." Alice patted Leslie's forearms locked across her chest. She smiled with relief at the potential solution to the problem, but something else left her unsettled. Why was she so distraught at the idea of Leslie leaving in the first place? She'd worked there for ten years without her and got along fine. And more importantly, why had she not wanted Leslie to let go of her at that moment?

Leslie leaned back in her seat with a sigh. "That's a relief. I mean, I know it's not a guarantee, but it's something."

"It's almost eleven o'clock. We better get going." Alice started the car, too distracted by her own confusion to rejoice with Leslie.

"Maybe you should bring it up to Mr. Engle as a hypothetical situation. What if he'd rather fire me for a girl with no children?"

"I'll tell him how fundamentally wrong he is and sic Cynthia, Kathy, and Dolores on him."

Leslie's eyes shimmered with admiration. "Boy, am I glad you're on my side."

"I'm not doing this for your benefit," Alice said with a smirk. "If you quit, I'll be stuck having lunch every day with that bubblehead Julie or Myrna the dinosaur. Some choice."

"Aww, it's so nice to feel wanted," Leslie said.

They elbowed each other playfully as Alice backed the car out and drove off.

❖

After Alice returned from her brief diversion at Branford Point, she thanked her sister for a delicious dinner by washing pans and loading the dishwasher. Memories of Leslie were still breaking out all over her face.

"I wish I could read your mind," Mary Ellen said. "Something awfully good's going on in there."

Alice blushed. "This visit's made me nostalgic."

"I'm sure. We'll have to open a bottle of wine and talk about it." Her sister took the dish towel out of Alice's hand. "Go keep Dave company. I'll have the coffee out in a minute."

Alice joined her brother-in-law, who was watching TV in the family room adjacent to the kitchen. He had on some Investigation Discovery program about murderous spouses.

"You're not getting any ideas, I hope," she said as she plopped on the couch.

Dave laughed. "Me? I'm learning what to watch out for from Mary Ellen."

"Don't worry about my sister," Alice said. "If she was going to kill you, she would've done it years ago."

"Quite true," Dave said. "Lord knows I've given her plenty of reasons."

Mary Ellen shuffled in with a tray of coffee mugs. "So if you decide to move back here, Dave and I have plenty of room until you find a place of your own."

"I don't know about that, Mare. It's a big decision." Alice sipped her coffee. "Maureen is up there."

"Her grave is up there, Alice. Her spirit goes wherever you go."

Alice glared at her sister. "I see you're still attending those hokey crossing-over seminars."

"I took one class on reincarnation and soul travel three years ago, and you still won't let me live it down. You should try not to be so analytical about everything."

"I'm an insurance actuary," Alice said, arching an eyebrow. "We're trained to be analytical."

Mary Ellen waved off her reply. "You're retired, and your family is here in Connecticut."

"All my friends are up in Boston."

"You have friends here, too, namely me. And what about Leslie? She needs you now."

"We're not close like we used to be. Besides, she has a very devoted family. Her ex-husband even comes to visit her."

"Now that's dedication," Dave said as he flipped through the channels.

"It's hard not to love Leslie." Alice cringed, hoping they hadn't interpreted that in the way she'd meant it.

"Apparently," he said.

"You know you'd do the same thing for Mary Ellen if you guys called it quits."

"Only if his second wife, Sophia Vergara, allowed it," Mary Ellen added and blew him a kiss.

"Well, I wouldn't blame Dave for obeying her," Alice said.

Dave raised his coffee mug in agreement.

"Please think about it," Mary Ellen said, still smiling at her husband. "I hate the idea of you alone in that big house."

Alice sipped her coffee, staring blankly at the television. The house had become too big. And empty. Living there alone, she found it almost impossible not to obsess about Maureen—so much of her style was in the decor of each room, so much of her heart everywhere else.

"Promise me you'll seriously consider it?" Mary Ellen said. "I'd love to have my big sister close by again."

Alice reached over and slapped her sister's knee. "I promise."

❖

By nine thirty, Alice was exhausted. She'd dozed off on the couch earlier, despite the blaring volume of the television. She finally went upstairs, crawled into bed in Dave and Mary Ellen's guest room, and put on her reading glasses. Was it too late to message Rebecca to check on Leslie? Was that too suspicious? Whatever. If she didn't pick up her cell phone and send the message, sleep would evade her well into the wee hours. Within five minutes she received a reply from Rebecca.

She's doing good, vitals are strong. Dr is still confident she's going to come out of it.

Rebecca ended her message with little prayer hands and heart emojis, and Alice replied.

Great news!!!! Mind if I come by tomorrow?

Please do. Don't even have to ask!!!

Alice smiled at her phone and sent Rebecca back a heart emoji. She placed the phone on the nightstand, switched off the light, and lay with her hands folded across her chest. As she waited for sleep, she watched the room transition from complete darkness into twilight as the moon filtered in through the blinds. If Leslie did wake up tomorrow, what would she say to her? Would she be happy to see her or bitter over their estrangement? Her stomach twisted at the thought of watching Leslie open her welcoming eyes only to find them cold and vacant. How could she bear it if she asked her to leave?

Why was she allowing those thoughts to contaminate her mind? Now she would never get to sleep. She flipped on her side into the fetal position and wandered back to Bill and Leslie's Memorial Day picnic.

May 1977

Alice was delighted to be celebrating with Leslie and her family. Sitting in an Adirondack chair, her eyes shaded by a hat and sunglasses, she watched Leslie's kids toss a Nerf football back and forth. They were striking renditions of their mother. Alice studied their sweaty faces and lean bodies, carefully matching angles of smiles, slopes of noses, and the hand-tic of Billy to the similar aspects of their mother.

When Leslie came outside carrying a tray of hamburger patties for Bill to grill, Alice marveled at how nice her legs looked in shorts. She had always hated hers, so skinny and white.

Alice stood up. "Leslie, let me help you with something."

"You're a guest. Stay there and relax."

"You say that every time I come over. I'm starting to feel like a bad relation."

Leslie flashed that dimpled smile. "Don't be a goof. Bill and I have this down to a science."

Although they weren't even touching, for some reason, Alice flinched at her proximity to him. "I insist," she said, suddenly restless. "I want to get out of the sun for a bit anyway."

Inside the house, Alice stood foolishly by the counter as Leslie scurried about packing a wicker tray full of mustard, ketchup, and relish. "Let me do something."

"Alice, I didn't invite you here to put you to work."

"Helping you set the table is hardly slave labor." She moved near Leslie, and the scent of her musky perfume mixed with the smell of skin on a hot day stirred something in her.

Leslie stopped for a moment and regarded her with sincerity. "Alice, you've been such a help, such a friend to me at work these last eight months, that I could never repay the favor."

"Nor should you feel like you have to. It's my job to properly train new hires. Plus you're my friend. I want to see you do well."

"Well, how lucky am I?" Leslie resumed scurrying around the kitchen.

"You have to stop acting like I saved you from a burning building," Alice said coolly, but secretly, she adored the role of heroine rescuing the lady in distress.

"I'm sorry for being so nerdy, but it's felt really good having a job again." She lowered her voice to a conspiratorial whisper. "Don't tell Bill or the kids, but I like having time away from my household duties."

Alice widened her eyes. "How do you live with yourself?"

"You're so fresh," Leslie said with a chuckle. In her flurry of activity, she bumped into Alice's shoulder. "Sorry."

"That's okay," Alice said softly.

Leslie's big eyes sparkled at Alice. "Here, since you're so eager for a job, you can carry this out." She thrust the tray of utensils into her belly.

Alice faced her with a serious look. "Boy, it didn't take you long to start ordering me around. I thought I was a guest."

Startled, Leslie reached for the tray. "I'm sorry. I thought you wanted—"

"I'm teasing." Alice held firm.

"Oh, you," Leslie yelped and lightly slapped her arm. "Just for that, you can stay and help me wash the dishes later."

She carried the condiments down the back steps to the picnic table, practically giddy at the thought of spending the night washing dishes side by side with Leslie.

"Ah, I see she got you, too," Bill joked from his post at the grill. He jerked his head toward the kids. "The only ones who ever get away with anything around here."

Something about his jovial voice and genuine eyes made Alice want to smash him in the forehead with his spatula.

"It's your job to cook it and their job to eat it." She winced at the sound of herself making small talk, never one for manufactured chitchat, but it was a necessary evil. For some reason, she felt so uncomfortable around him.

"You bet it is," he said. "They're bottomless pits. Leslie's paycheck goes mostly toward keeping the fridge stocked. Say, how about you? Burger? Dog? Both?"

Leslie stuck her head out the door. "Alice, would you mind bringing out one more thing for me? Then we can all sit down and eat."

"A dog, Bill," Alice said and flew up the stairs and into the kitchen. Leslie was all business at this point, but her intensity only made her more fascinating.

"Okay, you can take the napkins and condiments, and I'll bring out the pitcher of lemonade and glasses," she said, mostly to herself.

Alice watched Leslie whirl around the kitchen, fastidiously orchestrating every cookout detail with the exactness of a tornado. "Les, it was really nice of you to invite me."

"It was nice of you to join us. My brother and his family usually come for Memorial Day, but they're away in Baltimore this weekend. Besides, I wouldn't want you to spend it alone. You know you're welcome here any holiday you don't have plans."

"I've already spent Christmas, New Year's, and Easter Sunday with your family. I'm sure Bill must be getting tired of having to feed stragglers every holiday."

"Nonsense. You're not a straggler. You're my friend."

Alice didn't know if it was the end of the sliced onion on the counter or Leslie's wholesome sincerity that brought a tear to her eye.

"Besides, he's had his share of bachelor friends over for holidays, too. In fact, one's coming later, Frank. He's an electrician working with him on the subdivision."

"Yeah?" Alice said, feigning interest.

"Bill will kill me if he knows I told you, but we kind of thought you and Frank might hit it off."

A wave of dread hit her. "Oh, Leslie, another fix-up?"

"No, no," Leslie waved her hands for emphasis. "He didn't have plans this weekend and neither did you. You're both single, attractive people. There might be a spark. I hope you're not upset with me."

"No, I'm not upset." Alice fumbled for words as she processed her muddled thoughts and feelings. In the past, she would have been excited at the prospect of meeting an eligible man, but now, she had

an unsettling feeling about it, almost as if she didn't want Leslie to want her with someone else. "I just, well, if I had known this was a fix-up, I would've dolled myself up more."

"Don't think of it like that. It's a family barbecue. And you already look like an absolute doll."

Alice took off her sun hat and attempted to fluff her flattened hair. "My, but you are the diplomat. Don't blame me if Frank takes one look at me and books out through the woods."

"If he does, it'll be his loss."

"Mommy." Little Rebecca burst in through the door. "Daddy said hurry up. The meat is gonna burn."

"Okay, honey, we're coming."

Rebecca pulled on Alice's arm. "Alice, sit next to me, not Billy."

Alice looked down at Rebecca with a smile. "Groovy," she said dryly. "You can protect me from Frank."

Leslie rolled her eyes at Alice as they headed out with the rest of the picnic wares.

❖

On Tuesday morning, Alice stirred from bed feeling out of sorts. She'd had a fitful night sleep reliving images from Sunday's picnic. Leslie's husband was a handsome, affable man. Why did he irk her? And then the dream about Leslie—being close to her, touching her face, brushing her cheek against hers. Surely that must be because they'd become such close friends. Things sometimes got all muddled up in dreams anyhow.

Her disquietude vanished when she met Leslie in the lunchroom for ten-thirty coffee break. Her sunburned skin stretched into her broadest smile.

"So, did you enjoy yourself Sunday?" Leslie asked.

"I had a wonderful time," Alice said. "You have such a charming family."

"I've been blessed with good kids. I'm not just saying that because they're mine. For ten- and seven-year-olds, they're no trouble at all. They actually listen to us. And they just idolize their father."

Alice suddenly felt so envious of those kids. How could they not possibly idolize a mother who so clearly adored them?

"Have you heard from Frank?" Leslie said as she dunked a Lorna Doone cookie in her coffee.

"No." Alice began to fidget in her chair. "That's okay. He's not really my type anyway."

"That's too bad. He's so nice. And handsome."

"I don't care for the ponytail."

"I think it's kind of cute. He's a musician, too, you know. A guitarist. He auditioned for the Eagles a few years ago before moving back to Connecticut."

Alice laced her fingers together and stretched, no longer inclined to fake interest.

"I'll ask Bill if he said anything about you at work today."

"That's okay. Don't bug him about it. Men don't like getting in the middle of things like that."

"Bill doesn't mind. It's kind of fun playing matchmaker. You haven't had a date the whole time I've known you, Alice. That's tragic. You're too smart and too pretty to be single."

Alice contemplated the innocence in Leslie's eyes. "You know, Betty Friedan might say I'm too smart and too pretty to be attached. There's something to be said for true independence."

Leslie tilted her head. "I thought you said feminists can have husbands and boyfriends."

"Of course we can. We just don't need them to define us and validate our womanhood. Haven't you read The Feminist Mystique?*"*

Leslie shook her head.

"Boy, you really have been stuck in the kitchen too long. I'll bet you've never even burned one of your bras either."

Leslie protested. "I've had two kids. If I go around braless in public, these things will be headed in two separate directions."

Alice laughed as they headed back to the office. "Well, lucky for you, free-falling boobs aren't a crochet-club requirement."

❖

After morning break, Alice was unable to focus on work for the rest of the day. With the headphones in her ears and her boss's voice droning, she typed mindlessly, stealing glances at Leslie, feeling uneasy. What was happening? Was all Leslie's talk about the tragedy of being single getting to her? Was she turning into one of those women Betty Friedan talked about who ended up on Valium? Or worse, doing time in the booby hatch? Ridiculous. She had nothing to be anxious about. She worked for a secure company, lived in a well-manicured Cape that Tony agreed to let her keep, and had her Friday-night crocheting klatch every other week and her friendship with Leslie. So what if she was still single?

At ten past three, Alice timed her coffee break so she could walk with Leslie to the time clock to punch out for the day. As they were steeped in conversation about why Mr. Engle always waited till the last minute of the day to give Leslie "hot rush" letters, Alice followed Leslie to the ladies' room. From the stall, Leslie had determined he was resentful of her leaving earlier than the rest of the staff each day.

"No, I don't think that's it," Alice said as the water ran over her clean hands. "Being vindictive requires forethought."

"Maybe he just forgets I leave early."

"That sounds more like Engle."

Leslie pointed at her face. "Alice, can you check my eye? I think I've had a lash stuck in there all afternoon."

Alice's heart suddenly throbbed as she stood close enough to Leslie to pull at her eyelid and search for the errant lash. Leslie's breath hit her chin as she patiently allowed Alice's finger to poke at her eyeball. Even though she saw the tiny lash in the corner right away, Alice kept it there a second or three longer.

"Thank you," Leslie said, rubbing her eye. "That feels so much better."

Alice remained close to Leslie, her gaze fixed on her.

"What's the matter? Is something still there?" Leslie leaned closer to the mirror over the sink and inspected her eyes.

"No," Alice said, stepping back from the awkward exchange. "It's just a little bloodshot. It'll clear up."

"Thanks. You always seem to be saving me from something."

"I wish I was the hero you make me out to be."

"You're my hero." Leslie gave her a playful nudge in her side.

"Aww, shucks," Alice said and nudged her back.

They continued jostling each other.

"Hey, you just pinched my fat," Leslie said.

"Are you high? There's not an ounce of fat on you."

"I hide it well," Leslie said, gasping for breath. "It's stuffed inside my pantyhose."

Alice stopped suddenly when an unusual sensation thundered through her as Leslie pinched what she could grab of her sides.

Seemingly unfazed, Leslie adjusted the waistband of her skirt. "Getting these off the second I get home is my favorite part of the day. I don't care if 'nothing beats a great pair of L'eggs' when the elastic waistband is cutting me in half."

Alice laughed. "Why do you think feminists wear sandals and long skirts? Misogynists invented pantyhose and those pointy-toed heels."

"Who?"

"Misogynists. I'll let Cynthia and the ladies explain that theory to you on Friday." Alice smiled, and suddenly, Friday couldn't arrive fast enough.

CHAPTER FIVE

The next morning in Mary Ellen's kitchen, Alice squinted as the sun bounced off a glass patio table and pierced the sliding doors. Perched on a stool at the breakfast island, she stared into her fruit-on-the-bottom yogurt, stirring slowly, as if a genie might swirl up any minute and grant her three wishes. The first two wishes were easy, but what about the third?

Clarity. Yes, clarity would be her third wish.

"Are you turning into a vampire in your old age?" Mary Ellen shuffled toward the door and lowered the bamboo blind. "I was about to come in and put a mirror under your nose."

"We're full of jokes this morning," Alice said and sipped her coffee. "I didn't sleep well last night."

"I'm sorry. It must be so difficult seeing your friend like that." Mary Ellen sat on the stool across from her. "Any changes?"

"Not yet. Not that I know of anyway."

"Are you going to the hospital today?"

"I'm planning on it, but I've been there three days in a row. Her family's going to call security on the crazy old bat that keeps appearing at their mother's bedside. Like the grim reaper." She picked at her unkempt hair. "I think I even look like him this morning."

Mary Ellen flung her hand away and fixed the out-of-place hairs. "Her daughter contacted you. You came all the way from Boston to see her. I'm sure they appreciate it."

Alice shrugged.

Mary Ellen placed her hand over Alice's. "Familiar territory, huh?"

"Unfortunately. I pray the outcome is different for Leslie than it was for Maureen."

Mary Ellen nodded. "Hey, can I ask you a personal question?"

"Since when do you ask my permission?"

"I don't know. You always seem so awkward whenever I ask you questions that have to do with you being a lesbian."

"I'm not awkward about it," Alice said, but her cheeks felt like they were turning the color of her pomegranate yogurt. "Your questions were always inappropriately personal."

Mary Ellen sucked her teeth. "We're sisters. I would've answered any probing questions about me and Dave if you asked."

Alice grimaced. "Do you mind? I'm trying to eat."

"Did you know Dave doesn't even need Viagra?"

"Gross." Alice got up with her yogurt and newspaper, and walked out to the patio table.

Mary Ellen followed her outside.

After a moment of scanning the front page, Alice looked up. "What do you want?"

"The real story about you and your friend Leslie."

"What are you talking about? We were friends from work." Alice lifted the paper up to her face.

"Almost forty years ago. Must've been one hell of a friendship for you to come all the way down from Boston and visit her every day when she's not even conscious."

"I'm here visiting you and Dave."

Mary Ellen eyed her. "For someone who spent the better part of her life lying to everyone, you've never gotten very good at it. This woman obviously means a great deal to you."

Alice sighed and dropped the paper into her lap. "She does. I used to be in love with her, many, many years ago. Okay? Can I finish my breakfast in peace now?"

"I knew it," Mary Ellen said, sinking into a chair across from her. "Did she know?"

Alice found an article about the nutritional benefits of eating free-range chickens, mistakenly believing she'd actually be able to read it.

"Was she married at the time? Did you two have an affair?"

By her third attempt at reading the first sentence in the article, Alice lost her patience. "Can't you see I don't want to talk about this?"

"I'm sorry," Mary Ellen said in a pout. "Jesus Christ, I'm just excited to have my sister back for a while. You'd think I was asking you for a loan." She swept her empty coffee mug off the table and stormed off into the kitchen.

"Mare," Alice shouted. She got up and followed her in. "I'm sorry I snapped at you. It's just that, this is hard for me to discuss with you."

"Why? You told me about Maureen. Why is this different?"

"Because it is. I don't want you to think negatively of me."

"I thought we settled this when you came out. There isn't anything you could do that would change how I feel about you. You're my big sister."

"We had an affair, and she was married at the time," Alice blurted, her fists balled up with tension.

Mary Ellen was quiet for a moment.

"I had an affair with a married woman, Mare. How do you feel about your big sister now?"

"Sad." Mary Ellen's eyes brimmed with sympathy. "I feel sad for you."

"What for?"

"I can only assume it didn't work out."

"No, it didn't, but I certainly don't want or deserve your pity. I knew she was married, but it didn't stop me. It didn't stop her either."

"I'm not pitying you. I mean, did you set out to fall in love with her? Did you intend to have an affair?"

"No," Alice insisted. "I didn't even know I was a lesbian. It all came out of nowhere. I was in love with her before I even knew what was happening."

"Now it finally makes sense."

"What does?"

"Your nervous breakdown."

"I didn't have a nervous breakdown."

"It was something. You were so depressed for a year that I didn't know what you'd do. Don't you remember having these conversations about how worried I was about you? God, why didn't you just tell me?"

"Mare, it was the late seventies. We grew up going to church every Sunday. I'm the godmother of your son. How could I have told you any of it?"

"I don't know, but I wish you had." Mary Ellen draped Alice in a hug from behind.

Alice held on to her sister's arms, leaning her cheek on them for a moment.

Mary Ellen led her to the kitchen table. "So how did something like that ever get started?"

"We're really going to have this conversation?"

Mary Ellen rested her chin in her palm. "I certainly hope so."

Alice smiled at her sixty-seven-year-old "kid" sister. Why hadn't she come and stayed with her sooner?

"Quit stalling," Mary Ellen said, slapping the table.

"Mare, I have no clue how it got started. All I know for sure is when," she said, checking her mind's eye. "June of 1977. I knew something was brewing the night of our crochet get-together, right before the ERA rally in Hartford."

"I might've known," she said, teasing. "Leave it to a group of staunch feminists to turn a woman into a lesbian."

Alice mocked her with an exaggerated laugh. "Do you want to hear this or not?"

"Yes, yes. ERA rally, Hartford in '77. Go."

June 1977

Friday night, Alice rushed back and forth between the kitchen and living room of her small Cape Cod across from the beach in

West Haven. With patchouli incense lit, she arranged the fondue pot filled with Swiss-cheese chunks on her square coffee table, piling pillows around it for her guests to sit on. She felt particularly edgy for some reason. They'd all taken turns hosting their club meetings, so hostess duties were nothing new. The only explanation she found for her wired nerves was Leslie. But why? Leslie had been there a couple of times before when it was Alice's turn to host and always found something to compliment her on, whether it was her decor style or featured hors d'oeuvres.

Spotting an album jacket creeping out slightly from the otherwise flush row of records, she lurched to the credenza containing her stereo system and corrected the faux pas. The sound of a car door shutting summoned her to the door.

"Bella," Alice said after swinging the door open.

"Betty," Leslie replied excitedly.

They exchanged light kisses on the cheeks as Leslie entered with a tray of brownies.

"Don't shut the door," Leslie said. "The girls are right behind me."

Looking over Leslie's shoulder, Alice felt a twinge of disappointment when she saw that Dolores, Cynthia, and Kathy had also arrived five minutes early and were at the curb getting their things out of Cynthia's car.

"Your perfume smells so nice," Alice said. "Is it new?"

"Yes, it's Coty Wild Musk. Pretty, huh?"

"Very." Alice deserted the rest of her company walking up the sidewalk to follow Leslie's intoxicating scent into the living room. Realizing what she'd done, she returned to greet them as they filed in with wine bottles and bags of crochet supplies.

Once they all settled around the table with cocktails, snacks, and Kathy's small wooden trinket box that doubled as a joint case, Cynthia wasted no time in convening the meeting.

"Okay, sisters, as you know, next Saturday is the big ERA rally in Hartford," she said. "Governor Grasso is confirmed to speak, and I heard Senator Ribicoff might also be there. Bus transportation's been arranged, and it's leaving out of North Haven at eight a.m. sharp."

"Let's all meet at the diner off 91 for breakfast," Alice said. "I'll bring a thermos of mimosas for the ride."

"That sounds fabulous," Dolores said. "Leslie, you're coming with us, aren't you?"

Leslie, the only one actually crocheting, looked up from what appeared to be the front panel of a child's lavender vest. "Uh, I'll have to check with my husband first. Sometimes he does side jobs on Saturdays with my brother-in-law."

"Here's a talking point you may want to try when you check with him," Cynthia said. "If the ERA passes and women start earning the same pay for doing the same jobs as men, your husband probably wouldn't need to take side jobs on Saturdays anymore."

"Well, he doesn't do it every Saturday, and it's mostly to help out his brother. But I'll definitely try to make it."

Alice caught the furtive glances between Kathy and Cynthia. "Ladies, she's got young kids. Your kids are older or grown," she said, looking at Cynthia and Dolores. "She can't just run off any time the notion strikes her."

"Why not? It seems like her husband can," Kathy said. "And she's not just running off because she feels like it. Equality is the most important women's issue of our time."

"My sister-in-law says that if the ERA passes, women could be drafted into the army, and maybe even lose alimony rights," Leslie said.

"Your sister-in-law is an idiot," Kathy replied. "There is no more draft. They ended it four years ago."

"Take it easy, Kathy," Alice said with a scowl.

"Ladies, in-fighting is the last thing our cause needs." Cynthia stuffed an onion-dip-covered broccoli floret into her mouth. "Remember what Lincoln said about a house divided."

Kathy lit up a joint from her little wooden box. "All I'm saying is why does the entire burden of child care always have to fall on the mother? It takes two to make them. Shouldn't it take two to raise them?"

"Bill helps a lot," Leslie said. "He loves spending time with them."

"Don't mind her," Alice said. "She'll simmer down after a couple more hits." Then to Kathy, "C'mon, stop bogarting that."

Dolores reached over the coffee table, her fork aimed at the fondue pot. "I'm sure Leslie will be on that bus with us if it's at all possible. Look, I'm as dedicated a feminist as the next broad, but if my grown-up kids needed me, I'd drop everything for them in a minute."

"Same with me," Cynthia added. "We need to dispel the myth that feminism seeks to downplay the roles of wives and motherhood."

"That's right." Dolores said, twirling a chunk of bread in liquefied cheese. "Being a mom has been my most important and rewarding job. It's also made me want to eat my ex-husband's service revolver at times, but I still wouldn't trade it for anything."

"Not even the job of president of the United States?" Kathy said with a wink.

The ladies laughed at the absurdity and awesomeness of the thought.

"President?" Alice threw a pretzel at Kathy. "Someone get that joint away from her. It's obvious she's already high out of her mind."

Kathy sucked at the roach and passed it on to Cynthia. "Let's not forget those aren't the only roles women were born to have. I don't have any kids, but I'm very fulfilled as an educator."

"Hey, making sure the dodge balls are properly inflated is a vital part of the American education system." Alice mugged at her own joke and nudged Kathy over into a mound of pillows.

"You don't have to convince us of that, Kathy," Cynthia said. "We're all on the same side."

"We all know there's a lot of work still to be done," Dolores said, "but we'll accomplish it one step at a time. And Saturday we rally for the ratification of the ERA."

The ladies all raised their cocktail glasses and cheered.

After Cynthia and her carload drove off, Leslie and Alice began clearing the wreckage of empty glasses and dishes from the coffee table and surrounding end tables.

"Thanks for staying to help, but it's getting late. I can take it from here."

"I don't mind." Leslie's face seemed cut from stone as she covered the leftover cheddar-cheese plate and onion dip with plastic wrap. *"I bet you'll have to soak that fondue pot overnight."*

Alice picked up the crusty pot, scraping it with her fingernail. *"I wonder if Swiss cheese is a main ingredient in Krazy Glue."*

Leslie's tepid response aroused Alice's suspicion. *"Hey, is everything all right?"*

Everything in Leslie's posture said no. *"I have to give my two-week notice on Monday."*

"What?" Alice heard her clearly, but a single syllable was all she could manage after having the wind knocked out of her.

"I'm sorry," Leslie said as her eyes dimmed.

"I don't understand. I thought the part-time hours were working out."

"They were while the kids were in school. They've been out for a week now, and it's just been too much for my mother-in-law."

"Isn't there anyone else who could babysit?"

"My parents work. I mean, I could always hire a babysitter until three each day, but for what it would cost, it'd just be easier for me to stay home with them."

"Is your husband making you do this?" It took every ounce of reason for Alice to contain the resentment flaming up from her gut.

"Well, no, he's not making me, but we've talked about it, and I'm afraid he's right. It doesn't make sense to pay strangers to be with them when I can."

"But you like working. Didn't you tell him that? It makes you happy."

"Yes, he knows."

"He can't just order you around like you're his daughter."

"He's not," Leslie said, seeming resigned to an undesirable fate. *"I can't make a decision like this without considering his feelings or what's best for all of us. We've talked about other possible solutions, but we keep coming back to this one."*

"Of course. It's easier to control you when you're home, stuck in the kitchen."

"Alice." Leslie glared at her.

A rush of panic heated Alice's face the moment the words came out of her mouth. "I'm sorry, Leslie. I didn't mean that."

Leslie turned away from Alice, resting her hands on the counter.

"Boy, I think all Kathy's feminist propaganda is really getting to me," Alice said in a jovial tone as she moved closer to her.

"It's okay," Leslie said as she turned around. "I'm sick about it, too, but there's nothing I can do. The condition that I agreed to before going back to work was that I would do it as long as it didn't interfere with the family."

"I understand, but it's so unfair to you," Alice said, yet her sympathies were focused entirely on herself at the moment.

"I'm trying not to look at it that way. One of us has to quit, Alice, and it can't be Bill with me earning as little as I do in the typing pool. I know Bill. If I was the one who made the money we lived on, he'd quit and stay home with the kids."

Alice stewed quietly at Leslie's readiness to defend her husband as though she were the enemy. "You seem like you're okay with quitting." She hated herself for sounding so whiny.

"Of course I'm not okay with it." Leslie's chin dimpled as she fought back tears. "I love taking coffee breaks and having lunch with you every day. I also like the responsibility of my daily duties at work, but I just don't have a solid-enough reason to fight Bill on it any longer."

Alice deferred to the floor tiles, fresh out of will.

Leslie moved closer and took Alice's hands in hers. "Alice, please understand. It's not what I want, but I have to admit I've felt a bit guilty about leaving the kids ever since I started. We still have the crochet club. That doesn't have to change."

"Not until Bill decides that's getting in the way of your family, too." Alice worked her hands free and turned toward the window above the sink. The neighbor kids had left their makeshift bicycle ramp made of warped plywood over a milk delivery bin lifted off someone's porch in their driveway. If they were her kids, how would she feel about having to sacrifice the kinds of things Leslie had to? The very idea appalled her.

She sensed Leslie still behind her.

"Alice, is something besides my leaving bothering you?"

Leslie's perfume wafted into Alice's face as she stood before her, almost pinning her against the sink. She expected an answer but not the one confronting her at that moment. She was in love with Leslie. Deep, searing, shameful, terrifying love.

"No, no, nothing," Alice mumbled, flipping her hair behind her shoulder. "I'm tired and a little high. I just need to go to bed. I'll be fine in the morning."

"Well, okay." Leslie seemed unconvinced. "Call me tomorrow."

Alice agreed and followed Leslie to the foyer, anxious for her to go so she could breathe again. She closed the door, leaned against it, and shut her eyes to lessen the spinning in her head.

Mary Ellen sat at the kitchen table with her jaw hanging open. "I can't believe all this was going on, and I had no idea. Sounds like once you fell, you fell hard."

Alice gave a noncommittal shrug.

"So, when do we get to the juicy stuff? When did you kiss? When did you go to bed with her?"

Alice blushed. "Mare," she said in a singsong voice. "I'm getting in the shower now."

"Fine, but when you're dressed and ready, we're going for brunch. You can't just cut me off like this. It's cruel."

"It's a cruel world we live in," Alice drawled over her shoulder as she headed for the bathroom.

CHAPTER SIX

Standing by her threat, later that morning Mary Ellen had taken Alice to a cozy café across from the Branford green specializing in the most sophisticated breakfast and lunch offerings a townie from the Connecticut shoreline could ask for. At the moment, its charm was lost on Alice, who was picking at her tomato, avocado, and goat-cheese omelet.

"Have you given any more thought to moving back?" Mary Ellen asked.

"Mare, please." Alice sliced off a piece of her omelet with her fork.

"What do you mean, *Mare, please*? Is it so unreasonable to want my sister home again?"

"I told you I'd think about it, and I am. But right now, I have something else weighing rather heavily on my mind."

"Any news?"

Shaking her head, Alice ate another small bite of her omelet and then leaned back in her chair. "What if she doesn't wake up?"

"Honey, you can't think like that. She will."

Alice smirked. "That's what I keep telling her daughter—and with that exact same artificial conviction."

Mary Ellen sipped her cranberry juice. "All right. The woman's had a stroke. Maybe she'll never wake up. But it's only been a few days. Give it a full week before you have her in a permanent vegetative state."

"You're right," she said, glumly nibbling the corner of her wheat toast.

"Let's talk about something a little brighter, huh? Like your scandalous little field trip to Hartford."

No matter what the dilemma, Mary Ellen always knew how to get her to smile.

June 1977

As the afternoon sun baked Alice and everyone else in attendance in Bushnell Park, she smiled watching Leslie proudly wave her EQUAL PAY IS THE ONLY WAY picket sign and join the chorus of women and men chanting various "Ratify the ERA now" slogans. What a contrast to the woman who was about to quit a job she enjoyed to return to the drudgery of being a housewife.

"This is so exciting," Leslie said as she and Alice caught up to Cynthia, Kathy, and Dolores.

"What we're doing is so important, Leslie," Cynthia said. "We're carrying the torch lit by the original suffragists in the first wave. We can't let their struggles be in vain."

Leslie bowed her head in reverence.

"We're making a real difference," Kathy added.

"I don't know about that," Alice said as she chewed at the cuticle skin on her middle finger. Four heads whipped toward her in astonishment.

"What do you mean?" Kathy said.

"We're protesting in a state that's already ratified the ERA," Alice said, "and sweating our asses off in the process."

Kathy scowled at her. "Sorry we're making your mascara run, doll face."

"Yes, this is largely ceremonial, Alice," Cynthia said. "But we're here standing in solidarity with the movement. That's what's important."

"Yeah, Alice," Dolores chimed in sternly. "It's the support for the other states that counts." She leaned closer to Alice. "And frankly, I'd rather be here than down South in this heat picketing

for women's rights. We'd probably end up abducted by the banjo players from Deliverance.*"*

Alice and Dolores shared a private laugh.

"Well, I think it's great," Leslie said. "I love being a part of this. Wasn't Governor Grasso's speech so inspiring?"

"Far-out," Kathy said. "Connecticut's first female governor. It still gives me chills."

"She's married with kids and was still able to accomplish this," Alice said, her gaze falling on Leslie.

"Her kids are grown," Leslie fired back.

A breeze kicked up and blew her hair all out of place, and it took Alice's breath away. Standing beside her, their perspiring arms touching, Alice had to force herself to stop gazing at her.

"I wish I could've brought Rebecca," Leslie said.

"Why didn't you?" Dolores asked. "My daughters are milling around here somewhere, probably scoping out hippie dudes."

"She's only seven," Leslie said. "Besides, my husband took the kids to see some science-fiction movie. Star Wars, *I think it's called."*

She'd heard Leslie say "my husband" a hundred times, but lately, each time she uttered the phrase, it felt like an icepick jabbed into her ear.

"So if we do our activism jobs rights," Alice said, "by the time Rebecca is our age, equal pay for equal work will be a reality."

Everyone voiced boisterous agreement.

"Surely, even the federal government will have come to its senses by then," Dolores added.

"If not," Cynthia said, "it'll fall on us to incite the next revolution."

They all cheered and raised the empowerment fist in unison.

On the bus-ride home from the Hartford rally, Alice and Leslie absently leaned against each other in their seats as the school bus chugged along the entrance ramp to Interstate 91. They were tired, sticky, and full of burgers and beer from dinner at a nearby pub, but Alice couldn't remember feeling more alive inside.

Unable to stand the strain on her left eye from stealing so many sideways glances at Leslie, Alice turned to her. "Today was fun, wasn't it?"

Leslie tilted her head toward Alice and smiled. "I'll say. What a memorable day. It was worth the argument." She looked as though she'd let a secret slip.

"What argument?"

"No, it's nothing." Leslie turned toward the window across the aisle.

"Did you have a fight with Bill about going today?"

"No, well, I wouldn't call it a fight."

"What would you call it?"

"Just a little disagreement. He was uncomfortable about me going to any political rally—at first, I mean. I'm afraid he doesn't really get feminism, but I explained to him what the rally was about, and then he was okay with it."

"What's he afraid of?"

"He's not afraid of anything. He was just curious about why I wanted to go."

Alice's stomach knotted with anger at Bill. "You're a woman. You have a daughter. Why wouldn't you want to go?"

"He's fine," Leslie said. "I think he was a little uneasy when I first told him about our crochet meetings."

"Uneasy about what?"

"That maybe I wasn't happy being married anymore."

"Wow, talk about jumping to conclusions. I hope he's not going to try to talk you out of crocheting with us next."

"No, no, he knows I love it."

"We love having you. You've brought a wonderful new dynamic to the group."

"I'm so grateful to you girls. I've become so much more aware of the issues since I started coming."

"It wouldn't be the same if you stopped. It's going to be strange enough adjusting to work without you."

"Really? That's so sweet, Alice."

"Sweet? I felt like a big baby right after I said it."

Leslie nudged her in the side with her elbow. "Aww, you're not a baby. You're just being honest about how you feel."

"Listen, I'm sorry I made such a big deal about it the other day when you told me. I'm going to miss you like hell, but I support whatever you need to do."

Leslie's eyes melted into a smile. "Thank you for that, Alice."

Alice looked away, suddenly bashful.

"You know, I enjoy doing the job," Leslie said, "but if the truth be known, you're the reason I enjoyed going to work so much. Even though we haven't known each other all that long, I feel like I've known you forever."

"Me, too. I feel like I can talk to you about anything or nothing at all. I've had girlfriends for years I don't feel this comfortable with."

"Then it's divine intervention that I got hired at First American. We were meant to become bosom buddies."

Alice smirked and glanced at her own breasts, then at Leslie's. "Wow. That's pretty big. If God wants us to become best friends, then we better get right on it."

Leslie slapped her hand on top of Alice's as it rested on the seat between them. "We already are, you goof."

"We are?" Alice teased.

"Absolutely."

Alice held Leslie's hand and didn't let it go. Neither did Leslie.

Alice's phone began vibrating their table with a call from Rebecca. She looked at Mary Ellen as her heart sank. Rebecca had never called her before. They'd always communicated through text message. Something must be wrong with Leslie. She leapt up from the table and answered the call outside on the sidewalk.

"Hello? Rebecca? What's wrong?"

"Nothing, Alice. Mom's awake," she said, practically screeching.

"Thank God," Alice said as tears spilled down her cheeks. "How is she? What's she doing?"

"She seems okay, but they won't know for sure until they're done evaluating her. The doctor's in with her now. I have to get back in there with my brother, but I just wanted you to know."

"Thanks, thank you for calling," she said, exhaling into the phone. "Text me when it's okay for me to visit."

"You got it."

Alice ended the call and went back in the café, relief in full bloom on her face.

"What was that all about?" Mary Ellen asked.

"Leslie woke up."

Mary Ellen grabbed her hand. "I'm so happy for you."

"Her daughter's going to text me when I can go to see her."

"Are you nervous?"

"Of course I am. I have no idea what to expect."

"About what condition she'll be in?"

"That and how she's going to react seeing me for the first time in twenty-five years. What if she doesn't remember me?"

Mary Ellen wrung her hands in excitement. "This is just like in *An Affair to Remember* when Deborah Kerr is supposed to meet Cary Grant at the Empire State building, but she has that accident, and then he thinks she doesn't love him anymore."

Alice contemplated the analogy for a moment. "It's not like that at all."

"I mean because you're star-crossed lovers." Mary Ellen's eyes dazzled with optimism. "This may be your chance to get back together."

"Are you nuts?" Alice said and then remembered how her heart had dreamed of crazier things once.

"I don't see what's so nuts about it."

"For starters, I don't even think she's a lesbian. Her daughter said she was still dating men after her divorce."

"She was a lesbian for you once. I'm sure she could be one again."

"Mare, that's not why I came here."

"No? Then why did you come?"

"Her daughter asked me to. And you know what else? Maureen's only been gone a year. I'm not ready to pursue any romantic interludes. I'm still in mourning."

"You mean to say you wouldn't jump at another chance with your first true love?"

Alice shook her head in despair. "You ought to try watching something besides the Hallmark Channel once in a while."

Mary Ellen indicated Alice's plate piled with toast, hash browns, and half an omelet. "C'mon, finish your breakfast so we can go home and get you ready for your trip to the hospital."

"Get me ready? I'm not going to the homecoming dance, Mare. I have to wait until Rebecca texts me, and who knows when that will be? Her family is there, and the doctors are probably running all kinds of tests."

"Fabulous. Now we'll have plenty of time to shop for a new outfit for you."

CHAPTER SEVEN

The next morning Alice's eyes opened as the rising sun crept over them. She inventoried her surroundings in Mary Ellen's guest room, the former bedroom of her nephew, needing a moment to remember where she was and decipher reality from what she had dreamt last night. The text Rebecca sent as Alice was getting ready for bed had put her off sleep like she'd downed a pot of dark-roast coffee. It must've been three a.m. by the time she finally drifted off. She picked up her cell phone on the nightstand and checked to make sure Rebecca's text wasn't part of the dream sequence.

Can u come see Mom tomorrow, late a.m.? Can't wait 4 her to see you!!!

It wasn't a dream. Alice's stomach tumbled as a tentative smile stretched across her face. She sat up in bed and hugged her knees to her chest, trying to imagine what it was going to feel like seeing Leslie again. If the butterflies were any indication, it would feel like it did last night in her dream of their first kiss. She leaned against the headboard and closed her eyes, recalling the day that everything had changed for them.

Late July 1977

Although Leslie's workday at First American ended at three o'clock, on her last day she hung around the office awaiting the cocktail-hour sendoff at Finnegan's her coworkers had planned for her at five.

Curiously antsy all day, Alice busied herself clearing out all the tedious tasks she'd let pile up in her "in" tray since the beginning of the week. A strange onslaught of emotion percolated in her gut as Leslie flitted around the office dusting plastic ferns and making the in-house insurance agents fresh cups of coffee. When Leslie began cleaning out her desk, packing picture frames of her family, her candy dish, and an African-violet plant neatly into a cardboard box, Alice couldn't watch. She scuttled over to the bank of file cabinets across the large open office with a pile of paperwork.

When she'd completed her packing, Leslie approached her. "Why don't you let me do that? I've finished all my other work."

Alice shook her head.

"Mr. Dickerson put a file and letter draft on your desk," Leslie said. "He probably wants it done before you punch out for the weekend." She reached for the stack of files Alice had on the cabinets.

"Don't." Alice slapped a possessive hand on the papers, not looking up from the open drawer.

Leslie checked her surroundings. "Alice, what's the matter?"

"Nothing. I'm fine," she said softly, sliding her pile down with her to the next cabinet.

"You don't seem fine."

Alice took a breath, choking back the hazard of a breakdown. "I can't talk about it now, Leslie. Please, just let me do this."

"Okay." Leslie bowed her head and walked away.

Once the mountain of files had vanished into the drawers, Alice collected her keys from her desk and headed to Mr. Engle's executive washroom, a privilege she was granted whenever he wasn't in the office. She locked the door behind her, leaned forward against the vanity, and wept silently into her hand until the fear of being overwhelmed by her feelings stopped her convulsions. She surveyed her red eyes and swollen lips, and splashed cold water at them.

"Alice, open the door." Leslie's voice was accompanied by a gentle, persistent knocking.

Surprised that Leslie had found her, she opened the door and let her in.

"Honey, what is the matter?" Leslie pressed her hands against Alice's cheeks.

Alice draped her in a hug and cried silently on her shoulder.

"Alice, talk to me," Leslie said, stroking the back of her hair. "I can't help you if you don't tell me what's troubling you."

"Aren't you sad that you're leaving?" Alice said, still clutching her.

"Yes, I am." Leslie held Alice's shoulders and looked her in the eyes. "If you must know, I had myself a good, long cry in the shower this morning."

Alice reached for the box of tissues on the counter. "I must be losing my mind."

"Why? For getting emotional? You're allowed. Is it that time of the month?"

"I'm not usually an emotional person, Les," Alice said. "I really feel sad that I won't see you every day anymore. You've really become my closest friend over this last year."

"I feel the same way, Alice. I've enjoyed earning my own money and the independence of working here, but your friendship has been the best thing to come out of this. I don't want to lose it because I'm leaving. We'll still be friends, won't we?"

Adrift in the sweet vulnerability in Leslie's eyes, Alice kissed her on the lips, a lingering kiss that electrified her from her hair follicles to the tips of her toenails.

Surprisingly, Leslie didn't recoil. When Alice finally pulled away, Leslie opened her eyes and calmly asked, "What was that all about?"

Alice scratched at the back of her head in embarrassment. "Um, I don't know. I'm sorry. I mean, I'm not that way, you know, like Kathy, but I don't know. I just wanted to." Her hand trembled as she lifted it from the counter.

Leslie blotted Alice's lipstick off her lips with a tissue. "I suppose that's a stupid question to ask someone who's just kissed you."

"I'm sorry, Leslie. I don't know what else to say, except that it won't happen again."

Leslie reached into her purse and pulled out her compact. She stared straight ahead and powdered her nose in the mirror in an almost robotic fashion.

"Leslie?" Alice said, picking at her fingernails. "Say something."

Leslie looked at her through the mirror's reflection. *"I'm afraid to."*

"I promise I'll never do that again," Alice said with increasing agitation.

"That's not what I'm afraid of," she said, rummaging through her purse.

"Then what?"

"I liked it," she whispered.

"Leslie," Alice whispered back and kissed her again. Her emotions tumbled down in an avalanche of passion. What the hell was happening? She was kissing another woman, and she was enjoying it. She'd heard this sort of thing went on at swingers' parties. She'd even seen it at Studio 54 on a visit once with friends in New York City. As mod and forward-thinking as she'd considered herself, she'd never thought of playing an active part in the sexual revolution, and certainly not this part.

"We better get back to the office. It's almost five," Leslie said. She ran her fingers through her hair to fluff it up. *"I'm really looking forward to Finnegan's shepherd's pie. I've heard so much about it."*

Alice narrowed her eyes. Shepherd's pie? Was she serious? *"Uh, yeah, I had it once. It's delicious."*

Leslie's eyes lit up as she opened the door. *"Great."*

❖

As their evening of fond farewells with coworkers at Finnegan's was winding down, Alice's head pounded, and it wasn't from the tequila shots. Leslie had drunk more mai tais than her conservative constitution could handle, and they had produced the curious side effect of an unassuming, irresistible sex appeal. As she laughed *with some of the salesmen at the bar, her body swayed to the sassy rhythm of "You Sexy Thing."*

Alice couldn't take her eyes off her.

"Whoa, Leslie, if we knew you were this much of a hot tamale, we wouldn't have let you quit," Steve Briller said. "Right, Engle?"

Mr. Engle smiled and raised his Jack Daniels on the rocks. "Leslie, you're the woman I've been looking for my whole life. Marry me."

"Thank you, Mr. Engle, but I'm already attached." She waved her bejeweled ring finger at them.

"C'mon, Alice," Mr. Engle said. "Help me drown my sorrows in another shot."

She moved closer to the group. "No, thanks, Mr. Engle. I've reached my limit for the night." She found something so provocative about Leslie's delicate fingers as they cradled her cocktail.

"Here's my friend," Leslie slurred. She threw her arm around Alice's shoulder and jerked her close, nearly smashing their heads together.

The pub's loud music rang in Alice's ears as the shine on Leslie's lips whenever she licked them between sips of her drink had driven all rational thought from her brain. She worked free from Leslie's grip and rushed off to the ladies' room.

As she dabbed her face with a damp paper towel, her appearance unnerved her. She knew the face, but she didn't recognize the woman staring back at her. She sucked in deep breaths, trying to calm her racing heart.

"There you are," Leslie said as she peeked around the open door. "Are you okay?"

"Fine. Are you?" Alice tossed out the paper towel and regrouped.

"I'm spectacular," she slurred with conviction. "But I think it's time to go. The fellas are trying to get me to dump my husband."

Alice shook her head. "What comes after that? Engle dancing on the bar in his boxer shorts?"

"Heavens, I hope not." Leslie giggled as she held up the wall.

"Okay, Tiger, let's say our good-byes and get you home." She hooked her arm under Leslie's for support and led her out of the ladies' room.

Alice trudged alongside Leslie through the parking lot kicking stones as they headed to their cars. All evening, she'd managed to fend off vivid flashbacks from their moment in Engle's washroom earlier in the day, but at that hour, the will of the lonely was about as stable as gas prices during the '73 oil embargo. What had Leslie thought about it? Had she thought about it at all since? Through a haze of Miller High Life, Alice considered that maybe what had occurred between them meant nothing more to Leslie than an affectionate exchange between friends. She'd certainly been acting that way all night.

"I had such a good time tonight," Leslie said when they stopped at her car. "We should've done this with the crew more often." She fanned herself through the humid July-night air.

"I'm sure we could do this again some Friday night. I won't have to twist any of their arms to join us."

Leslie hiccupped and let out a sigh. "I have more fun with you than anybody, Alice."

"Me, too," she replied instantly.

They stared at each other for an endless moment.

"Listen, about what happened earlier..." Alice said.

Leslie waved her off. "Don't worry about that. It was nothing."

It didn't feel like nothing, but then Alice should've been grateful for the pass Leslie was presenting her.

"I just feel a little silly. And I want to make sure we're okay."

"Of course we are," Leslie said, swaying a bit. "Outta sight, sister," she added with a chuckle.

"Hey, you don't seem ready to drive home yet."

"I don't? How come?"

"Close your eyes and stand on one foot."

Leslie snorted with laughter. "Okay. I can do that." She made the attempt and staggered into the side of her car.

Alice led her by the elbow. "We're going down the street to the diner for some coffee. C'mon. Let's take my car."

"You don't have to go through all this trouble on my account. It's so late."

"It's nine forty-five," Alice said, checking her watch as she led Leslie to the passenger side of her car.

"You're a sport," Leslie said as she settled into the bench seat in Alice's Ford Galaxy. "I can't thank you enough."

As Alice turned the key in the ignition, Leslie hooked her arm around Alice's neck and pulled her into a kiss on the mouth—not as deep as O'Neal and MacGraw in Love Story, *but delayed enough and moist enough to destroy any room for interpretation.*

Alice tasted Leslie's gloss on her lips. "If you keep thanking me like that, you're going to get us arrested." She checked her rearview mirror for coworkers or anyone else who might have been wandering out of Finnegan's.

"I'm sorry," Leslie said through a hiccup. "I think I've had too many mai tais."

"I think so, too. What do you say we get some black coffee in you?"

"If you insist."

Alice flung her arm on the seat behind Leslie as she backed out of the parking space. Driving to the diner, she fought to stop gawking at Leslie, whose eyes sparkled in the flash of each passing streetlight. She was happy Leslie was in no condition to drive yet. Despite a dizzying evening filled with alternating flares of panic, confusion, and shamefully wonderful lust, she didn't want the night to end. The thought of Monday morning and every other weekday morning without Leslie crushed her.

She pulled into the diner parking lot, threw the gearshift into park, and slapped her thighs. "Two cups of black coffee coming right up."

"Can we throw some Bailey's in it?" Leslie asked as she climbed out of the car.

"I like your style." Alice smiled at her.

"I like yours, too," Leslie said. "I want a Denver omelet."

Leslie rested her head on Alice's shoulder as they walked through the parking lot toward the diner's entrance. Alice made a secret, solemn vow then that what she'd done earlier that day in Engle's washroom would never happen again.

But it did.

August 1977

Alice had been crawling out of her skin all week, a consequence, she'd assumed, of Leslie's absence in the office after working together for ten months. Finally, Friday had arrived, and thank Hera, it was a crochet Friday. Alice had deliberately taken her time getting ready, knowing Leslie would be as punctual as a tax bill and would have to come in and wait.

As Leslie sat on the edge of Alice's bed filing her fingernails, Alice scurried around her bedroom collecting the finishing touches—a spritz of perfume, a dab of hand lotion.

"I'm sorry for making you wait," she said. "I should've called you when Engle asked me to stay late. I had to make some phone calls for him about a shady claim."

"I'm surprised," Leslie said. "Doesn't he always try to cut out early on Fridays?"

"Why do you think he asked me to make the calls?"

"Typical," Leslie said.

"You want a glass of wine?" Alice asked as she put on her earrings.

"I'll just have a sip of yours. I'm sure we'll be having cocktails at Kathy's."

"I'm sure we will, too." Alice handed her the glass of merlot resting on her dresser.

Leslie swirled the wine over her tongue before swallowing it. "I'm actually glad you're the one running behind. I hate being late, that awful look hosts always give when you finally show up. Tonight I can blame it on you."

"Oh, I see how you operate," Alice said and dropped two pairs of sandals on the floor. "Which ones?"

"They're both nice. Which ones are more comfortable?"

"Ah, you're learning. Comfort over sex appeal."

Leslie perked up like the student who always had the right answer. "Misogynistic sandals are as big of a threat to the feminist movement as constricting panty hose."

"Your newfound social awareness is impressive," Alice said. "The ones with the rubies are more comfortable." She slipped her feet into them and tossed the other pair into her closet.

"Perfect. Those are also the sexy ones."

"Hey, you said you just wanted a sip. It's almost gone."

Leslie leapt up from the bed as Alice approached her. "I'm sorry. It's so smooth, it went down too easy."

"I think we have time for another," Alice said as she slipped the glass from Leslie's hand.

She gazed at her, surprised by the intensity in Leslie's eyes. She leaned in and tasted the peppery berry in the wine on Leslie's lips. Reaching behind, she placed the empty wineglass on her dresser and swept Leslie up in her arms.

They kissed slowly, as though experiencing an exotic food for the first time, savoring the new flavors and sensations. Alice slid her hands down Leslie's waist, trying to pull her closer, but their bodies already hadn't an inch between them. The scent of Leslie's skin, the warmth of her breath consumed Alice as they kissed long and hard, apprehending like a wild mustang their first real moment alone. As Alice shuffled her toward the bed, the only thing that could've broken the spell was the sudden ringing of the telephone.

"Kathy," she said. "Ah shit, I forgot to call her." She scrambled over the bed for the phone on her nightstand. Amid profuse apologies, she assured her they were on their way.

Leslie smoothed down her peasant blouse and gingham shorts, flushed and embarrassed.

They hurried out of the house without a word, but on the ride over to Kathy's, Alice fidgeted in the passenger seat as the silence grew oppressive. "We're really late," she said, clutching the bottle of wine in her lap to keep her hands still.

"I know, but the girls will understand. You couldn't help having to work overtime." She sat straight up to the steering wheel, her eyes glued to the road.

Is that why Leslie thought she was jittery? How could she be so calm right now when it was only Kathy's phone call that had kept them from landing on her bed and then who knew what from there? She wanted Leslie to say something, to at least acknowledge what they'd done in Engle's washroom, in the parking lot, and then earlier in her bedroom, but obviously, something stopped her. Alice was afraid to broach the subject since she wasn't sure what it all meant.

All she knew was that she was thinking about Leslie a lot. Frequently. Constantly.

❖

Cupping a gift-wrapped African violet in her hand, Alice marched like a soldier from the parking garage, through the hospital's main entrance, up the elevator, and down the hall toward Leslie's unit. But as she approached the doors to the ICU, she slowed her pace nearly to a shuffle. In the past week, she'd thought of Leslie again as frequently and with almost as much fervor as she had when she'd first fallen in love with her. But why? Had she been sucked into a whirlwind of mere nostalgia, or had the fire in her heart for Leslie never truly burned out? Regardless of which scenario, was this really a road she'd want to walk down again? Fear assailed her, stopping her in the hall only yards from the doors that could reopen every wound she'd thought Maureen had healed in her decades ago.

"Alice," Rebecca said as she came up behind her. "Perfect timing. I just ran to get my mom a cup of coffee from the cafeteria. It's better than what the kitchen delivers."

Without a word, Alice looked down at the straw sticking out through the lid of the Green Mountain Coffee cup.

"She has some issues with fine motor skills," Rebecca said in response to Alice's expression.

"Is she paralyzed?"

"No, but her left side was affected. She's going to need physical and occupational therapy to get her back into shape. They want her to use a straw until her hand is stronger."

Alice felt like sliding down the wall and bawling on the linoleum.

"Don't look like that, Alice," Rebecca said with a smile. "She's awake and she's talking and, best of all, she's leaving here."

"When?"

"The doc said the sooner they discharge her and get her into a rehab facility, the better her chances for a full recovery. We're just waiting for the word."

Alice stood there, crinkling the wrapper on the plant.

"Alice, don't you want to see her?"

"Yes." Alice relaxed into a cautious smile. "Yes, of course."

"Let's go."

Alice followed Rebecca single-file through the doors, her heart grooving wildly in her breast, her mouth puckering with dryness. They rounded the corner into Leslie's room, Rebecca first, Alice peeking over her shoulder.

"Mom, I got your coffee," Rebecca said.

Leslie opened her eyes, unaware of Alice standing in the background.

"Thanks, babe," Leslie said softly and clicked the button to raise the back of her bed. That was when their eyes met.

"Alice," she whispered.

"Hey, Bella," Alice said, stepping around Rebecca. Without contemplating the consequences, she bent over and kissed Leslie on her cheek.

A frail giggle made its way out. "Hiya, Betty."

Alice clutched her hand and sat in the chair by her bed. Leslie attempted to sit up but couldn't manage it.

"Let me help you, Mom." Rebecca and Alice helped her reposition herself higher in the bed.

"Listen, if now isn't a good time or you need to rest, I'll just…"

"Alice, stay," Leslie said, her voice raspy. "I'm just a little pooped from physical therapy. They've already started with my arm and leg, and I haven't even gotten out of bed yet. Can you believe it?"

"It won't be so bad once you've built up your strength," Rebecca said.

Alice and Leslie stared at each other like identical twins who hadn't known of each other's existence until that moment.

"Uh, Jake, honey," Rebecca said. "Let's go down to the cafeteria for some ice cream."

"Okay." He stood up, still focused on playing a game on his tablet. He kissed Leslie on the way out.

"Thank you, baby," Leslie said.

"He's a doll," Alice said.

"Thanks. All three of them are. I got lucky with my kids and grandkids."

"I'm sure luck had something to do with it, but you raised your kids right, Leslie. It's clear to see how much they adore you."

Leslie offered a humble smile. "It was so nice of you to come down from Boston, Alice. Rebecca said you've been here every day since you arrived."

"I had to make sure one of my sisters was okay, Bella." She raised the empowerment fist playfully. "I'm so glad you are."

"I feel like I've been run over by a bus a few dozen times, but I'm grateful it isn't worse."

"Someday you'll have to explain to me how you could've been in a stroke-induced coma and still come out looking beautiful."

Leslie waved off the compliment. "Even after three days in a coma, I can't believe that. But thank you."

Leslie's smile was springtime to Alice's dormant heart. Everything inside her was coming alive, and it terrified her.

"So now that you know what I've been up to," Leslie said, "let me hear about you."

"There's not a heck of a lot to tell. I'm retired, turned the big seven-oh last year, and I've been getting in some traveling here and there."

"How is…oh, forgive me. I forget your partner's name."

"Maureen. She passed last year. She had MS."

"I'm sorry to hear that."

"As much as I miss her, it's awful watching someone you love suffer like that and not being able to do a thing for them. The powerlessness was unbearable."

"I can't even imagine."

Alice nodded in appreciation. "Have I mentioned how relieved I am that you woke up?"

Leslie smiled. "Have I mentioned how surprised I was to see you standing behind my daughter?"

"I bet for a minute you thought you were having another stroke."

Leslie laughed herself into a brief coughing fit. "Oh, Alice. Nobody's ever made me laugh like you do."

Nobody's ever made me feel like you do was on the tip of Alice's tongue, but luckily, she managed to stop it from leaping out into the room.

"Well, I should let you get some rest before your next round of therapy. It says on the board they're coming in at three."

"How much longer are you in Connecticut?"

"I haven't thought about it. My sister and brother-in-law don't seem to mind me staying with them. Maybe I'll hang around there until I wear out my welcome."

"Please stop by again before you go home."

"I think I'll have to. If I hang around their house all day, they're going to cut off my free accommodations by the shore."

"Thank you for coming," Leslie said.

"Any time."

When Alice bent down to hug her, Leslie lifted her left arm and gave her a feeble squeeze, her arm trembling from the effort. "Take it easy, Bella." She stopped and turned at the door. "By the way, did it affect your long-term memory?"

Leslie frowned. "A little bit here and there. Why?"

"Do you remember what we..." She waved her index finger between the two of them.

Leslie closed her eyes as though sniffing a single fragrant rose. "A stroke's got nothing on what we had."

"You get better, friend," Alice said. "I'll be in touch."

Alice grinned all the way to the elevator, her heart a garden of secret hope. She took a deep breath and hoped the feeling would pass. Quickly.

CHAPTER EIGHT

Alice woke early the next morning, not from the anxiety that had been her alarm clock for more than a week, but from pure excitement. Leslie was moving to the rehab facility, and that meant she was one step closer to recovery, to being herself again—whoever that was. Alice had to admit that after all these years she was aching to find out. And what about after her recovery? Again she shut down the thought before it grew wings and jetted her off to a region that she didn't want to explore. Now was the time to be there for Leslie in friendship, and in the spirit of sisterhood, she vowed to leave it at that.

After a quick shower, she went downstairs and made a cup of coffee with the Keurig, imagining herself as Leslie's one-woman therapeutic cheering squad as she sipped.

"Hey, you." Mary Ellen came in from the patio with her coffee cup and breakfast dish. "Don't tell me you're off to the hospital already. It's not even nine o'clock."

"Not the hospital, the rehab. I'm going there later for moral support."

Mary Ellen narrowed her eyes as she rinsed her dishes at the island sink. "Somebody's got a little crush. You gonna carry her schoolbooks for her, too?"

"Physical therapy is grueling. She needs all the support she can get to stay motivated. Besides, with me there, her kids don't feel so pressured to be there 'round the clock."

Mary Ellen eyed her with suspicion. "Well, gee, isn't that thoughtful of you."

"I'm a very thoughtful person," Alice said and smiled into her coffee mug.

"Hey, are you going to be around for dinner tonight? I figured we could order Thai or something."

"Uh, I'm not sure. I was going to see what Leslie was doing tonight. You know, it's Friday."

"The woman's in a convalescent home. I'm pretty sure a night on the town is not on her agenda."

"It's not a convalescent home. It's a rehab facility, one from which she'll be leaving in no time. I just want to make sure she's not alone in case her kids can't come by."

"So you're just going to hang around there all day and night? Make sure nobody mistakenly admits you."

"Mare," Alice said, studying her. "Are you upset about something?"

"No," she said, hesitating. "Well, yes, sort of. You've been here a week, and we haven't done anything together. You're always off visiting Leslie. I hate to sound selfish, but don't you want to spend any quality time with me?"

"Of course I do," Alice said, hoping she wasn't going to drag out this conversation for too long. "Let me see how today goes. It's her first full day there. She may be so tired tonight, she won't want any company."

"Sister, dear, who wouldn't want your company?"

Alice smiled and hugged Mary Ellen tight. "Thanks for understanding. I'll make it up to you, I promise."

"You better."

Mary Ellen gave her a firm whack on her butt before Alice gathered her small purse and keys and headed out the door.

❖

Alice slipped her arms into the sleeves of the light hooded jacket she'd had around her shoulders in the air-conditioned physical-therapy room. She'd been sitting there shivering for nearly thirty minutes watching the young redheaded PT drill Leslie through a battery of exercises for the mild hemiplegia in her shoulder and arm.

Leslie looked over as Alice rubbed the back of her arms to generate body heat. After wiping her brow with her forearm, she flipped Alice the bird.

Alice laughed and called out, "I'm sorry, but it's freezing in here."

"That's it, keep rubbing salt in my wounds," Leslie said, panting.

"Okay, Mrs. O'Mara," her PT said. "You're done with your top half for the day. Great job. We'll work your leg this afternoon."

"Thank you, honey," Leslie replied. "I feel better already. I think I'm ready to be discharged." She wiped her face with a hand towel, and her therapist helped her up off the exercise mat and into her wheelchair.

Her therapist smiled. "Not quite yet, but you're getting there."

"You must be starving after that workout," Alice said. "How about some lunch?"

"Sure. Where to? A seafood meal with an ocean view?"

"How about the cafeteria?" Alice said, smiling at the PT. She turned Leslie's wheelchair around, and they headed down the hall.

"Alice, this is so nice of you to come here and spend time with me. But I'm sure you have other less-depressing places you can be."

"And miss the chance to chauffeur you around in this bitchin' set of wheels?"

"Well, it'll be wonderful to have lunch with you again, even if it is at a convalescent home."

"Don't call it that. It sounds so permanent. It's a rehabilitation facility. You'll be leaving soon. You haven't moved in."

"Whatever," Leslie said. "Do you remember when we used to have lunch together every day at work?"

They chose a table near a large window overlooking a marsh. The sun glistened on an active osprey nest rising out in the middle of swaying grass and cattails.

"I remember very well." Alice helped Leslie transfer from her wheelchair into her seat. "They were some of the best days of my life."

"Mine, too," Leslie said, her blue eyes as mesmerizing as ever. Alice let her eyes dally on Leslie's for a moment. "So, uh, what would you like to eat?"

"Surprise me."

Alice raised an eyebrow and strolled to the counter. Surprise me, she said. The whole last week and a half had been one mind-blowing surprise after another, beginning with Rebecca's Facebook message that the love of her life had been in a coma. Now two weeks later, they were together again, having lunch—and it almost felt like no time had passed at all. Almost.

She browsed the containers of the featured lunch entrees in the glass case, none of which looked appealing, and opted for a couple of slices of pizza and two side salads.

As she approached the table, she noticed Leslie's profile as she gazed out the window at the summer landscape. She was breathtaking—a silent portrait of beauty and grace. What she would've given to capture that exact moment on film to keep forever.

"Pizza," Leslie said. "This should be interesting."

"Tell me about it," Alice said. "I still have several items left on my bucket list, but nursing-home fish sticks is not one of them."

Leslie wrinkled her nose. "That explains what I was smelling."

They grimaced at each other playfully.

"Is pizza okay?" Alice asked, suddenly panicked. "Can you eat it? I'm sorry. I'll get you something else."

"No, no, it's fine. I need the practice." She smiled, lifted the square piece of pizza with her left hand, and nibbled the corner.

"It's no Zampano's, but it's not bad," Alice said.

"I heard they make delicious pizza."

"What do you mean, you heard? You've had it," Alice said. "That night I ordered pizza before we were supposed to go to Dolores's."

"Alice, I'm sixty-nine years old. Even if I hadn't just had a stroke, how would I remember pizza from forty years ago?"

A blush scorched Alice's cheeks. Maybe bringing that up hadn't been the smartest idea.

Leslie stared at her expectantly.

"Well, let me put it this way," Alice said. "The most memorable part of the evening wasn't the pizza."

Alice's blush was apparently contagious, infecting Leslie as she furrowed her brow, clearly trying to recall the night.

"Oh, my," she said after a moment. "I think I remember."

August 1977

Alice paced by her kitchen window, checking every few seconds for Leslie's car. Her stomach flipped like a cheerleader's waiting for the captain of the football team to take her to the prom. Why did Leslie make her feel this way? It didn't make sense. No woman had ever affected her like this. On the other hand, no man ever had either. Whatever was going on with her, she'd resolved to get to the bottom of it with Leslie that night.

"Thanks for coming over early."

"It's my pleasure," Leslie said. "With the kids at my mother's and Bill bowling, it's the one night I can get out of the house without having to do a million things first."

"Sit down and help yourself. I ordered half pepperoni and half mushroom."

"Two of my favorites." Leslie opened the pizza box and inhaled the aroma.

Alice filled their glasses with Tab soda and paced around the kitchen, gathering grated cheese, napkins, and red-pepper flakes.

"Hey, aren't you going to sit down and eat?" Leslie pulled out a slice of pepperoni, folded it, and bit off a large chunk.

"Yeah, uh, in a minute." Alice hovered behind Leslie's chair. "Listen, Les. I wanted to talk to you about something, something that's been weighing on my mind."

"Well, okay," Leslie said, twisting her body from side to side to find Alice. "Come sit down and talk." She dabbed her lips with a napkin and regarded Alice with the attentiveness of a psychoanalyst.

Alice sat, staring at Leslie. She'd had this conversation in her head for several days, but now the words abandoned her like a partner in crime fleeing as the authorities closed in.

"I was wondering..." Her throat suddenly dry and scratchy, she paused for a sip of soda. *"I mean, I want to know what you..."*

Leslie appeared to be anticipating every syllable. *"What I what?"*

"I was wondering if...if...you think I should paint in here." Alice shoved a slice of mushroom pizza into her mouth in defeat.

Leslie inspected the entire kitchen. *"I like the mustard yellow. It matches the avocado-green appliances so nicely."*

"Hmm, it does, doesn't it?"

"You could try some new curtains. Whenever I need a change but don't want to spend a lot of money, that's what I do."

"And that's what does it for you?" Alice said dryly.

"Usually." Leslie tore apart two slices of mushroom. *"Is something else bothering you?"*

Alice shrugged as she nibbled the crust of her pizza, disappointed she hadn't had the courage to start the conversation she'd wanted so badly to have with Leslie. Maybe the solution was to taper off their friendship—stop calling her so often, showing up at the field when Billy had a baseball game, and joining her family for holidays.

"I think I know what the problem is." Leslie got up and started clearing the table. *"You need a man in your life. You're too young for this spinster routine."*

"Spinster? Now wait a minute," Alice said. *"Why is a single man my age called a bachelor and applauded for his independence? Do you know how many times I've seen those cats get slapped on the back and congratulated for avoiding the 'old ball and chain' for so long?"*

Leslie gave her the high eyebrow. *"How many times?"*

"Well, twice," she said, sheepish at first. *"But that's twice more than I've heard it said to a woman."*

"Point taken," Leslie said. *"But I still think having someone to go out with on the weekends would lift your spirits, someone other than friends."*

"Hey, don't undervalue the power of friends to lift your spirits." Alice shuffled around Leslie as she put away the condiments and sponged off the table.

"I would never," Leslie said with a smile. "I've come to understand it better than ever over the last several months."

When Alice turned back from the sink, she bumped into Leslie. Their eyes locked, and they hesitated for a long, agonizing moment before their lips met. What was it about Leslie that drew her like a magnet to steel? For that matter, what was it about her that seemed to have the same effect on Leslie? Alice grasped her around the waist and towed her along until she backed up to the counter. When Leslie cupped her face in her hands and kissed her passionately, Alice nearly crumbled into a heap on the floor.

Slowly they made their way into the living room and onto Alice's couch, where they grew increasingly tangled up and sweaty. Leslie's bag of crochet hooks, patterns, and yarn lay nearby on a chair. So enthralled in making out, they didn't check the clock until they were already a half hour late.

"Leslie, it's seven thirty," Alice finally whispered.

"Oh, God." She sprang up from under Alice. "We're so late. How are we going to explain it?"

"I'm surprised Dolores hasn't called. Don't worry. We'll come up with something," Alice sat up and straightened her twisted bell-bottom jeans. "I got it. You had to wait for your husband to get home from work."

Just then Alice's phone rang. She dashed into the kitchen and answered it, stretching the cord as she walked to the living room and signaled to Leslie.

"Sorry, Dolores. I meant to call. Leslie and I won't be able to make it tonight. I'm not feeling well, and she called earlier to let me know she couldn't find a sitter."

Leslie looked at Alice in surprise.

"Okay, yes, thank you. We'll see you ladies here in two weeks." Alice replaced the receiver and sauntered back to the couch next to Leslie. "I'm sorry. I don't know what made me say that."

Leslie fought a smile like a sinner in church. "I'm glad you did." She traced the curve of Alice's jaw with her fingertips. "This is so strange. It feels like I'm in a dream when I'm alone with you."

"The most amazing dream," Alice whispered. She stroked the ends of Leslie's hair as though Leslie were some priceless museum piece she'd been forbidden to touch. "I'd always known women could be close with their girlfriends, but not this close."

Leslie's smoky blue eyes focused on something across the room as they seemed to puzzle out their situation. "Have you ever been this close to a friend before?"

Alice shook her head.

"Me either." She tightened her grip on Alice's hand.

Alice shut her eyes and closed Leslie's hand between both of hers, relieved to hear her finally acknowledge that something was simmering between them.

"I love kissing you," Leslie whispered as though someone might be listening.

Alice's eyes popped open. "I do, too," she whispered back. "I don't know why, but it was never like this with my husband, or anyone else, now that I think of it."

She wondered if Leslie had thought about her as often as she had when they weren't together. But a profound sense of caution held back that confession.

Leslie rested her head against Alice's. "I'm so confused."

"I am, too," Alice said. She lifted Leslie's chin, and they kissed slowly for a while.

"Alice, I..." Leslie looked down.

"Tell me." Alice stroked her hair for reassurance.

"I've never felt like this with Bill either, not in fourteen years with him. I don't understand it because I love him. He's a good husband." She bent forward, elbows pressing into her thighs, and covered her face with her hands. "I'm so ashamed to admit that."

Alice patted her on the back, struggling to find a way to comfort her as her heart hemorrhaged at Leslie's confession. After a moment, she pried Leslie's hands away from her face. "Don't feel ashamed, Leslie. We're friends. I'd never tell anyone."

"I know you wouldn't. It makes me feel awful to hear myself say it out loud."

Alice inhaled as a slow panic brewed in her. "We should stop doing this, whatever it is. I don't know what we were thinking."

Leslie wiped the tears from her cheeks. They sat as still as pet rocks for what seemed like forever.

"Kiss me one more time," Leslie whispered.

The sibilance in the word kiss broke the silence, startling Alice. She searched Leslie's glassy, fretful eyes for a moment, fighting the energy drawing her to Leslie's lips. "What's happening with us?"

"I don't know." Leslie closed her eyes and pulled Alice's head toward her.

Feeling like it would be the last time she'd ever see Leslie, Alice slid her hand up Leslie's thigh, her skin hot and damp. Leslie let out a soft moan of surrender. As she unzipped Leslie's cut-off denim shorts, the scene was so surreal, she felt like a voyeur.

"I'm falling in love with you," she breathed in Leslie's ear.

"Don't say that, Alice," Leslie whispered as she helped Alice lower her shorts over her hips.

"I'm sorry," she said and bit Leslie's earlobe.

Leslie moaned louder as she squirmed beneath Alice. The taste of her tanned skin grew sweeter the lower Alice journeyed with her mouth.

They moved together in a fluid motion, exploring each other like their bodies were rare, precious finds.

After they made love, they lay in each other's arms on the couch in silence. What could either of them possibly say to lessen the seriousness of what they'd done? Alice's arm had gone numb under Leslie, but shame had her paralyzed anyway. This was all her fault. Why had she ever kissed her in the first place? People had urges and impulses all the time that they never acted on. Why had she? She couldn't bear to think what Leslie was feeling at the moment.

Finally, she said the only two words she could string together. "I'm sorry."

Leslie looked up at her. "What are you apologizing for? I should've stopped you."

"I shouldn't have touched you."

Leslie got up on her elbow. "Alice, I wanted you to. I've never been touched like that before, or that turned on."

"Well, neither have I," Alice said, almost insulted. She sprang up and scrambled to get her jeans on. "I've never felt like this for anyone before, much less a woman. And I certainly haven't done anything like this." She tossed Leslie's clothes at her.

"Me either," Leslie said. "My husband is the only other person I've been with. I never even played doctor when I was a kid."

Alice rolled her eyes. "If only that's all this was."

"We can't be the first girlfriends who've done this," Leslie said as she dressed, mirroring Alice's frenetic motions.

"No, we're not, but they're called lesbians."

"Lesbians?" Leslie's face contorted like a tarantula was crawling up her leg. "We can't be lesbians. We were both married. I'm still married, happily, I thought. Bill and I don't have any problems. I mean, none more serious than the average couple."

Alice glared at her. "You're not making me feel any better about this."

"Oh, God, did I just commit adultery? My husband—what if he finds out?"

"Hey, hey, calm down. He's not going to find out," she said to reassure them both. "It won't happen again."

"It won't? We let it this time."

"Well, maybe we've been spending too much time together."

"You're not saying we can't be friends anymore?"

"No, no," Alice stammered, surprised that was Leslie's main concern at the moment. "We'll just have to, you know, not skip crocheting anymore."

"Right," Leslie said. "That was a mistake."

Alice looked at the clock on the wall. "You better get going. Crocheting probably broke up about fifteen minutes ago."

"Crap, you're right. Bill's not home yet, but I want to be home before him, so it won't look suspicious."

"Leslie, you have to relax. If you go home all flipped out, then it will look suspicious."

"You're right, you're right." She absently gathered her crochet bag and her purse. "Where are my keys?"

"Les, please don't panic," Alice said as she felt her own panic rising.

"That's easy for you to say," Leslie said, dragging her fingers through her wild hair.

"No, it isn't," Alice said. "I just don't know what else to say right now."

"We'll make believe this never happened. That's simple enough." Leslie's eyes were dilated with fear as she ruffled through her purse for her car keys.

"Sure, sure, whatever you want," Alice said helplessly as she followed her to the door.

With her hand on the doorknob, Leslie whirled around with tears in her eyes. "Please don't say anything."

"I promise, Leslie. I don't want anyone to find out about this either."

Alice leaned toward her to kiss her good-bye, but Leslie disappeared out the door. Resting her head against the closed door, Alice almost heard the crack in her heart at the rejection.

After a moment, Leslie barged back inside. "I don't think I can pretend this never happened." She kissed Alice with a slow burn that sealed that night in Alice's memory forever.

Alice peered through the chintz curtains as Leslie backed her station wagon out of the driveway. Her eyes pooled. Although her body still trembled and her mind whirled from their night together, the ache in her heart watching Leslie drive away troubled her the most. She stood at the window long after Leslie's car had vanished down the road.

❖

When Alice finished sharing her recollection of that night, Leslie had turned to her from the cafeteria window, melancholy eclipsing the sun filtering in on her face. "God, Alice, I haven't thought about that for years."

"Neither had I," Alice said. "It's amazing what the mind is capable of when it needs to protect the heart."

"After we broke up, I used to pray to God to help me understand why you came into my life if I was only meant to lose you."

"What was His reply?"

Leslie smirked at Alice's irreverence.

"Rebecca and I were talking the other day," Alice said. "She was grilling me about you. She even asked if you and I were ever involved."

"Did you tell her?"

"No," Alice said, mildly offended. "But she's a lesbian. Why haven't you ever mentioned it to her?"

"That I had an affair while I was married to her father?"

"That's not exactly the angle I'd use first, but I can appreciate your concern. She said she wishes you two were as close as you were when she was younger."

"I know what she means," Leslie said, wistful. "I wish that, too, but where do I start when I've had to conceal this part of me for so long? Secrets are walls meant to keep others out."

Alice fought to conceal her growing frustration. All these years later and Leslie still felt the need to hide. She was single and her own daughter was a lesbian. How much better could her coming-out circumstances possibly have been?

She checked her wristwatch. "I should get going now. I have to meet my sister."

"All right," Leslie said, her voice flavored with disappointment. "Well, thanks again for coming. This was nice."

Alice wheeled Leslie back to her room, steering the conversation away from any other dangerous recollections. And leaving without any future promises.

CHAPTER NINE

Once she got back from the rehab facility, Alice spent what was left of the afternoon in a chaise lounge on Mary Ellen's patio in a malaise of summer heat and disappointment. It was her own fault, really. She'd been an old fool for even allowing the slightest germ of emotion for Leslie to form beyond friendship. What's more, Maureen had only been gone a year, but Alice had been directing all of her energy toward Leslie.

"Alice?" Mary Ellen called as she stepped out onto the patio. "There you are. Are you coming out with Dave and me tonight?"

"Where are you going?" she mumbled from under the sun hat resting on her face.

"We decided to try this new place in the center of Branford. Dave likes the local beers."

"Didn't you say this morning you were ordering in?"

"Well, since we're going to play drag-queen bingo tomorrow night at the Annex Club, we thought we'd go out for dinner tonight."

Alice pulled her hat off her face. "Did I hear you right?"

Mary Ellen chuckled. "It's a fund-raiser for the Gay Men's Chorus. The Birnbaums took us a few months ago. It's a riot—a bit raunchy but fun."

"And Dave goes?"

"They serve alcohol."

"Let me think about tonight," Alice said, replacing her hat on her face.

Mary Ellen huffed. "By all means, take your time. What do I care that all I am to you is a sunny patio between visits with Leslie. Apparently, I'm running a flophouse for wayward widows with a Vitamin D deficiency."

Alice stifled a laugh. "You're an amazing sister and human being."

"Don't fall asleep. We're leaving at six."

"Roger that." Alice turned over on her side and wanted to finish the memory she'd begun exploring earlier at lunch with Leslie.

August 1977

Waking early the morning after she and Leslie had made love, Alice threw off the covers but lay in bed listening to the birds chirping as the sky lightened. She'd never really fallen into a sound sleep the night before anyway—too many thoughts crowding her mind, or was "worries" the more appropriate word?

She wanted, more than anything, to be with Leslie.

She wished Leslie's son Billy had a baseball game so she could show up and park herself on the bleachers next to Leslie like nothing was different between them. Maybe she should call her up later in the afternoon and discuss whether they would watch Starsky and Hutch *or* The Mary Tyler Moore Show *like they'd sometimes done on Saturdays.*

What if Leslie didn't answer the phone? What if she told her to stop calling? Alice's skin crawled as all the horrific possibilities swarmed her imagination. She hastened out of bed and gathered her laundry from the hamper. Physical activity was the only thing to keep her from totally losing her mind. As badly as she wanted to call Leslie, she concluded that if they were to talk, Leslie should be the one to call.

That night, after a long day of waiting for a phone call that never came, Alice met her cousin, Phyllis, for dinner before going to the movies to see Annie Hall. *At the Greek diner across from the theater, Alice dug tracks into her mashed potatoes with her fork.*

Phyllis pushed a strand of wiry, graying hair that escaped her tortoise-shell hair clip behind her ear as she broke off another piece of chicken pot pie with her fork. "Why did you order that big meal if you weren't hungry?" She jabbed her fork into a mound of cooked carrots on Alice's plate.

"I didn't know I wasn't hungry until I started eating." Alice dabbed her mouth with her napkin and leaned back in the booth.

"What's the matter?" Phyllis asked.

"Nothing. Everything." Alice looked out the window into the diner parking lot.

"Everything all right at work?"

Alice nodded.

"Man troubles?"

"Not even close."

"Are you gonna give me a hint?"

"I'd rather not," Alice said. "There's nothing you can do anyway."

"That's true with most problems, but the payoff comes with getting it off your chest."

"This is big, Phyllis." Alice's full attention finally made its way back to the table. "The kind of problem people stop talking to you over."

"Really?" Phyllis seemed intrigued. "Have you stolen Carter's Little Liver Pills? Joined Patty Hearst in the Symbionese Liberation Army?"

Alice chuckled. "Phyllis, I'm serious."

"What then? I've known you since you were born, babysat you till you were twelve. You couldn't do anything bad enough for me to stop talking to you."

"I think I'm in love with a woman. No, I am *in love with a woman."*

"Oh." Phyllis dug her fork into the remains of her chicken pot pie.

Alice sighed. "See? Told you."

"Knock it off," Phyllis said. "The crust is my favorite part." She pulled out the last big chunk of flaky piecrust with her fingers

and stuffed it into her mouth. "What does this woman think about you being in love with her?"

"I think she feels the same way about me."

"That helps. So now what?"

Alice sipped her ice water. "Nothing."

"What do you mean, 'nothing'? If you both think you're in love, what's stopping you from finding out for sure?"

"Her husband."

Phyllis waved her finger in the air. "Check, please."

"I told you there wasn't anything you could do. And frankly, getting it off my chest didn't help much either."

"Boy, when you get yourself into a pickle, you don't mess around, do you?"

"Hey, you're talking to a woman who only got straight As for effort in school."

"Have you told your sister?"

"Are you out of your mind?" Alice said. "If Mary Ellen knew her big sister fooled around with another woman, much less a married one, she'd have a conniption fit. I'm a horrible person, aren't I? I can't imagine what you're thinking about me right now."

"I'm a professor of nineteenth-century literature. In Romanticism, we're not big on passing moral judgments. Obviously, you're not going to pursue it."

That was obvious to Alice's intellect but not to her heart. At the moment, she wasn't quite sure which one was calling the shots.

"You're not going to pursue it, right?" Phyllis said louder.

"No, of course not."

"Good. I didn't think you were into exercises in futility."

"This whole thing is as surprising to me as it is to you, you know."

"It's not really that surprising." Phyllis picked at her teeth with her pinky fingernail. "You've avoided men since Tony, and then, you know, all those feminism meetings."

"What are you talking about? You got me into feminism. You're the biggest feminist I know, and you're not a lesbian."

Phyllis tilted her head at Alice's sensitivity. "I'm teasing you."

"*Ass.*" *Alice whipped a balled-up napkin at her.*

"*Do you think you're a lesbian?*"

"*I don't know, maybe,*" *Alice said, trying not to sound exasperated.* "*One minute I'm a divorcee minding my own business, going to work each day like anyone else, and the next I'm in love with a married woman who's awakened me in every imaginable way—emotionally, spiritually, and especially physically. Good Lord.*" *She shuddered, revisiting the passion of the night before with Leslie.* "*Do you think that makes me a lesbian?*"

Phyllis shrugged. "*It's the seventies.*"

"*Is that supposed to make me feel better?*"

"*Since I'm not a lesbian, I'm not the best person to ask what constitutes being one, but I will say this: viva la sexual revolution.*" *Phyllis pulled her wallet out of the brown and orange crocheted purse Alice had made for her.* "*Dinner is on me tonight.*"

August 1977

Alice had survived the weekend not calling Leslie. That Monday morning, she arrived at the office early, fatigued from her sleepless, emotional wreck of a weekend. The days at work were still lonely without her cohort, but that morning she was relieved Leslie had quit. How could she have faced her and then gone about business as usual knowing they'd made love only a few nights earlier?

As she shuffled papers on her desk, she overheard Julie and Marianne discussing the latest scandal on As the World Turns—*Adrienne's salacious affair with the married Haden. The girls chattered away about how exciting and immoral it was. What kind of woman would do that? Had that conversation occurred only a month earlier, Alice might've jumped right in and offered a resolute,* "*A slut, that's who.*"

As she eavesdropped, she wondered if her relationship with Leslie amounted to the same thing. Was Leslie cheating on her husband? Alice wasn't a man and, therefore, didn't do to Leslie what her husband would do. They were friends, after all. What they had wasn't like an affair on soap operas. Was it? Alice was in love with her and thoroughly enjoyed making love with her, more than with anyone else. Did she actually prefer women to men, or was it just Leslie?

"Hey, Alice, I need that policy. The customer is coming in any minute." Mr. Engle was standing in the doorway of his office.

"I'm sorry, Mr. Engle," Alice said, flustered, and began rifling through the clutter on her desk. "I have it right here."

"Then please bring it in," he said.

"Here I come."

When she finally located the forms, she took them into the office with her tail between her legs, unaccustomed to disappointing her boss in any way. Enough of this foolish daydreaming about Leslie. She returned to her desk with her head fully into her work and spent the rest of the morning typing dictation, her ears, mind, and fingers working in precise harmony.

Around lunchtime, she applied some Wite-Out to a document. As she was blowing it dry, she looked up to see the mirage of Leslie walking toward her desk with a smile fresher than a meadow on Little House on the Prairie. *She placed a small African violet in gift-wrap cellophane on Alice's desk.*

"Do you have any plans for lunch?"

"Leftover meatloaf and mashed potatoes," Alice replied, entranced.

"Gee, I hope the idea of lunch with me is more tempting than leftovers."

Alice smiled, trying to keep her face from shimmering like Donna Summer's gold-lame hot pants. "Let me take these into Engle, and then we can go across the street."

"Take your time," Leslie said. "I'll say hello to the girls."

When Alice came back to her desk to collect her purse, she overheard the conversation Leslie was having with Julie and Marianne.

"How groovy that you can stay home, Leslie," Julie said as she pressed a fake eyelash back into place. "I hope I can soon. I miss watching my stories every day."

"*First you gotta snag yourself a husband, Jule,*" *Marianne said, then turned to Leslie.* "*So how are you keeping busy now that your days are free? Getting into all kinds of far-out trouble?*"

The girls laughed, and Alice bashed her leg into her open desk drawer.

"*The usual routine. Laundry, cooking, the kids' orthodontic appointments,*" *Leslie said.* "*Are you ready, Alice?*"

Alice glared at her, rubbing her shin.

"*That was smooth,*" *Leslie mumbled as they entered the elevator and the doors closed.*

"*Marianne's comment caught me off guard,*" *Alice said.*

"*You? How do you think I felt? I was right in the line of fire.*"

They relaxed into easy smiles and gazed into each other's eyes.

"*This is the best surprise,*" *Alice said.*

Leslie surprised her further with a kiss and embrace that lasted until the elevator hit the ground floor.

At the sandwich shop across from the office, they sat at the crowded lunch counter eating soups and sandwiches. Alice had so much she wanted to talk to her about, but the venue bustling with hungry blue-collar and office workers on their lunch breaks precluded an intimate discussion.

"*So, are you getting used to retirement?*" *Alice slurped some beef-barley broth off her spoon.*

Leslie shrugged. "*I'm having a tougher time readjusting than I thought.*"

Because of me, Alice wanted to ask but instead opted for the less incendiary "*Why?*"

"*Well, the kids aren't babies anymore. They don't need me as much as they used to. Billy's been attending basketball camp every day for four weeks, and Rebecca is always off in her girlfriend Karen's pool. Besides, I got accustomed to using my brain every day. I miss having that challenge. I mean, how many cakes do you think you need to bake before you know the recipe by heart?*"

"*How many?*"

"*Four hundred and fifty,*" *Leslie said dryly.*

"*Really?*"

Leslie rolled her eyes. "No, not really. I have no idea."

Suddenly, Alice was like a scientist witnessing a successful experiment. "Do you know what all this sounds like?"

"What?"

"Betty Friedan's 'The Problem that has No Name' essay."

"The what?"

Alice scoffed. "Don't you listen at our crochet meetings? Dolores was talking about it. It's at the beginning of The Feminine Mystique. *I let you borrow that book months ago. Haven't you read it?"*

"I haven't had time," Leslie said sheepishly.

"Haven't had time? You don't work."

"Just because I don't work doesn't mean I have time to lounge around reading books all day."

"That's exactly why you should read it. It's an essay that explains why so many women in the 1950s were depressed and popping Valium like candy from a Pez dispenser. Being a housewife is boring."

Leslie looked offended. "I know it's not the most glamorous life, but it's not boring. It has its moments."

"Of course it does," Alice said, trying to be sensitive. "I didn't mean to—well, come on, Leslie, be honest. When was the last time something provocative went down at the orthodontist?"

"Last Wednesday. I had the sheer pleasure of witnessing Dr. Santello lace into Billy for not wearing his elastics. I kept on telling him, but he'd just 'yeah, ma' me to death."

Alice stared at her for a moment. "How are you not a Quaalude addict?"

Leslie laughed. "I miss hearing your one-liners every day." Suddenly, the glint in her eyes faded. "I just don't smile as much now."

Alice stirred her soup, letting pieces of barley plop into the broth. "When you worked here, I would actually have fun at work. Now I'm back to the old grind of mindless office procedures and avoiding the people I dislike."

Leslie smirked, apparently familiar with that list. "I love having lunch with my kids, but they're not really big on discussing current events. I miss that, too."

"Do you know what I miss?"

Leslie shook her head.

"You."

Leslie poked at the pumpernickel bread on her sandwich. "I can't stand the idea that our next crochet club isn't for another two weeks."

"God, me, too," Alice said. "Hey, do you want to go shopping or something this week? I mean if you can get a sitter."

"A sitter's never a problem. My parents love having the kids on a Friday night. Bradlee's is having a big linen sale this week, and if you want, we can try that new Italian place in the Annex first."

"Sounds mint." Alice delighted in Leslie's enthusiasm. "We should get going. Some of us are still on the clock."

"Don't rub it in," Leslie said as she stepped down off the stool. "Where are you off to now?"

"I have to pick up Billy at basketball camp, and then I'm going home, making a nice pitcher of iced tea, and sitting outside on my chaise lounge with The Feminine Mystique.*"*

"You keep talking like that, and I'm not going to feel sorry for you anymore."

"Oh, really?" Leslie looped her arm through Alice's as they crossed the street. "I'll call you up and let you listen the next time Billy and Rebecca are having a battle royal over the television. You'll feel plenty sorry for me then."

"Something tells me they could burn your house down, and you'd still worship the flowers they trample on."

"You know me too well, Alice," she said. "I'll come up with you, so I can use the ladies' room."

In the restroom, Alice loitered at the sink rinsing her soapy hands until Leslie came out of the stall. Their eyes connected in the mirror's reflection. The air grew thick with awkwardness as water trickled over their hands. Leslie was the first to look away, drying her hands on the towel hanging from a dispenser.

"I thought of you all weekend," Alice said quietly.

Leslie sighed.

"I'm sorry, Leslie. I shouldn't have said that."

All through lunch, Alice had heaved thoughts of Leslie's tender lips from her mind, shaming herself unmercifully for allowing them to creep in. Although their night had been the most exquisite experience she'd ever had, it had come as a frightening surprise.

"You don't have to apologize," Leslie said. "Why do you think I'm here?"

They leaned toward each other and kissed, vigilant to keep their bodies from touching.

"Why can't I stop thinking of you?" Leslie whispered, resting her forehead against Alice's. "It's driving me crazy."

"I thought it was just me," Alice said.

Leslie shook her head. As they stared at each other, the apprehension in Leslie's eyes wrenched Alice's heart. She'd never intended to cause her any distress with her first misstep. But how were they to know any of this would or could ever happen?

"Do you want me to leave you alone?" Alice said, bracing for the answer.

Leslie blotted the tears under her eyes with the sides of her index fingers. "No, I don't want you to. That's the problem."

Alice bit her lip so Leslie wouldn't see her coming apart. "Me either."

"Your friendship means so much to me, Alice. Let's not ruin it."

"Yours does, too, but I don't know how to be just your friend since..."

"Sure, it makes things a little awkward," Leslie said. "But we can get past it. Everyone makes mistakes."

Before Alice could respond, they jumped apart when Julie stormed into the bathroom.

"Alice, Mr. Engle wants to know where you are. Your lunch hour ended fifteen minutes ago."

Alice glanced at Leslie. "It's like I'm still married to Tony."
She then turned to Julie, sweetly. "Tell him I'm coming back right now."

After Julie left, they traded smiles and a smoldering kiss before emerging from the sanctuary of the ladies' room.

❖

Alice sprang up in Mary Ellen's lounge chair, almost as if from a bad dream. The feeling she'd had with Leslie earlier today was identical to those days right before she'd fallen helplessly in love with her. She'd better go out to dinner with her sister and brother-in-law before she slid so deep into thoughts of Leslie, she'd never be able to climb out.

CHAPTER TEN

After dinner in Branford center, Alice walked with her sister and brother-in-law down Main Street to Common Grounds, a regular stop for Dave and Mary Ellen whenever they ate in town. Dave had brought two cappuccinos to Alice and Mary Ellen, seated on a worn leather loveseat in the corner, and announced he was going to have his coffee with some of the regulars gathered at a large table in the center of the coffeehouse. His wife did not object.

"All right, now that he's over there, start explaining," Mary Ellen said, licking foam off her lip.

Alice was taken aback by her directness and played it cagey. "Explaining what?"

"You spent the day with Leslie, and then you came home sad and mopey. What's the matter? Did she take a turn for the worse? Does she have a second husband you didn't know about?"

"Second husband?" She glared at Mary Ellen incredulously. "No, she's fine. She had some nerve damage on her left side, but she's definitely improving. They have a terrific therapy staff where she is."

"Then why are you in a mood?"

Alice sipped her cappuccino and took a moment to appreciate the eclectic artwork and murals on the walls. "I don't know if I should keep going there every day."

"You're not obligated to. You said she's getting better, and she has family, which by the way, so do you."

"It's not that I feel obligated. The problem is I want to."

"Christ, are you falling for her again?"

Alice smiled at her sister's dramatic ways and then said softly, "I don't think I ever stopped loving her."

"How could that be? You and Maureen were a great couple."

"Maureen was an exceptional human being. She was easy to love."

"But Leslie was the love of your life?"

It pained Alice to hear Mary Ellen say that and know it was true. She loved and respected Maureen so much, but as happy as they were, she'd never quite felt with Maureen that special something Leslie had stirred in her—and was stirring again.

"Am I a horrible person if I admit that?" Alice said.

"No," Mary Ellen said. "If things were different back in the seventies you probably would've ended up with Leslie. But that doesn't mean what you had with Maureen was anything less than genuine. We love different people differently."

Alice took a moment to absorb her sister's wisdom. "How are you so wise to the nuances of romance? You've been with Dave since high school."

"Haven't you ever watched *Super Soul Sunday* on the Oprah Winfrey Network?"

"Uh, no," Alice said. "I'm sorry to say I've missed that one."

"So how do you think Leslie feels?"

"Well, I thought she might have been flirting a little, but in a convalescent home, how do you tell the difference between light flirting and heavy gratitude?"

Mary Ellen chortled into her cappuccino foam.

"I don't know," Alice went on in a more serious tone. "It's such a strange context to be talking about second chances. It's been over twenty-five years since we've even seen each other. We're so old, she's not well…"

"Alice, age has nothing to do with love. I would think you know that. You're seventy-one, not a hundred and seventy. You're vibrant, active, and still look amazing. If you're trying to talk yourself out of having feelings for her, you'll have to come up with a more persuasive argument."

"Perhaps I'm making too much of the situation. I live in Boston, after all. I'm just here for a visit. If my feelings become overwhelming, I could just hop in my car and drive away."

"Right," Mary Ellen said. "Far, far away from your problems just like you did thirty years ago."

"I wasn't running away from my problems. I got a better job."

"You became an insurance actuary. You could've stayed in Hartford. You didn't have to move two and half hours away from everyone."

"We're not going to get into how I wasn't there for Mom again, are we? I offered to move her in with Maureen and me when she couldn't live on her own anymore."

"You knew damn well she wouldn't have gone up there."

"For God's sake, she died twenty years ago. When will this argument be over?"

"It's not even about Mom, Alice. Don't you get it? You didn't just run away from Leslie. You ran away from me."

"It was a decision I needed to make. I never stopped being your sister, and I never will."

"I miss how you used to share things with me. After you met Leslie, everything changed."

"Because I did. I didn't know I was a lesbian until I met Leslie."

"That's a whole chunk of your life I know nothing about. I wish you'd tell me something."

Alice took another sip of her cappuccino. "All right, I'll tell you something. How about a time when coffee landed Leslie and me in trouble?"

Mary Ellen smiled with delight. "Sounds delicious."

August 1977

Alice picked up Leslie that Friday night with the noblest of intentions. As originally planned, they'd split an antipasto salad and an eggplant-parmesan sub at a new Italian restaurant in the

Annex section of New Haven, trading details of work and home life with kids. But noble intentions were no match for what simmered wordlessly between them. For her part, Alice had investigated the contents of the antipasto until her eyes ached from concentration. The pickled carrots and cauliflower, marinated mushrooms, roasted red peppers, Genoa salami, imported ham, and cubes of table cheese kept her in check. If she looked up for too long, she'd fix her eyes on Leslie and so would end the casual chitchat between friends she was making a heroic effort to maintain.

"So Rebecca and I had a long conversation today about playing with her brother's racetrack and model airplanes," Leslie said as she pulled a strand of mozzarella from her half of the eggplant sub.

"Why? Did she break something," Alice asked, still not looking up.

"No, but she's got her own toys. Barbie airplane, Barbie camper, Barbie beauty shop—you name it, Barbie does it. I think Mattel will go out of business once she grows out of them."

Alice, still plucking various items from the antipasto with her fork: "Maybe she's bored with Barbie. A racetrack sounds like a lot of fun."

Leslie paused, skewering Alice with her glare. "Haven't you eaten anything today?"

Alice finally came up for air. "I'm sorry. Here, have some more." She pushed the platter toward Leslie.

"No, I'm getting full," Leslie said, peering inside her sub. "I started taking these diet pills this week, and they really work."

"What do you need diet pills for? You've got an amazing figure." Alice hadn't meant to make her blush, but if anyone knew the truth about Leslie's figure...

"I don't know. I'm pretty sure I've put on weight. Some of my slacks are uncomfortable now." She glanced around the restaurant as if the solution to life's most puzzling riddle was hidden somewhere behind the grimy wall paneling. "I don't know. I just feel like I need to do something."

They were roaming away from casual-friend chitchat.

"Is everything okay?"

Leslie offered the smile Alice had figured out was Leslie's Carol Brady smile of the mom whose problems always resolved themselves after the last commercial break.

"Are you sure?" Alice said.

She nodded.

"You ready to blow this taco stand?"

"Yes. I think some shopping is in order after a meal like this." Leslie counted out her half of the check and rose from the booth.

"You hardly ate anything."

"I'm fine, Alice. It just means more room for dessert." Leslie's smile was more reassuring, but Alice still wasn't convinced.

As appetizing as shopping sounded, they never quite made it to the linen sale at Bradlees. After leaving the restaurant, and without saying a word, Alice had steered her car toward the onramp of Interstate 95, going in the opposite direction.

"Um, Bradlees is back that way," Leslie said, poking her thumb over her shoulder.

"I like the one near me in West Haven better. Then we can stop at my house for coffee or something if you want. I picked up a nice Danish ring at the bakery after work today." Alice felt Leslie's eyes studying her profile as she drove over the Q Bridge.

"Okay." Leslie rested her hands in her lap.

They drove in thorny silence for the rest of the way until they reached the exit in West Haven.

"I have an idea," Leslie said. "Why don't we have coffee first?"

"That's a great idea." Alice clasped the steering wheel tighter. Her real appetite was finally going to be satisfied.

As soon as Alice closed the door behind them, they thundered down the hardwood hallway like a freight train, crashing into walls, knocking family photos to the floor. Through deep, steamy kisses, they peeled off articles of each other's clothing as they headed to Alice's bedroom.

When they slid into Alice's cool sheets, Leslie's body molded to the contour of Alice's. She flung her arms around Leslie, and her palms soaked in the supple softness of her upper back. They gazed at each other between slow, sensual kisses, eyes conveying what couldn't be expressed in words. But what were they expressing? What Alice was feeling defied explanation. Did this prove beyond a doubt she was a lesbian? She'd loved and been loved before by two caring, passionate men, but it had never felt like this—so electric, so consuming, so complete.

After nearly two hours of making love, they lay quietly face to face, heads sharing the same pillow, legs and arms entangled in sheets torn out from beneath the mattress.

"I can't believe the way you make me feel," Leslie whispered.

Alice melted in the dreamy look in Leslie's eyes. "I can't believe any of this."

"It scares me, Alice."

"No kidding. Feel my heart." She placed Leslie's hand on her bare chest.

"Mine beats like that, too."

"Really?" Alice said. "When?"

"Whenever I'm waiting for your car to pull in my driveway or I dial your phone number and count the rings until you answer or I just happen to catch you looking at me the way you do."

Alice slid out from under Leslie's arm and propped herself up on her elbows. "Leslie, I know you don't want me to say this, but I have to, just this once. I'm in love with you—madly, passionately in love with you."

"I know the feeling, but I don't understand it." Leslie sprang upright, tugging the sheet up to her neck. "I've never felt anything like this before. I've been with my husband for fourteen years, since the summer after I graduated high school. He's my first love. How is it that I've never felt this way with him?"

Alice popped up, too. "How the hell should I know? Tony and I had our problems, but I loved him. I didn't want to split up." Alice scratched at the side of her head through her messy hair. "At least I don't think I wanted to. I mean, I was pretty devastated going through it. But then, I don't know, I also felt this strange sense of relief."

"Maybe this really isn't what we think it is," Leslie suggested. "Maybe we were so upset about not working together anymore, we just got all mixed up."

Alice narrowed her eyes. "Upset about not working together anymore? Do you always go to bed with your coworkers when you quit a job?"

"Well, you don't have to act like I'm stupid."

"You're not stupid. That rationale is stupid."

"Excuse me, Dr. Freud. That's the best I can come up with in my present state of mind."

"Jeez, I hope I never need you for an alibi."

Leslie groaned and fell back on her pillow, throwing an arm over her eyes. "We can't keep doing this, Alice."

Alice fell back and lay next to her, staring at the ceiling. It ground her up inside to hear Leslie say that, but she was right. They couldn't keep doing it, for a million reasons, not the least of which was the ache that only bored itself deeper after each time Leslie left. She could already feel her stomach tightening.

"I'm sorry. This was all my fault," Alice said. "I have no idea if the Bradlees near me is better. I've never even been to the one in East Haven."

"No, it's my fault. I'm the one who suggested we have coffee first. I've just been thinking about you so much since...well, you know. I think I wanted it to happen again, to experience all of it."

"I'd say we experienced all of it this time." Alice reached for an extra pillow and hugged it close to her chest.

"Oh, Alice." She moved the pillow and rested her cheek on Alice's chest, embracing her with her whole body.

Alice squeezed back, eliciting an involuntary whimper from Leslie's diaphragm. "Can't I kidnap you and keep you here forever?"

"I'd love to be your prisoner," Leslie said softly. "I feel like I already am. My heart is your hostage, for sure."

"I hate driving you home more than anything." She pressed her lips into Leslie's hair as the clock on her nightstand flipped to nine fifty-five. "We better get up. It's late."

"Can I have one last kiss?"

Alice melted in the innocence in Leslie's eyes. She caressed Leslie's cheek with her fingertips before pulling her in for a tender good-bye kiss.

When Alice dropped her off, she stayed in the driveway and watched her walk through the side entrance, turn on a light, and pass through the kitchen. Moments later her husband's car pulled into the driveway. She threw the gear shift into reverse, but he made eye contact and gave her a friendly wave before she could back all the way out. She waved back and hit the gas pedal as her stomach pitched in shame. What kind of twisted cosmic prank was this that something could make her feel so euphoric one minute and like such a creep the next? Her eyes blurring like a rain-soaked windshield, she pulled into a convenience-store parking lot and blotted them with a napkin from her glove box.

August 1977

A few days later, Alice experienced the same mirage at work as the previous week, only this time it wasn't so magical.

"Aren't you happy to see me?" Leslie's eyes darkened as she hovered over Alice's desk.

"Of course I am," Alice whispered. "But if you keep showing up here, people are going to suspect something."

"What's so suspicious about two coworkers having lunch together?"

"Nothing, except you and I aren't coworkers anymore."

"You know what I mean. Friend, coworker, what's the difference anyway?"

Alice tried reassuring herself she was only being paranoid. "You're coming here every week, sometimes twice a week. It might start to look funny to some people."

Leslie looked appropriately chastised but… "Alice, I can't wait until Friday to see you," she said in a grave whisper. "I'm going crazy thinking about you and missing you all week. Don't you feel the same?"

"Constantly," Alice said. "How about from now on, we'll meet at the restaurant. Then nobody will be the wiser."

"But then we can't kiss in the ladies' room. I need to kiss you."

The urgency in Leslie's eyes sent a tingle through Alice that electrified her in all the right places. "Let's go get some supplies for my desk." With a tilt of her head, she motioned for Leslie to follow her down the hall to the storage room.

She unlocked the door and, after whipping her head side to side to ensure the hall was clear, shoved Leslie inside the room and then shut the door behind them. She leaned against the metal shelving stocked with pens, steno pads, Wite-Out, and pink message slips and clutched Leslie by the blouse. They kissed hard, Alice's heart pounding. At any moment one of the other girls might be by to replenish her desk supplies. She wrapped her arms around Leslie's lower back and pushed her closer, weakening from the heat of Leslie's body.

"I can't stand this, Les," Alice whispered. "It just makes me want more."

"I know. I'm sorry." She kissed Alice insatiably, groping at her breasts. Was she overcome with desire, or was it just an effort to evade the same ugly conversation they'd had nearly every time they were together?

Alice gently pushed her back. "Are you?"

Leslie seemed confused as she wiped her smeared lipstick from the corners of her mouth. "Am I what, sorry?"

Alice stood anticipating what she'd always feared after pursuing this line of questioning.

"Yes, I'm sorry. Do you think I enjoy having to sneak around? Kissing you in a supply closet?"

"You have to admit it's a hell of a diversion for a bored housewife—the seventies version of sneaking around with the milkman."

"Do you really think that about me?" Leslie flung Alice's hands away from her. "This is not about me being a bored housewife. I'm in love with you, Alice. There's no other reason on earth I'd betray my husband like this. A good reason doesn't even exist, but I can't *help myself around you." She turned and leaned against the supply shelf. "I feel like such a horrible person."*

"I'm sorry," Alice said, pulling her into a hug. "I didn't mean it. I swear." She kissed Leslie's head as she cried.

"We should get out of here," Leslie said, wiping her face with the back of her hands. "I shouldn't have come. I won't anymore."

Alice apprehended her hand as Leslie reached for the door. "You mean into the office, right? We can still meet for lunch."

"No. Let's just keep it to crochet night. We have to stop, Alice. It's just getting too hard."

Panic charged through her. Had Alice pushed too far? Leslie seemed serious this time. "Les, let's go to lunch, and we can talk about it. I didn't mean to start trouble between us."

Leslie's face was stone. "Alice, let go of the doorknob."

Alice swung open the door at the precise moment Steve Briller was walking by.

"Afternoon, ladies," he said, his buckled ankle boots scuffing the carpet. "Your powder room out of order or something?"

"Something like that," Alice snapped and kept walking.

"You can always come and gossip about the other girls in my office if you need to," he sang. "Nice seeing you, Leslie."

As Alice headed to the elevators, Leslie followed.

"Alice, please don't be mad at me," she whispered. "I couldn't stand it if you didn't speak to me anymore."

"I'm not mad at you." Alice stared straight ahead as she repeatedly jabbed at the down button. "I don't want to lose you."

"Do you think that's what I want?"

"I have no fucking idea what you want," Alice spat. "Every day it's something different. I can't keep up with it anymore." She took off toward the staircase, and once more, Leslie was on the move behind her.

On the landing between floors, Leslie finally caught her by the arm. "Alice, I'm sorry."

"It's so goddamn easy for you to walk away, isn't it? Back to your happy home with your perfect family."

"I'm not walking away from you. I just don't know what else to do. I'm making you so unhappy with what little I can offer you." She pulled Alice closer. *"I want you so much, Alice. I crave you. But there's nothing I can do."*

Alice yanked her arm free. "There is something you can do. You just don't want to do it." She stared into Leslie's eyes, searching for anything she could cling to.

"You have no idea how badly I want to do it."

How many times had Alice heard that? Yet each time she found a gossamer thread of hope to grasp in Leslie's words.

"You have to go now before someone smarter than Steve Briller overhears us. I only have twenty minutes to get something to eat."

"I'll call you this week, okay?"

Alice stared at the grime on the green-speckled floor tiles of the stairwell. *Tell her no,* she thought. *Tell her no right here and now and free yourself from this trap.*

"Alice, I'll call you, okay?"

She looked into Leslie's eyes so full of love and fear. *"Okay,"* her mouth said before her brain had a chance to suppress it. She pushed open the door to the lobby, and after parting with Leslie on the sidewalk, she spent the remainder of her lunch hour bawling in the seclusion of her car in the parking garage.

September 1977

It had been nearly two weeks since Alice had spoken with Leslie. To her surprise, she'd found a store of self-control that prevented her from picking up the phone and begging Leslie to see her again. Still, one day blurred into the next as her sadness over missing her showed no signs of ebbing. Tired of making up excuses to everyone, she agreed to spend the afternoon with her sister, who was eager to get out of the house and enjoy a Saturday respite from her two young sons. All during lunch at the restaurant, Alice had been systemically tortured by an assault of songs, all relating in some form or another to love, piped into the bar. Abba's *"Knowing Me, Knowing You"* was her current nemesis.

"Would you ladies like anything else?" the waitress asked, ready to hand them their check.

"Yes, I'll take another Miller High Life," Alice said, and immediately noticed her sister's expression. "What?"

"Three beers at lunch?"

Abba's singers taunted her about this is where the story ends, about saying good-bye.

"It's been a rough week," Alice said, twisting what was left of her napkin.

"Work?" her sister asked.

Alice shrugged languidly.

"Don't you want to talk about it?"

Alice shook her head.

"Ally, why don't you ever want to talk to me anymore?"

"What do you mean? What have we been doing for the last hour?"

"We've been eating, and I've been doing all the talking."

"So? You have a lot to talk about."

"How many tales about your nephews' macaroni art projects and projectile vomiting at three a.m. can you stand? For God's sake, I'd like to converse about what people are doing out in the real world for a change."

"Is this what your life has come to?" Alice said, fighting the urge to mock her. "Living vicariously through me and my mundane work stories?"

"I don't care about your work. I've been waiting patiently for a juicy romance. Why aren't you dating?"

Abba sang about it being time they faced the fact that they were through.

Thanks for the burn, Alice mentally told the band. She squirmed and peered over her shoulder. "Where the hell is our waitress?"

"Not that I'm not enjoying watching my big sis drink herself into cirrhosis, but we should get going. We can get some shopping in before Dave and the boys get home from the game."

"Ugh, Mare, I don't have the energy for one of your frenzied shop-athons. Can you do it without me?"

"Now I really know something's wrong with you. Please talk to me."

"Nothing's wrong. Can't I just be tired from a busy workweek?" She hated lying to her sister. They'd always shared everything. Maybe she should confide in her. Mary Ellen had a talent for lavishing her with comforting words in any situation.

"I admire you, Al," Mary Ellen said, taking cash out of her wallet. "You're so good at the British stiff-upper-lip bit. You'd make our Nanny Prudence proud."

On second thought, telling Cousin Phyllis was one thing. She tripped to her own pied piper anyway. Telling her baby sister was another. How could she inform the one person who'd always looked up to her that she was a homosexual homewrecker? Mary Ellen would never recover from the disappointment.

"Okay, you win," Alice said. "Let's hit Malley's downtown. I could use a new pair of dungarees."

"That's the spirit," Mary Ellen said as they headed out. "You can wear them tonight to the Knights of Columbus dance with Dave and me."

"I already told you I'm not interested in being the third wheel on your date with your husband. I still haven't recovered from the last one watching your perverted rendition of 'The Hustle' in your matching Donnie and Marie outfits."

Mary Ellen looked up as she unlocked the driver's side door. "That was an isolated incident. Dave was drunk."

"Sure, Dave was drunk." Alice sucked at her cheeks.

"Please come with us. There are always lots of foxy guys there. Last month I could swear I saw Erik Estrada's twin."

"I'm going to pass, thanks. I want to watch that new show, The Love Boat." It sounded dumb the minute it came out, but Alice had been out all day with Mary Ellen. She wanted to be home in case Leslie had called earlier and would try her again at night after the kids went to sleep.

"You're going to stay home on a Saturday night to watch a TV show?"

"How the heck can I watch it if I don't stay home?" Alice huffed. "Would you mind unlocking my door, please?"

They got in the car and waited a minute for Mary Ellen to apply a fresh coat of lipstick.

"Ally," Mary Ellen said. "Promise me you'd confide in me if anything was wrong."

Alice replied with an earnest smile, but it was a promise she knew she couldn't keep. As a beer belch tickled its way up her throat at two in the afternoon, she wondered how much lower she could go. Her affair with Leslie was tearing her in two, filling her heart and body with pleasure she'd never dreamed possible and transforming her into a liar and a schemer. If she felt like that, how must Leslie feel having to lie and scheme while looking someone she cared so much about in the face?

"Thanks, Mare," Alice said, smacking her sister's leg. "I'm fine."

She couldn't wait for the day to end so she could sit on her couch next to a telephone that wouldn't ring.

❖

"Wow," Mary Ellen said, leaning forward with her empty cappuccino cup dangling by the loop from her finger.

Alice waved her hand in front of Mary Ellen's face to extricate her from her apparent trance. "Wow what?"

"That reminds me of a porno movie Dave used to hide from me in the late seventies."

"Seriously? A porno?" Alice said excitedly and then lowered her voice. "Do you know how devastated I was that day you dragged me shopping all over creation?"

"That's what you get for not confiding your troubles in your dear, trusted sister. I could've comforted you."

"Yeah, right," Alice said with a smirk. "You couldn't even watch a dirty movie with your own husband back then, and you were going to counsel me on the lesbian affair I was having with a married woman?"

"I eventually watched one with him," Mary Ellen said discreetly, smoothing down her blouse. "The eighties were a particularly dull decade for us in the bedroom."

"Well, congratulations," Alice said. "Anyway, you'll have to forgive me for keeping you in the dark about my illicit affair."

"It's okay—as long as you tell me everything now."

"There's nothing else to tell."

"Not yet anyway." Mary Ellen raised encouraging eyebrows and crunched into the last piece of the biscotti they were sharing.

CHAPTER ELEVEN

A lice needed a day off from Leslie, if for no other reason than to slap her head on straight again. Age might've had the power to bring on cancer, strokes, and forgetfulness, but one thing it couldn't do was conquer the heart. When it wanted to beat again with passion and vivacity for someone, it did just that no matter what the calendar read.

Earlier in the week, she'd looked up Cynthia and Kathy, and they had arranged a lunch date at a winery closer to Cynthia's house, as her eyesight wasn't up to long-distance driving. Seated on the deck overlooking an eternity of verdant grounds and tangles of grapevines, they snacked on gourmet cheeses and crackers, an umbrella shading them from the mid-July sun.

"Here's to Dolores," Cynthia said after pouring everyone a glass of Estate chardonnay.

Alice and Kathy raised their glasses, and they sipped in honor of Dolores's memory.

"Goddamn ovarian cancer," Kathy spat. "One of the greatest feminists we had the privilege of knowing, and she was taken out by the body part that most represented womanhood. How do you like that?"

Alice and Cynthia exchanged looks.

"Cancer took her out," Cynthia said. "Not her ovaries."

"You're missing the symbolism here," Kathy said.

"Personally, I'm an ass woman," Alice said dryly.

The ladies laughed and hoisted their glasses in another toast.

"I can't believe she's been gone six years already," Cynthia said.

Kathy frowned. "It goes by too fast."

"And Leslie's stroke," Cynthia added. "How's she doing?"

"She's okay," Alice said. "Thankfully, it wasn't severe. She's got some recovery time ahead, but she seems to be responding well to the physical therapy."

Cynthia made the sign of the Trinity. "We have to do this again as soon as she's up and about. It'll be nice for all of us to catch up."

Alice agreed. "Let's actually do it, not just say we will."

"Did you stay in touch with her all this time?" Kathy asked with what Alice detected was a note of suspicion in her voice.

"Who, Leslie?"

"Who else are we talking about?"

"After I moved to Boston, it was challenging to stay in contact with everyone," Alice said.

"I'm surprised. You became so much closer to her than the rest of us."

Alice glared at her. "What's that supposed to mean?"

"Nothing," Kathy said. "It's just an observation."

Cynthia chuckled. "Dolores once said you and Leslie acted like an old married couple."

"So that's what you all did when we weren't there?" Alice spat. "Talked about us behind our backs?"

"You two were there the night Dolores said that," Kathy said. "It was the night the abortion discussion got really weird. At first we thought you'd brought a stash of bunk weed, but then we remembered you always supplied primo stuff."

The wine, the summer heat, and Kathy's line of cross-examination had Alice's head in a whirl. She was a sip or two away from telling her to piss off with her nosy insinuations, but instead she licked her dry lips and said, "It was a touchy subject that made Leslie emotional."

"You were both pretty emotional that night," Cynthia said. "I only remember because the tension between you two was palpable.

Dolores's comment wasn't meant as a dig. It was more to ease the uncomfortable vibe in the room."

"What exactly do you two want to know?" Alice turned a searing gaze on Kathy, as if protecting Leslie was her sworn duty. "By the way, Kath, when did you finally find your way out of the closet?"

"Look at me," Kathy said, spreading out her arms. "Does a jet need the word 'airplane' scrawled across it for you to know what it is?"

Cynthia almost sprayed her wine across the table, and Alice fought cracking a smile out of principle.

"I don't know why you're getting your Depends in such a bunch," Kathy said. "You've been out for years, too. We're your friends. We're just wondering if there was anything between you and Leslie you want to share with us now."

Yes, Alice had wanted to share it with her friends. She'd stopped lying about her personal life so long ago that remembering how to do it now required some finesse. And since spending time with Leslie had unearthed the relics of complicated feelings she'd buried long ago, she could use some objective opinions. But would confiding in her friends a part of her own history mean she was betraying Leslie?

"Thanks, ladies," Alice said, placing a hand on each of theirs. "I appreciate your concern, but the three of us are here together right now. Let's enjoy the present before this becomes another part of our pasts we'll never get back."

"Oh, please, is this what we've become?" Cynthia drawled. "We used to exchange profound insights on one of the most influential social movements in American history. Now we're spouting catchphrases from corny greeting cards."

Kathy and Alice laughed.

"Really?" Alice said. "You think my words of wisdom are good enough for greeting cards?"

"Yes, but I wouldn't go around bragging about that," Cynthia said.

Kathy leaned back, stretching her legs to the chair across from her. "This is the life. I gotta bring Gretchen here."

"I hope you'll come around more often now, Alice," Cynthia said. "I'm sorry we hadn't heard about Maureen. We would've come to the service."

Alice gazed out at the haze the sun cast over the winery's landscape. "It's my fault," she said. "When Maureen got sick and then started failing, I isolated myself from everyone, my family, too." A smile suddenly brightened her face. "It's good to be back."

Kathy raised her glass again. "Here's to the second wave of the Second Wave."

After they clinked glasses, Cynthia's eyes widened with enthusiasm. "We have to have a reunion meeting one night with Leslie—crocheting, hors d'oeuvres, the works."

"The works?" Alice asked out the corner of her mouth.

"The works," Kathy replied with a mischievous grin.

"Hmm, what will our feminist topic be now?" Cynthia said, already contemplating it.

"You ask that like things have changed so radically for women in the last forty years," Alice said. "How about how Republicans are still trying to climb into our uteruses?"

"How about the Equal Pay Act?" Kathy said. "Can you believe that fucking thing still hasn't passed?"

They shook their heads in collective despair.

"It's like Simone de Beauvoir wrote back in 1950," Cynthia said. "'Women are the other,' and the codes of law were set up against us. Unbelievably, it hasn't changed much."

"That's unbelievably depressing," Kathy said.

"It is," Cynthia added, "but we're also closer than we've ever been to electing a female president."

"Super," Alice said, refilling everyone's glass. "When she gets elected and realizes she's making only seventy-eight percent of the last president's salary, maybe an executive order will settle it once and for all."

They toasted again.

"I can't wait for our next meeting," Cynthia said, and her smile spoke for everyone.

As Alice drove home to Mary Ellen's later that afternoon, her mind wandered back to the night Kathy and Cynthia had mentioned, the night she and Leslie had almost blown their cover in Cynthia's bathroom.

October 1977

Alice stood in the kitchen rolling joints as an early autumn breeze ruffled the curtains over the sink. She licked the edge of the paper and twisted it between her thumb and forefinger, realizing she was looking forward to the first hit a little too much. Several weeks of not speaking with Leslie was wearing on her, and time, apparently, had her low on the waiting list for wound healing. Now she had to muster the stamina to fake being fine around the girls— no way that was happening straight. She held up the last of her creations and twirled it around, admiring its tightness, symmetry, and all-around craftsmanship.

"Alice, hurry up with the party favors," Kathy called out from the living room.

Suddenly, their voices rose to an excited pitch. At first Alice assumed they were cheering in anticipation of her handmade accoutrements, but when she walked in the room, the girls were taking turns hugging Leslie, who'd just made a late and surprise arrival.

Alice gritted her teeth, simultaneously compelled to jump into her arms and bolt out the back door before Leslie spotted her.

"Hi, Alice," Leslie said, her blue eyes speaking words only Alice could comprehend.

She exhaled and forced a smile. What a buzzkill. Good thing she wasn't buzzed yet. She sat down across from her and sparked up a doobie.

Her strange aloofness and eagerness to smoke were too obvious to pass unnoticed.

"Jeez, tough day, Alice?" Cynthia asked and sipped her wine.

"Yes, you might say that." Alice fought the urge to look at Leslie, her throat burning from the billow of smoke she'd sucked down.

"Well, then, let's get down to business," Dolores said as she unwrapped a platter of Spam, tomato, and cheese squares.

"It was my turn to pick," Cynthia said, exhaling smoke. "So I went for a real hot-button issue, but it needs to be addressed."

"Let me guess," Dolores said with a grimace. "Abortion."

Cynthia glowered at her. "I'm sorry. I know this is an unpleasant topic and one we'd like to avoid, but it's a crucial issue that speaks to women's basic civil rights."

"Right," Kathy said, sipping her beer. "The right to choose what happens to my own body."

"If you ask me," Dolores said, "abortion is just another social construction that helps men avoid responsibility. Think about it—no shotgun wedding, no eighteen-year financial commitment, and best of all, they're not the ones who have to have the god-awful procedure."

Alice leaned into Dolores's face and stared for a moment. "Whoa. You just blew my mind with that one, Lucretia."

Dolores nudged her into a pile of pillows. "You dope. You're stoned."

"I'll say she is." Leslie's glare and the bite in her voice were a clear response to the freeze-out Alice had been giving her since she'd arrived.

"Wasn't this argument settled four years ago with Roe versus Wade?" Alice said and reclined against a pile of pillows as the herb worked its magic.

"Only in the sense that women don't have to die getting back-alley, illegal abortions anymore," Cynthia said. "But women in most states still have to face the indignity of having to justify why they need one. And there are still restrictions in place that create a real financial burden on the woman, like having to travel to another state to have one."

"Leslie, you're awfully quiet on this," Dolores said.

She looked around like she was afraid to answer. Finally, she took a deep breath. "I don't believe in abortion."

"None of us believe in abortion," Alice said softly. "This is a civil-rights issue."

"What about the baby's civil rights?"

"You mean the fetus?" Kathy asked. "A fetus depends solely on the woman to grow into a baby, and if that woman isn't ready or is incapable of handling it, she should have the final say."

"She could put the baby up for adoption," Leslie said.

Cynthia poured another glass of wine. "And have to live with the knowledge that her child is out there in the world, hopefully being taken care of properly and not hating her for giving it away."

"Do you want women to revert back to being mutilated by unqualified quacks who'll do anything for money?" Kathy said.

"I don't want anyone or anything to be mutilated," Leslie said, visibly upset. "Excuse me for a minute. I have to use the bathroom."

Alice's eyes trailed Leslie until she disappeared around the corner. She then glared at them. "Smooth move, Kathy."

"What?" Kathy protested. "Are we a feminist group or a bunch of Mormons?"

"We're friends first," Alice said and looked at Dolores. "Why didn't you open your mouth? You're on her side."

Dolores raised her palms helplessly.

"Look, I have kids, too," Cynthia said, "but I had them with a loving husband. This is about reproductive freedom. Do you know how many women end up stuck in situations with the wrong guy because they can't handle the financial burden alone?"

"They could always kill them for their life insurance," Alice drawled.

"Here's a unique idea—women shouldn't sleep with the wrong men," Dolores added.

"What the Christ is wrong with you two?" Cynthia barked. "I can't believe what I'm hearing."

"Seriously," Kathy said. "Alice, can't you ever contribute anything besides sarcasm to these discussions?"

"This is getting way too heavy," Alice said, standing up. "I'm gonna go check on Leslie."

She meandered over to the bathroom and tapped on the door. "Les? Leslie?"

A muffled "what" came through the door.

"Are you okay?"

"No," Leslie said through sniffles.

Alice jiggled the locked doorknob. *"Will you let me in?"* she said gently.

After a moment, she heard the click of the door unlocking and walked in to find Leslie sitting on the toilet lid wiping her face with a wad of toilet paper. She crouched in front of her, resting her hands on Leslie's knees. *"Hey, Bella, don't take this so hard. It's just a philosophical exchange of ideas. We're all either high or drunk or both every time we have them."*

"That's not why I'm crying, you dummy," Leslie said. *"You're ignoring me tonight, like you can't stand looking at me."*

"I can't," Alice said, wiping some of Leslie's tears with her thumb. *"One look at you and it kills me. Reminds me how desperately I love you and can't have you."*

"I miss you," Leslie said as she cried softly.

"I miss you, too, baby." Alice pulled her off the toilet onto the floor where they sat and cried onto each other's shoulders.

"I want to be with you, Alice." She kissed her with wet, salty lips.

"God, I want that, too," she whispered, pecking her gently, sensually. *"Leave Bill and be with me."*

Leslie's tears smeared across Alice's cheeks, but she had no answer. She just clutched Alice tighter and devoured her in a kiss.

"Are you ladies okay in there?" Cynthia asked through the door.

Alice wiped her face, remembering she hadn't locked the door behind her. *"Yes, fine. Be right out."*

"Are you sure?" Cynthia asked.

"Yes," Alice snapped. *"We'll be right there."*

They scrambled to their feet, dried their tears, and took a moment to pull themselves together.

"I can't stand not seeing you, not talking to you," Leslie whispered.

"But you said being together was too hard."

"It is, Alice, but not being with you is torture. Please don't leave me." She embraced her again, clinging so tightly she was shaking.

"I won't, baby," Alice said in her ear. "We'll figure something out."

"Promise?"

"I promise," Alice said, trying to dislodge herself from Leslie's grip. "We better get back out there before they move the meeting in here."

Leslie's hands slid over Alice's hips and groped at her ass. "I wish we could sneak out and go to your house."

"Holy shit, me, too." Alice pressed her lips on Leslie's, pushed her against the sink, and ground her hips into her.

A fist pounded on the door. "What the hell are you doing in there, wiping each other?" Kathy bellowed. "Come on. This beer is going right through me."

Leslie pushed Alice away, causing her to stumble against the door. Alice opened it and found Kathy's eyes scrutinizing them.

"Now I know what you were doing," she said, nodding.

"We weren't doing anything," Alice said.

"Come on, it's obvious. Have you two looked in the mirror?"

Alice and Leslie examined each other in a near panic.

"So who puked and who held her hair back?" Kathy asked.

They both grumbled with nervous laughter.

"Can't put anything over on you, Kath," Alice said, patting her on the shoulder.

After the controversial klatch broke at the usual time, Alice and Leslie stood chitchatting over the roof of Alice's car in Cynthia's driveway. When Kathy and Dolores finally drove away, the tone of the conversation shifted.

"I wish you didn't have to go home," Alice said.

"I don't want to," Leslie said.

"I wonder if there's a diner around here," Alice said, then added, "Or a cheap motel."

Leslie's eyebrow shot up as she fondled her car keys in her hand. "I'll settle for either as long as I don't have to say good-bye to you yet."

Alice consulted her wristwatch. "Follow me off exit sixteen. We'll stop at whichever we come to first."

Leslie's headlights were steady in her rearview mirror on the highway all the way to the exit. Alice took a left off the ramp and drove for about a mile before spotting the orange neon sign of a 24-hour diner. She pulled into the parking lot and drove all the way to the back of the lot bordered by a wooded area. Leslie pulled in a few spaces away from her and waited for Alice to walk over to her.

"C'mere for a minute," Alice said, leaning against her car door, eyeing her as though she were a prisoner about to have a conjugal visit.

Leslie walked to her, her smile inching wider as she got closer. "Aren't we going in?"

"Get in my car," Alice said. "If I have to stare at your lips another moment and not kiss them, I'm certain I'll die."

Leslie scurried around the car and jumped into the passenger seat, and Alice wasted none of their precious time before laying a sensual kiss on her.

"What if someone sees us?" Leslie whispered.

"It's late," a kiss; "it's dark," another kiss, "and I don't care," a deeper kiss that settled the protest.

Leslie didn't seem too concerned either as she slid under Alice on the smooth vinyl, bench-style front seat.

Alice cradled Leslie's head in her hands and kissed her like fire racing through a barn, pressing her body into Leslie's as though they could melt and then fuse into one. What she wouldn't do to make time stop in this moment when they were the only two people in the world.

She worked at the clasp of Leslie's bra, anticipating resistance, but Leslie moaned softly and arched her back to accommodate her fingers. Unbuttoned, unhooked, and uninhibited, they made love feverishly as headlights flashed intermittently through the fogged-up windows. Somewhere in Alice's distant mind lurked the fear of being discovered by the fuzz or worse, a group of hoodlums, but her body and heart were so consumed in Leslie's softness and the ravenous response of her body that common sense hadn't stood a chance.

Afterward, they sat up sweaty and disheveled, their skin an exotic mixture of perfumes and pheromones. Alice ran her fingers through her damp hair, shaken by the intensity between them, the high she felt whenever she was in Leslie's arms.

Leslie had rolled down the car window and was fanning herself with the cool but stagnant night air. "You make me crazy, Alice," she said quietly, with resignation.

"I know it makes you uncomfortable when I say this, but I'm in love with you. Completely." Alice stared into the blackness beyond the wall of pine trees. "You're an addiction. You're unhealthy for me and can get me in all sorts of trouble, but I can't resist you when you're in front of me."

"And what about when I'm not?"

Alice turned and looked at her face, so beautiful in the glow from a distant parking-lot light. "Then I'm jonesin' for you like a fiend."

"I don't know what to do," Leslie said.

"About what?"

"I want you, Alice. I want to be with you so bad, but—"

"I know, I know," Alice said brusquely. "You've said this many times, but it's not that you don't know what to do. You just won't do it."

"You don't understand. I've got so much more to lose than you do."

"Yes, you're right. My heart, my pride, and my sanity are frivolous luxuries I can certainly live without."

"Alice, you know I didn't mean it that way. Please, let's not fight over this again."

Alice took her hand. "I'm sorry, baby. I don't want to fight. These last few weeks without you were unbearable—I don't know." She shook her head and suppressed the rise of familiar angst.

"I should go," Leslie said softly.

Alice nodded.

"Can I call you this week?"

"If you don't, I will," Alice said, managing a smile.

Leslie leaned over and gave her a kiss Alice felt tickle her soul. "I love you, Alice—more than you'll ever know."

She got out of the car before Alice could respond. A fast break. Alice hated them, but they were a necessary evil.

On the drive home, Alice blasted the radio in an attempt to extinguish the emotion smoldering in her even as her body still tingled from car sex with Leslie. But the driving beat of Rita Coolidge's "Your Love Has Lifted Me Higher" couldn't tune out the cacophony in her heart that her swift departure so soon after another torturously short interlude had caused.

She'd grown accustomed to the bouts of sadness that alternated with the ecstasy of making love with Leslie or simply a moment of stolen kisses, even finding comfort in the familiarity, but now it seemed the sadness was lasting longer and occurring sooner than before. Meeting Leslie at the diner hadn't been the brightest move, but it was one she wasn't ready to stop herself from making.

CHAPTER TWELVE

A lice relaxed in a lounge chair with a glass of lemonade keeping her lap cool. She watched her sister watching her son, DJ, and his son and daughter chase each other around the yard with lacrosse sticks in the afternoon sun.

"I'm getting heat stroke just looking at them," Alice said.

"DJ, you better take a break," Mary Ellen shouted. "You're going to have a heart attack in this heat."

DJ walked over to them, drying his hair with a beach towel. "Nothing to worry about, Ma. I'm a young forty-six. Those two keep me young." He dropped down in a chair next to them and broke open a bottle of water.

Mary Ellen's ten-year-old granddaughter, Madison, ran over and landed in her lap. "Grammy, I'm starving."

"Pop's getting the grill fired up, baby," she said, brushing sweaty bangs off the girl's forehead. "Are you gonna have some barbecued chicken?"

Madison bobbed her head excitedly as she sipped her father's water.

"Let me go help him," DJ said and headed over to the patio.

"It's so great having everyone together," Mary Ellen said. "It's been too long since we've all done this."

"I'm having an amazing time." Alice smiled at her grandniece as Mary Ellen stroked her ponytail.

And suddenly, like a curious butterfly, Madison flew off Mary Ellen's lap to see what her father and brother were up to at the grill.

Mary Ellen raised an eyebrow at Alice. "If it's so amazing, why is that phone in your hand?"

"What? Oh." Alice placed the phone on the small glass table between their chairs, truly unaware she was holding it.

"Why haven't you gone to see her since Friday?"

"I've been busy," Alice said.

"Bullshit. You were there every day since last weekend, for hours, even when she wasn't conscious. Now that she is, and it seems like she's going to recover, you're suddenly too busy to visit her?"

Alice lifted her sunglasses to address her sister. "I hope we're not going to have to start checking out homes for you."

"What?"

"You've been complaining that I'm not spending any quality time with you, and now that I am, you're asking why I'm not with Leslie."

"If you want to be with her, Ally, go be with her. I didn't mean to bully you into staying here."

"Bully me? I'm having the best time here with you and Dave and the kids. I wouldn't want to be anywhere else."

Suddenly, Alice's phone chirped and vibrated as Rebecca's name and number flashed across the screen. She snatched the phone off the table and ran into the kitchen to answer it.

"Hi, Alice," Rebecca said. "I hope I'm not calling you at a bad time."

"No. Is everything okay?"

"Yes, fine. I was just wondering if everything was okay with you."

"Me? Yeah, why do you ask?"

Rebecca seemed to hesitate. "Well, Mom said you had a really nice time reminiscing over lunch Friday, but you haven't been by since—I mean not that you have to come at all. I just wanted to make sure everything was okay with you."

Alice exhaled into the phone. Rebecca seemed genuinely concerned, but how could Alice tell her what was really going on? She'd been having a hard-enough time getting a handle on it herself.

She was in love with Leslie all over again, and it had only been a year since her partner had passed.

"Okay," Rebecca said softly. "I won't keep you—"

"Rebecca, wait," Alice said before she ended the call. "Listen, um, I had a wonderful time with Leslie on Friday. I so enjoyed reminiscing with her."

"Apparently, she did, too. She hasn't stopped talking about you since."

Alice's smile stretched her tight, sun-kissed skin. "As it turns out, I was planning to pay her a visit tonight after my family picnic," she said, a smile lingering in her voice.

"Oh, that's, uh…Mom'll be happy about that. Listen, I'm sorry I panicked and called you in the middle of your picnic."

"It's no trouble," Alice said. "I appreciate your concern."

She smiled again after they ended the call, her mood entirely transformed. What a trip to contemplate that all these years later, one of the two reasons she and Leslie couldn't be together would be playing matchmaker for them now.

After an uplifting afternoon of grilled chicken, mixed-berry trifle, and water-balloon fights with her nephew's kids, Alice took a quick shower, stopped at the florist, and was on her way to the rehab facility. At a traffic light she checked her reflection in the rearview mirror, noting the pronounced smile lines around her mouth and eyes. The decision to come back to Connecticut had been a good one. Time spent with family, old friends, and Leslie had been the salve she'd long needed.

Maureen's illness and death had carved a cavernous wound in her over a five-year span. By the time she'd laid her to rest, she hadn't recognized herself anymore. Only twice in her life had something affected her so profoundly as to change the essence of her being: leaving Leslie and losing Maureen. Now it seemed she'd been given the chance to reclaim one of those losses. But to what degree?

As she rolled into Sunday traffic, she reminded herself to breathe and flashed back to a time when another of Leslie's family members had tried his hand at matchmaking.

October 1977

After their steamy night in Alice's car, social gatherings at Bill and Leslie's had gone from awkward to downright unbearable. At their Halloween party, Alice sat sipping a Jack and Ginger, flipping through a TV guide, yawning repeatedly—as inviting a party guest as the clap. She'd been actively avoiding the cat in the pirate costume, Vic Howard, a handsome plumber with weathered hands and a dimpled grin rivaling Leslie's in its beauty. That fucking husband of Leslie's. Why couldn't he ever bring around someone ugly, missing teeth or fingers, any hideous defect that would provide an easy excuse for her not to date him? Maybe the solution lay in her own hands. Maybe she should take a page out of Kathy's beauty regimen—no more makeup to accentuate her full lips and thick eyelashes, no more outfits that emphasized her shapely figure—only clothing and shoes that readied her for a hike in the mountains at a moment's notice.

As she knocked back the last drop of her drink, she saw Vic wave at her. Damn it. She whipped around toward the fireplace, smeared her mascara with her finger, and messed up her hair as he made his way over.

"There you are." He smiled, as charismatic as Omar Sharif in Doctor Zhivago. *"Say, who are you supposed to be again?"*

She raised the zipper on the front of her royal-blue jumpsuit and pressed down the square tinfoil packets of wires stuck to her forearms. "The Bionic Woman." She lifted her arms to his face.

"Of course. Well, I hope your bionic hearing didn't catch me telling everyone how foxy you look in that jumpsuit." A goofy laugh accentuated his compliment.

"Hmm, wouldn't I love to be able to pick up conversations across the room." She scanned the party guests, trying to locate Leslie's short Little Red Riding Hood dress.

"Looks like I found you just in time." He indicated her empty glass. *"What are you drinking?"*

"Jack and Ginger." She handed him her glass and looked directly at him to ensure he noticed her newly disheveled appearance. As he walked toward the makeshift bar, she was confident he wouldn't hang around too long after returning to drop off her fresh drink.

"You have an intriguing smile," he said when he returned.

"How do you know? I haven't smiled all night." She snatched the drink from his hand and took a healthy swig.

"Yes, you have—before, when you were talking to Leslie. She must've been telling you one hell of a story. Your face lit up like their Jack-o'-lanterns. Except your teeth are much nicer."

"Thanks." She damned her parents for being able to afford orthodontics. *"Speaking of our hostess, where is she?"*

"Probably in the kitchen. So why haven't you smiled all night? That's like a plant refusing to give off oxygen."

She inspected his glassy brown eyes. *"You're the most poetic plumber I've ever met."*

"Don't let the years of toil on these hands fool you," he said. *"I'm a thinking man. How about you let me take you out to dinner some time and prove it?"*

"I'm fine taking your word for it," she said.

"Come on, Alice. It's a valuable thing to be on a first-name basis with a plumber."

"I've had pretty decent luck with the Yellow Pages."

Vic smirked. *"Do you always work guys over like this before saying yes?"*

Alice zeroed in on Leslie across the room as she came out of the kitchen. She carried a platter of hors d'oeuvres over to Bill, who looked like a big dope in his Big Bad Wolf costume. He said something in her ear, producing that lone, killer dimple on Leslie's cheek. Alice's blood boiled as her imagination conjured all sorts of horrific possibilities.

"You know what, Vic?" she said as though spiting Leslie. *"Let's go out to dinner some time."*

"Really? Oh man, righteous. Okay. Let me find a pen to take down your number."

Alice smiled like a silent-film villain as she walked over to Leslie. *"You and Bill look like you're having a smashing good time."*

"There you are," Leslie said. *"Where've you been hiding?"*

"Well, I was hiding from Vic the poetic plumber, but it turns out he's a better detective than you."

"Only because I've been busy in the kitchen. I didn't expect this many people."

"What was so funny between you and Bill?"

"What do you mean?"

"When you came out of the kitchen, he whispered something to you. What was it, something romantic?"

"No, no," Leslie said, flustered. *"He said we're lucky that Fat Tommy showed up, or we'd be eating pigs in a blanket and that salmon mold for dinner for the next week."*

Alice gulped the rest of her drink, trying to wash down a pungent pang of jealousy. Leslie had been Bill's girl for so long, they had so much history, so many inside jokes, a bond Alice could never compete with, and not for lack of will.

"That's very cute," Alice said. *"Bill's a funny guy."*

"Alice, are you upset about something?"

"It sucks enough seeing you and Bill together. Can't you save the cutesy lovebird stuff for when I'm not around?"

"Honestly, it wasn't like that at all," Leslie said discreetly. *"I've told you before, we've never had that kind of relationship. He's not really a lovey-dovey kind of guy."*

"Who picked out your costumes? Talk about a misogynistic rape-fantasy cliché."

"A what fantasy? Alice, they're nursery-rhyme characters. We bought them for a costume party three years ago."

Alice sipped her drink, refusing to look at her.

"I'm sorry. I..." Leslie stammered. *"Maybe inviting you was a bad idea."*

Alice's eyes couldn't conceal the sting from that one. *"Well, I'm sorry my presence here is cramping your style."*

"Baby, that's not what I meant," Leslie said. "I mean, you know, now that we're involved, maybe...I don't know."

"You mean now that we're in love, we have sex..."

Leslie chewed her lip. "Alice, what am I supposed to do?"

"Nothing, Leslie. You don't have to do anything. I, however, have to use the bathroom."

Once Alice was securely concealed behind the bathroom door, she plotted ways to escape the party without giving Vic her phone number. As she washed her hands, she was startled by her reflection. Ratty hair, tire-mark mascara circles under her eyes, and contemplating fleeing a party by climbing out a tiny window over the toilet. Not exactly the Bionic Woman's finest hour.

Once she pulled herself together enough to walk out of the bathroom and execute her escape by an actual doorway, she searched surreptitiously for her purse. Upon identifying the target on the floor next to the recliner, she dove into the shag carpet and crawled like a Marine to apprehend it.

"Hey, Alice, come over here," Bill's voice beckoned.

So much for a clean getaway. She walked over to Bill, standing with Vic, Leslie, and somebody's cousin. "What can I do for you, Bill?"

"Why are you giving my friend, Vic, here a hard time? He just wants to take you to dinner. Afraid the feminists will string you up by your eighteen-hour bra if you go?"

"Bill, please," Leslie said.

He'd obviously had a few more drinks than usual, and Alice didn't care for his antagonistic tone or Leslie's limp attempt to admonish him. "If you must know, Bill, we are permitted to have dinner with men...every third Friday if it falls on an odd date and the moon isn't full."

Bill and Vic exchanged perplexed looks.

"I already told him I'd go out with him, but thanks for your help, Yente. By the way, I think there's a fiddler on your roof."

She walked away, fishing for her car keys in her purse.

Leslie looped her arm through Alice's and pulled her into the kitchen. "Please don't be upset with me."

"Your husband's drunk, and I'm going home. If Vic asks you for my number, give it to him."

"You're not okay. Please stay a little longer and sober up."

"Thanks, but this evening's been sobering enough." She motioned toward the door, and then turned back to Leslie, planting a long, wet kiss on her, to the point where Leslie had to push her away.

"Not here, Alice."

"Right. Not here, not ever."

Alice blew out the kitchen door like a storm before her ability to reason was completely gone. What was it about Leslie that reduced her to a lovesick teenager? The whole situation was absurd, impossible, and when they were alone together, the most powerful drug she'd ever experimented with.

She bargained with herself not to call Leslie anymore, pleaded, in fact. She had to stop. Cold turkey. No gradual tapering off. It simply wouldn't work that way. Their relationship was wrong for so many reasons, not the least of which was the complete loss of her emotional stability.

November 1977

A week later, as Alice sat at her kitchen table waiting for Vic to pick her up, she found little consolation in honoring her vow not to speak with Leslie. Each day slogged along more slowly than the one before as she missed the sound of Leslie's voice, the scent of her hair more and more. Now she struggled to summon the enthusiasm for a date with someone she had no interest in having dinner with. Against all reason, Leslie was the only person her heart beat for.

Alice soothed her nerves with a glass of white wine as she listened to the radio. She'd switched to a hard-rock station after being ambushed once again by several sadistic love songs. Aerosmith, Lynyrd Skynyrd, and Kiss had lulled her into a false sense of security with raunchy lyrics and screaming guitar solos. And then it happened: *"Love Hurts"* by Nazareth. She seized the battery-operated transistor radio and hurled it into the dining room. It took out a plastic ficus tree before skidding to a stop against the baseboard.

As she poured a second glass of wine, she couldn't remember a time she felt less excited about doing something any woman would sacrifice her left nipple for. The handsome, dimpled plumber was taking her to dinner at an upscale restaurant in downtown New Haven and then to hear a symphony at the Palace Theatre—not too shabby. If her mind and heart hadn't still been so spellbound by Leslie, she, too, might've been willing to offer up her left one for the chance.

The chime of the doorbell broke the silence. She gathered her purse, house keys, and a shawl for the evening, and slapped on a smile as she pulled open the door.

"Leslie."

"Why haven't you answered your phone?" Leslie walked past her into the house.

"You can't stay. Vic is coming to pick me up any minute."

"Fine. Now that I know you're not dead, tell me why you haven't answered my calls, and I'll go."

"Do you really need to ask?"

"Because of the party? Look, I know it was awkward but—"

"It's more than that, Leslie."

"Is it Vic? Do you really like him?"

"Leslie, I love you, I desire you."

"Then why are you going out with him?"

"For one thing, you said I should so people, like Bill in particular, won't get suspicious. Remember?"

"Are you going to sleep with him?"

"I just met him. Why would I sleep with him? And so what if I did? You sleep with Bill."

"I have to," Leslie shrieked in protest.

"Let's get one thing straight, Leslie. This is a free country. No one has to do anything."

"I just can't stop having sex with my husband, not unless I want to end my marriage."

"So you'll be free to be with me, the one you supposedly truly love? No, of course you wouldn't want to do that."

"I wish it was as simple as you think it is."

"What exactly do you think is so simple for me? Missing you desperately? Being in love with someone I'll never have, someone who has sex with someone else? Yeah, it's a real piece of cake."

"You knew I was married when we started this."

"And you knew I'm single, so I'll screw anyone I want without running it by you first."

Leslie shrank like an abandoned puppy. *"Why are you acting like this?"*

"It's over, Leslie. We made a mistake. We never should have let it get this far."

"That's obvious, Alice, but it did get this far, and now I don't know how to get out of it without completely falling apart."

Alice sighed, barely holding her own broken pieces together. *"We can't see each other anymore, not even as friends."*

Leslie's eyes filled with tears as the doorbell chimed.

"That's him," Alice said. *"You have to go."* She extended her hands to assess how badly they were shaking.

"Can't we talk about this before you make any drastic decisions? Call me tomorrow," Leslie said. *"Promise you'll call me tomorrow."*

"Les, you've wanted to end this, too. Why are you fighting it now? Because it's me breaking it off, not you?"

"No, Alice. I know we can't go on like this, but we owe it to each other to talk this out calmly, not when you're about to go out on a date."

"What's the point? Unless you're going to leave Bill, there's nothing else to say. Now you have to go."

"Alice, please," Leslie said, blocking her passage to the door.

The doorbell rang again.

Startled by Leslie's vehemence, Alice acquiesced. *"Okay, I'll call you. Now pull yourself together. I can't keep him waiting any longer."*

When Alice opened the door, Vic presented her with a bouquet of flowers and an innocent smile. *"Hey, Leslie,"* he said when she moved around Alice toward the door.

"Hi, Vic," she said quietly. *"Have a great time."*

"Thanks." He watched her walk away and then looked at Alice.
"I hope I didn't interrupt anything important."
"No, no, just girl talk. Thanks for the flowers. Pour yourself a
drink while I put them in a vase."
She indicated the cocktail cart so he wouldn't follow her into
the kitchen. She let the running water overflow the vase as tears
streamed down her cheeks. How was she supposed to enjoy a fancy
dinner with Vic when she felt like leaning over and barfing her guts
out in the sink? She watched the small, dead rose leaves circle the
drain as she tried to force Leslie from her mind.
"Can I give you a hand in there?" Vic asked from the living
room.
"No, thanks. Be right out." She rubbed the black tear streaks
from her cheeks with a dishtowel.
As they walked to the door, he placed his hand lightly on her
back and led her out the door like a gentleman.
"I think this is going to be a groovy night," he said.

The next morning Alice had waked wondering if the night
before had been the kind of dream you have after a particularly
wild acid trip. After getting drunk at the Japanese restaurant and
cackling several times and then napping through the symphony, she
hadn't expected to hear from Vic again. She'd considered sending a
thank-you note to the waiter who kept bringing her sake, thus saving
her the unpleasantness of the "I don't think this is going anywhere"
conversation when Vic requested a second date.
Her hangover had abated in time for a Saturday evening out
with her cousin Phyllis, a fortune Phyllis might not have found so
fortunate. Alice pouted as she dragged the same long French fry
through a blob of ketchup in her plate.
"Would you please stop moping?" Phyllis said, dropping her
grilled cheese onto her plate. "I want to feel sorry for you, but it's
hard to when someone jumps into a raging inferno and is surprised
when their ass catches fire."

"I don't expect sympathy," Alice said. "I'm well acquainted with the error of my ways. But you don't have to berate me for feeling sad. I can't help it. Haven't you ever been in love before?"

"Yes, I've been in love. Frankly, it was more trouble than it was worth. But in your case there are mitigating circumstances."

"Exactly."

"I mean you didn't know you're a lesbian, so how could you have possibly predicted that you and Leslie were on a collision course toward an illicit, tawdry affair?"

"Exactly," Alice repeated excitedly and then dropped her greasy fry onto her plate. "Wait a darn minute there. It wasn't tawdry. It was beautiful, poetic, tragic. And let's not jump the gun with the lesbian thing. I'm dating a handsome plumber named Vic," she lied.

Phyllis shook her head. "There's another fire you've set for yourself."

"What do you mean?"

"Why are you dating him?"

"He's nice and very handsome."

"Sounds like an ideal diversion."

"Maybe that's just what I need right now. I miss Leslie so much. These past few weeks have been torture. I reach for the phone at least three times a day."

"I'm proud of you for showing such remarkable restraint. It'll get easier in time. In the meantime, do you think it's wise to string this poor man along?"

"You know, dear cousin, it would be nice if, once in a while, instead of being the voice of reason, you'd support me in my quest to do the wrong thing that will eventually end badly for everyone involved."

Phyllis smiled. "I can't do that, dear cousin. Besides, you seem to do well enough in that department without my support."

Alice pushed her plate away and sat back in the booth.

"Here's a radical idea," Phyllis said. "Why don't you find another woman? A single one."

"I don't want another woman. I want Leslie."

"Okay, fine." Phyllis blotted the corners of her mouth with her napkin. "You let me know how that works out for you." She signaled for the waitress.

Alice considered the suggestion. Another woman was out of the question. Another woman could never measure up to Leslie— her smile, her high-pitched laugh that tickled everyone around her, those lips, that buttery smooth skin. She'd destroy another woman with comparisons. She could be with Vic. She knew how to be with men, even if she could never love one the way she loved Leslie.

"Vic is a nice guy." Alice handed Phyllis cash for the bill and wondered if she hadn't written him off a little too soon.

"Yes, so you've said."

"I think I can make it work with him," Alice said, nodding. "It's certainly worth a try."

"I have a strange feeling dinners with you are going to start being painful for me."

"What's that supposed to mean?"

"Alice, I'm seriously beginning to worry you're losing your grasp on reality. Deal with your feelings for Leslie before you dive into something else, especially with a man. I think you need to admit to yourself that that train's left the station for good."

"Phyllis, please stop trying to make me a homosexual. Can't you see I have enough on my plate here? Trying to forget Leslie is already more than I can handle."

Phyllis rolled her eyes. "Okay, I promise to stop making you a homosexual if you promise to start including your brain when making important decisions."

"I think I've proved I'm quite capable of that these past few weeks. Do you know how easy it would be for me to call Leslie and concoct an excuse to get together with her?"

"That reminds me of a quote. Proust, I think it was, said, 'So few are the easy victories as the ultimate failures.'"

Alice smirked at her. "Save your brainy literary quotes for someone who needs them. I've got everything under control."

They left the bistro and began walking up Chapel Street.

"See, that's where you lose me, Al. You've got nothing under control, and if I may extend my inferno metaphor, sleeping with a married woman is playing with fire. How much longer do you think she can get away with it before he catches on?"

"We're very careful," was Alice's mousy reply.

"That's reassuring," Phyllis drawled. "After he comes home, finds you in bed with his wife, and shoots you in the head, I'll be sure to put 'they were very careful' on your headstone."

"We don't do anything at her house. We don't do anything at all anymore. I've ended the affair."

"Ah, yes, hence the tragic mood. Well, you ought to really enjoy this play tonight."

"What are we seeing?"

They stopped on the sidewalk near the Yale Repertory Theatre, and Phyllis pointed to the marquee.

"Othello," *Alice said.* "Marvelous."

CHAPTER THIRTEEN

As Alice walked down the hall of the rehab center toward Leslie's room, her heart fluttered with the same raw anticipation it used to on her way to pick her up on crochet night. She switched the mixed bouquet of flowers from one hand to the other, shaking her nerves out through her free fingers as she rounded the corner. Rebecca and Leslie were sitting at a small table having coffee and crumb cake as Jake navigated a *Star Wars* spaceship around the room.

"Hey, kids," Alice said, peeking into the room. Something was different as she walked in.

"Hi, Alice." Rebecca jumped up and hugged her. "Mom, aren't you going to say hi to Alice?"

With the support of the chair's arms, Leslie lifted herself, gripped the rolling walker by the table, and shuffled toward Alice. "Hey, Betty."

The wheelchair was gone. Alice's eyes watered as she gently wrapped her arms around Leslie. "When did this happen?"

"Yesterday," Leslie said. "I couldn't wait to show you."

Alice glanced at Rebecca, who eyed her knowingly.

"I'm so happy for you," Alice said. "Perfect timing, too. Cynthia and Kathy want a reunion of the old crochet klatch, and we can't have it without you."

"I'll be thrilled to join you," Leslie said and headed back to her chair.

"Mom, Jake and I have to get going. Billy's coming tomorrow after work, but call me if you need anything."

"Thanks, baby," Leslie said, cupping Rebecca's face when she bent to kiss her.

"Gram, wanna see what this can do?" Jake flew his spacecraft over to her.

"Let me see, Jakie." Leslie put her arms around his waist as he dazzled her with its flashing lights and screeches.

"Come here for a second?" Rebecca whispered, and they stepped outside the room.

"What's up?" Alice asked, eyeing Leslie from the hall.

"I know you've said there was nothing more than friendship between you and Mom, but all I know is I haven't seen her this pumped about anything since Jake was born."

"Well, sure, she's pumped. She's walking again after she thought she was paralyzed."

"Alice, that's not why."

"I'm afraid I don't know what you're suggesting."

Rebecca studied her for a moment. "All right. I'll humor you if you really want me to, but the chemistry between you and my mother is so obvious. It's like when she woke from her coma, she was reborn, and I know it wasn't from some white-light experience."

Alice admired the pastel floral wallpaper to hide the blush of a schoolgirl learning her crush liked her back.

"Alice," Rebecca said gently. "What do you still have to hide?"

"I don't have anything to hide, honey, really," Alice said. "My wife died a year ago, and I'm here as a friend to support your mother as she recovers. That's what she needs to focus on right now."

Rebecca smiled with understanding. "I'm sorry, Alice. My romantic imagination seems to have ridden off the rails. I didn't mean to disrespect your grieving process."

"You didn't," Alice said. "I was an active participant in every phase of my grief, believe me. This visit to Connecticut has been a welcome respite, just what the doctor ordered."

"It's nice that you could both be there for each other again. I hope when you go home, you'll stay in touch."

"I won't make the same mistake twice."

"Anyway, I should be focusing on my own disaster of a marriage instead of pressuring you about dating my mother."

"How are things going with Sage?"

"She's coming back home, and we're going to give couples' therapy a try."

"That's a positive step. I'm rooting for you."

Rebecca hugged Alice. "Thanks." She stuck her head in the room. "Come on, Jake. Let's get going."

Alice walked back into the room and sat at the table with Leslie. "You want to put on some sensible shoes and take a walk outside?"

"No, thank you," Leslie said. "I was outside earlier with Rebecca and Jake, and I'm kind of wiped out from today's therapy."

"Would you like me to go and let you get some rest?"

"You just got here." Leslie's mouth drooped like a kid whose recess had just been cancelled. "I've been hoping you'd come by."

"I'm sorry I didn't make it yesterday. I figured I'd give you a break. Or give your family a chance to visit with you."

"They have plenty of time to visit me. But please don't feel obligated to come, Alice." Suddenly, a mischievous glint appeared in her eyes. "Just because I gush over how much I enjoy your visits."

"I enjoy them, too, more than you know."

Their eyes locked for an uncomfortable moment, conveying more than they had since Leslie regained consciousness.

"Will you still want to visit when I get out of here? I mean until you go home."

The phrase *go home* was a tricky one. This week Alice had felt more at home in Leslie's presence than she had in the entire year since Maureen passed.

"I can't wait till you walk out of here, and yes, I'll come to see you." Alice looked over her shoulder out into the hall. "Say, does Bill come around?"

"He showed up at the hospital a couple of times, but after he knew I wasn't going to die he hasn't bothered."

"Does that disappoint you?"

"Not at all. We're friendly, but we've had our own lives for a long time."

"It seems strange to be with you and not have the specter of your husband hanging over us. I think for me, it's still there."

"I'm sorry it was so difficult back then, Alice. I don't know if I'll ever be able to apologize adequately for what you went through."

"You have nothing to apologize for. We were both adults. I can't fault you for doing what you believed was best for you and your kids."

"It was such a confusing time."

"I'll say. It sure changed me."

Leslie clutched the bouquet of flowers, burying her nose in it as she gazed out the window.

"Did you ever date another woman after me?"

"I thought about it." Leslie turned back to the table. "But it took me so long to get over you that...I don't know. By the time I did, I was so used to being on my own that I never bothered pursuing it."

"I'm sorry, too." Alice closed her eyes and for a moment stopped battling her heart against the rush of abandon it wanted to feel. "Over the years I sometimes wished we'd never met just so you wouldn't have had to endure such a painful struggle."

Leslie smiled. "Do you want to know something strange?"

"I'd love to," Alice said with a flirtatious lilt.

"Of all the things I've wished for in the last thirty years, that was never one of them."

"How could that be? What we had almost destroyed us both."

"And it reshaped me into the kind of woman we talked about and admired in our feminist meetings, the woman I never felt I was capable of being."

"I keep thinking about that time we met for lunch in Boston when you told me you were going to divorce Bill. I didn't believe you'd go through with it."

"You were with Maureen then."

"I can't help but wonder what would've transpired if I had believed you. If only you'd called me a year earlier..."

"Alice, if I didn't have kids, I never would've let you go in the first place. God, I was so in love with you. But I'd made a commitment to keep my family stable until my children were on their own. I raised two caring, reasonably well-adjusted human beings who love and respect me unconditionally. I don't bother with regrets."

Alice smiled with pride. "You've come a long way, Bella."

Leslie squeezed Alice's hand and stifled a yawn. "Sometime you'll have to tell me about Maureen."

"I'd like that," Alice said, standing. "But right now I'm going to let you get comfortable and relax. You look exhausted."

"Don't go," Leslie said, surprising them both with her eagerness. "I mean if you have somewhere to go, of course, but if not, it's still early."

Alice sat down again. "It is nice not having to rush off by a certain time."

"It's wonderful," Leslie said.

"Although I will have to get out of here at a decent hour, or they may think I'm a patient and force me to do those sadistic exercises that make the veins in your neck bulge out."

They shared an easy laugh, and Alice reveled in the simple pleasure of just being with Leslie—without the complications of sex, secrecy, and the insanity of first love.

"My God, that was awful." Leslie said. "Every time I wanted to cling to you forever, I'd look at the clock and have to go."

"I wanted to smash that damn clock with a hammer," Alice said. "But that's because I never wanted you to leave my side—especially to go home to someone else."

"I knew it was hard for you," Leslie said, "and that you were hurting."

"I realized you were, too, even though sometimes I didn't act like it." Alice grew sullen, losing her sense of balance as Memory Lane began icing over.

"Alice?"

She exhaled deeply. "I was so hurtful to you that night."

January 1978

After they'd made love on Alice's sofa and then quickly dressed, Alice let a recurring curiosity lead them into a conversation neither was prepared to have.

"Do you think of me when you're with Bill?" she asked, stroking Leslie's forearm with her nails.

"I think of you all the time—when I'm with Bill, the kids, at the grocery store, listening to the radio."

"No, I mean when you're in bed with Bill."

She sighed. "Alice."

"Why does that question make you uncomfortable?"

"The whole idea of talking about Bill when I'm with you makes me uncomfortable."

"I just want to know if you think of me while you're making love with someone else."

"It's not the same as it is with you, Alice."

"I know that. I remember what it was like with Tony. Your chest isn't nearly as hairy as his."

"You know that's not what I meant. I've never felt the emotional connection to him that I feel for you. I didn't know it then because I had nothing to compare it to. Alice, nothing compares to you."

"So you don't enjoy it as much as you do with me?"

"No, I swear."

"But you still do it with him."

Leslie's hands quavered under Alice's scrutiny. "I have to. I can't just stop. Then he'll really know something's the matter."

Alice gritted her teeth with jealousy. How could she be intimate with someone else when she'd professed her undying love for her? She struggled to work it out in her head. Alice had felt no desire to be with anyone but her since the moment it began. It left a bad taste in her mouth to even think of it. Then the second part of Leslie's response registered.

"What do you mean, 'then he'll really know'?"

"It's nothing." Leslie hesitated. "Lately he's been asking what's wrong with me." She burrowed her head into Alice's armpit.

"What is wrong with you?"

She sprang up and glared at Alice. "You mean apart from being devoured by guilt? Alice, I'm living a double life. I'm so preoccupied thinking of you, wanting you, missing you that I miss half the conversations that go on in my house. The other day I almost made the kids tuna sandwiches with Roscoe's canned cat food." She paused and then said in a soft, shaky voice, "You'd be surprised how often I cry myself to sleep."

"Why do you cry?" Alice tried to keep an analytical tone, but the thought of it slashed her apart inside.

"Why do you think, Alice?"

"I don't know," she said calmly as tension began billowing up between them. "That's why I'm asking you."

"I'm betraying him. I love him, but I don't want to have sex with him anymore."

"Then stop."

"How can I stop?"

Alice's lip twitched with jealousy. "Just stop."

"I can't do that. I'm already being so unfair to him."

"If you deny him, maybe he'll go out and have his own affair. Then we'll have more time together."

"I can't do that. It'll ruin my marriage."

"That would ruin your marriage?" Alice wrestled with Leslie's logic. "You don't think being here with me right now is ruining your marriage? Or is it that as long as you go home and spread your legs like a good little wife, everything's fine?"

Leslie's eyes watered. "Alice, why are you being so cruel?"

"I don't know. I'm sorry." She got up and paced beside the sofa. "I don't know what I'm doing anymore, Leslie. I haven't had a decent night's sleep in weeks. All I do is think of you. The only thing that interests me is being with you. I don't understand why I'm so lost in you."

"That's the thing you're not getting, Alice. I feel the exact same way about you."

"Then move in with me, you and the kids." The suggestion escaped before Alice realized the folly in it.

"You know that's not a possibility."

Leslie's tone offended her.

"Why can't it be? Times are changing. Miss Estabrook and Miss Lyons have been living together for years just a few houses down from here."

Alice stated this as if it were as common an occurrence as ants at a picnic. Of course, she neglected to include how all the neighborhood kids made sport of tormenting them, stealing their newspapers, digging up their lawn with their bicycle tires, and bombarding their house with eggs and rotten tomatoes every Halloween like they were launching aerial raids against the Viet Cong.

"Were those neighbors married when they met? Did they have children?"

"I don't know. I don't think so."

"We've been over this before. I can't leave Bill."

Hearing that yet again lit the fuse on Alice's anger and frustration. *"I know why you can't,"* she spat. *"You don't want to because you're still attracted to him. I'm just some lonely housewife's afternoon delight now that your kids aren't babies anymore."*

"Alice, why do you keep saying that? Please tell me you don't really believe it."

"Give me one reason why I shouldn't."

"I'm in love with you." Leslie's voice sounded strained as she pleaded. *"Deeply, truly in love with you. Can't you feel it when we make love?"*

"It's the seventies. That's no longer a prerequisite for screwing around."

"It is for me, Alice. What I feel for you isn't only about sex. We have so much more than that, something so much deeper."

"Don't kid yourself, Leslie. We have sex. You have something much deeper with your husband."

"I wish I could make you understand," she said in quiet resignation. She collapsed on the couch and cried into her hands. *"I'd have to break up my family to be with you. My kids would be devastated. My family would never forgive me, especially if I left Bill for a woman. They'd never get over the embarrassment."*

Alice picked up her wineglass and pitched it across the room with a guttural cry, sending it crashing into the wall and Leslie recoiling back. She dropped onto the loveseat and sat quietly, her diaphragm hiccupping from crying as she tried to catch her breath.

"Alice," Leslie whispered.

She ignored her, boiling in the pot of insignificance Leslie had poured her into. No matter how badly she desired it, she would never mean to Leslie what she'd wanted to. She'd never be as important as she was to her. She wanted to scream at her, more hurtful things than she'd said before, if that was possible. How dare Leslie get to have her cake and eat it, too, while Alice lurked in the shadows starving for whatever crumbs Leslie threw her?

"Say something." Leslie kneeled in front of her, weeping as she rested her forehead on Alice's arm. "Please say something, Alice."

After gulping down a stomach full of tears and humiliation, Alice sat up, trying to make herself big again. "I understand. I really do."

"You do?"

Alice closed her eyes against the rising disgrace. Leslie threw her arms around her and squeezed her almost to the point of suffocation.

"Oh, Alice," she said, continuing to sob. "I love you so much, I can't stand it. My heart is breaking."

Alice pulled her up to the loveseat and held her, shushing her whimpering as she stroked her hair. What was she thinking, lashing out at her like that? What gave her the right? She felt like some deviant prowling outside their home, intruding on their privacy, threatening their happiness as a family.

"I'm sorry I said those things, Les," she finally said. "I was way out of line."

Leslie looked up and wiped her face with her sleeve. "I don't blame you for wanting that. I want it, too, but I just can't hurt my kids like that. Their happiness means everything to me."

"Obviously." Alice didn't want to sound sarcastic, but she'd absorbed all she could about why the love of her life refused to be with her.

"If you had children, you'd know what I mean."

She glared at her. "I know what you mean. Even though I've never fulfilled my womanly destiny of giving birth, I'm not some insensitive bitch."

"I know you're not, and I didn't mean for it to sound that way." She stroked Alice's chin. "I should go home. I can't fight with you anymore. It's killing me."

"I don't want to fight either. But please don't go home yet. It's still early." The desperation in her voice startled her.

Leslie embraced her again, clinging to her, sniffling softly in her ear.

Alice kissed the back of her hand and blinked away what little pride she had left. As their love built on secrets and lies started to crumble, she wanted to savor every moment with Leslie she had left before it collapsed entirely.

Alice and Leslie sat quietly for a moment, digesting the difficult memory. Alice fondled a thread on her Bermuda shorts while Leslie caressed her coffee cup. Finally, they looked at each other and smiled reassurances and hope for a new beginning—or a long-awaited closure.

CHAPTER FOURTEEN

A lice coasted into the gravel driveway around nine o'clock, hoping her sister would be asleep on the couch so she could sail in and up the stairs without having to debrief anyone on her visit with Leslie. She turned off the ignition and remained in the car for a moment. Her head throbbed slightly now that the adrenaline surge from being with Leslie had subsided. Leslie was under her skin again, but how deeply? The question had begun to constrict Alice like polyester slacks in the summer heat. Maybe her feelings were merely fond nostalgia for an old friendship. Or not. Was it possible that Leslie was thinking as much about their past as Alice had been?

She walked into the house and toward a flickering light coming from the patio. Dave and Mary Ellen were sitting around a small fire pit, a bottle of white wine chilling in an ice bucket. Suddenly, she was grateful they hadn't fallen asleep in front of the TV.

"Hey, sissy," Mary Ellen said, tapping the arm of the vacant chair beside her. "Care for a cold one?"

Dave leaned forward and poured her a glass of sauvignon blanc. "So how's your lady friend?"

Alice glared at her sister as she reached for the glass. "What did you tell him?"

"That you've reconnected with an old flame," Dave said. "Good for you. I hope it works out."

"Hope what works out?" Alice said.

"That you get to pick up with her where you left off," Mary Ellen said.

Alice scoffed. "Nobody truly gets to pick up where they left off, especially when it's been nearly forty years."

"I disagree," Mary Ellen said. "I believe wholeheartedly in second chances."

"What a lovely thought, but I'll never get one with Maureen." Alice sipped her wine and stared into the fire as Dave pushed the graying logs with an iron.

"Not in this lifetime," Mary Ellen said, "but maybe it'll come in a different realm."

Alice looked over at her brother-in-law. "She's cut off after that glass."

Dave chuckled and winked at his wife. "Maybe the point is that you have another chance now, in this life."

"Maybe I don't want another chance with Leslie," Alice said. "Maybe it was exactly what it was meant to be back then, and that's it. Maybe loving her the first time around tore my heart out, and now there's nothing left."

Mary Ellen regarded her for a moment, then said gently, "How did you love Maureen as much as you did if your heart was torn out?"

"Okay, it was half torn out from Leslie. Maureen took the half that was left with her when she died."

They all sat quietly for a moment, staring into the crackling flames. Alice wondered if what she'd just said was true. If it was, then why was she so invested in Leslie now?

Dave downed the last of his wine. "Well, this is becoming one of those sister moments that make me very uncomfortable. Call me when you want the fire out."

"Chicken," Alice said, smiling.

He patted her on the head and gave his wife a peck on her cheek. Once he was inside and had closed the sliders, Mary Ellen emptied the bottle into their glasses.

"What did you and Leslie discuss that put you in this mood?"

"We finally stopped dancing around the topic of our affair and actually had a conversation about something specific. It was a painful time." Alice shook her head as if that would expel the memory.

"What did you talk about?"

Alice poked at the logs as the flames ebbed. "How heart-wrenching it was always having to say good-bye. She didn't want to leave, I didn't want her to, but that was always the inevitable conclusion."

"How long did you two go on like that?"

"About a year, on and off. I can't tell you how many times we broke up. We just couldn't let go."

"Boy, that explains so much," Mary Ellen said. "I remember that weekend in February after the blizzard. Everyone was out celebrating Valentine's Day, and you were miserable. You passed it off saying you missed Tony. I knew you were full of crap, but I couldn't imagine what the real story was."

"That was not a good day." Alice gulped her wine and stared into the flames.

"What happened?"

Late February 1978

After a three-week hiatus thanks to the blizzard, the next crochet klatch was at Dolores's house, where they sat around the living room snacking, sipping, smoking, and crocheting every so often when their hands were free to pick up their needles. Alice sat on the sofa with the makings of a beret she'd wanted ever since she saw Mary Tyler Moore toss one into the air during the opening of her favorite TV show. She was unusually quiet, smoking more than normal to dull the ache of Leslie's absence. Aside from the initial surprised inquiries about her absence when she'd arrived, the ladies hadn't dwelled on it—until they'd run out of inequities to be indignant about.

"Where's Leslie?" Kathy asked. "She hasn't been to a meeting since when, January?"

Yeah, that's right. Thanks for the reminder, Kathy.

"Maybe she and her husband went out for a romantic dinner," Cynthia said. "A belated Valentine's Day."

Thanks for the reminder, Cynthia. *Alice pulled at the collar of her turtleneck sweater.*

"No, they're doing that tomorrow night," *Dolores said.* "That new Italian place on the hill."

Cynthia and Kathy oohed and ahhhed.

"How do you know?" *Alice asked tartly.*

"She called me this afternoon."

"How do you not know?" *Kathy asked.* "You two know when you're getting your periods."

Cynthia turned to Alice. "Is she not coming anymore?"

"I'm sure she'll be back," *Alice said. She could only hope Leslie would, but it seemed she'd laced into her about leaving Bill hard enough to keep her away for the time being.*

"Say, is her husband behind this?" *Kathy asked.* "Did he get wind of our feminist agenda and forbid her to come?"

"Bill's not like that." *Why was she sticking up for him when she'd frequently fantasized that he would tumble into a cement mixer at a construction site? Especially with this news of a romantic dinner tomorrow night. Either she was high off her ass or she'd already lost her mind.*

"Cut her some slack, Kathy," *Dolores said.* "Her kids are young. Running off and setting the world on fire whenever the mood grabs her isn't an option right now."

"Must I always get a lecture on the noble sacrifices of motherhood at the first whiff of feminist oppression? I was just wondering if she was skipping meetings against her will."

"Of course she is," *Cynthia chimed in.* "That's part of the noble sacrifice. Do you know how many times I've had to skip doing things I wanted to do because the kids were sick or had some homework project I had to help with?"

Kathy rolled her eyes. "Alice, you want to help me out here. I fear our movement is rapidly losing ground."

"Look, I wish she could be here, too, but she can't," *Alice said.* "We need more wine."

She hoisted herself off the sofa and went into the kitchen, fleeing from the ghost of Leslie that seemed to pursue her no matter where she went. Her eyes clouded with tears as she worked the corkscrew into a bottle of merlot. She inhaled and whispered, "Keep it together, Alice," as she exhaled.

Kathy stuck her head around the swinging door in Dolores's kitchen. "Hey, Betty, are you okay?"

"I'm fine. This bitch of a cork doesn't want to come out."

Kathy took the corkscrew from her and worked around the damage she'd done. "Listen, I know something's been bothering you, and I have a feeling it involves Leslie."

"Well, aren't you a regular Kreskin? Am I a little bummed out that my friend hasn't been around? Yes, I am. Anything else I can help you with?"

Kathy smirked as she wiped out the last fragments of cork from the mouth of the bottle. "Matter of fact, there is. If this is just about you missing a friend, why the hell are you getting so defensive with me?"

Alice glared at her. "If you've got something to say, stop beating around the bush and say it."

Kathy looked over her shoulder and lowered her voice. "You've got a thing for her, don't you?"

Alice's face flamed like the towering inferno. "You're out of your mind. You ought to lay off the gonga. It's making you hallucinate."

"Okay. You don't want to talk about it. I dig that. But if you ever want to, I'm a good listener and a discreet one."

"Is that right? How come you've never revealed your secrets? It's not like anyone would be surprised."

"I was trying to be a friend to you. I'm sorry you were so offended by that." Kathy grabbed the wine bottle and sulked off to the living room.

Feeling like a grade-A heel, Alice went back in and sat next to Kathy, offering a pat on her shoulder as an apology. But she wasn't able to shake off the funk dogging her that night and left early, feigning a headache from the cheap grass Kathy had brought.

Instead of going home, she drove by Leslie's house. At that hour, her husband was still out bowling with the guys. Maybe her children were sleeping over at their grandparents', as they usually did on crochet nights. Would it be so bad to stop in and say hi? Time and distance were supposed to help her move on from their doomed love affair, but at that point the only sign of movement was her climbing the walls, missing Leslie to the infinity of her soul.

The light in the living room was on as Alice drove by at a crawl. She spied in to see if she could spot Leslie—just a quick glimpse that might ease some of the yearning that had weighed down her heart for the past month. No sign of her. She turned around down the street in someone's driveway and headed back toward Leslie's, slowing conspicuously as she approached the house. She hit the brakes and stopped in the middle of the lane when she noticed a figure in the kitchen. It was only Billy. She kept her eyes on the window as he rummaged through cabinets. A moment later, Leslie padded into the kitchen and interacted with him before opening the refrigerator. Transfixed on Leslie's every move, Alice hadn't noticed the approaching headlights of a car behind her. The car's horn blared as the driver maneuvered around her. Startled, Alice drove on, circling the block and heading back to the house again. Maybe if Leslie noticed the car, she'd come out and say hello. She rolled up in front of the mailbox, out of the main lane of traffic, and stared into the window again, her lights still on, car idling.

The next set of headlights caught her attention as they slowly grew brighter in her rearview mirror. Her heart beat double-time as the car nearly came to a full stop behind her before turning into the driveway. It was Bill, home from bowling. She hit the gas and tore off with a squeal down the street. She focused on Bill's car in the rearview mirror to make sure he hadn't decided to follow her, but when she returned her eyes to the road, she jerked the steering wheel to avoid sideswiping a parked car in front of a neighbor's house.

She swallowed hard against the sandpaper in her throat and held the wheel tighter. She drove home in the dark silence, fearing not only the radio DJ waiting to ambush her with one of their songs but also who she was becoming.

Saturday, February 25, 1978

The next morning, Alice woke with a mother of a hangover, courtesy of the bottle of Asti Spumante she'd drunk before passing out sprawled across her sofa the night before. After putting on a pot of coffee, she visited the bathroom and had a prolific puke. In the kitchen, she found relief in a cool, wet paper towel against her face as the percolating coffee mimicked the sounds she'd made moments earlier in the tiled acoustics of her commode. Credit for some of her nausea went to her behavior after leaving Dolores's, stalking Leslie's house like a burglar and then her near run-in with Bill. If he'd confronted her, she would've needed a mystery writer to come up with a plausible explanation for why she was staked out by a snow pile in front of his house.

Why had Dolores needed to announce to everyone that Leslie was going out for a romantic Valentine's dinner with her husband that night? Wasn't missing Leslie punishment enough? Now she could add to her agony the indignity of knowing Leslie would be "celebrating" the lovers' holiday with her husband, not the woman she was supposedly madly in love with.

As a quiet rage steamed inside, Alice threw on a pair of sneakers, hoping a run in the crisp morning air would settle the Valentine's Day goblins taunting her with visions of champagne glasses, Jacuzzis, and velvet, heart-shaped beds from those offensive, beautiful Mount Airy Lodge TV commercials.

Saturday Night, February 25, 1978

Alice's first mistake that night was turning down the invitations she'd received from her sister and one of her married girlfriends to occupy the sidecar on their dinner dates with them and their husbands. Even Cousin Phyllis, who usually railed against the capitalists' shameless commercialization of love, had plans with a young, long-haired associate professor at the university.

She sat Indian-style on her sofa slurping lo mein noodles her chopsticks pulled out of a carton. A glass of wine on the end table and the weekend edition of the evening news were her company. A more depressing evening she couldn't have imagined. When the news and her third glass of wine were over, she determined she would have to leave the house or her lifeless body wouldn't be found until Monday after she'd failed to show up for work.

She could've easily gone for a brisk walk along the boardwalk in West Haven only a few miles from her house. That would've made the most sense, but instead she hopped on the Interstate toward Branford Point—or so she'd convinced herself. Of course, it was only a coincidence that she'd have to drive by the restaurant Leslie and Bill were dining at—well, "have to" in the sense that if she took the East Haven exit instead of the Branford one, she'd have to pass right by it.

She pulled into the restaurant parking lot and scanned the rows of cars for theirs. Maybe they'd had an early reservation and were gone now. She clenched her teeth at what they'd have time for if they finished dinner so early. Or maybe they'd changed plans and were at a different restaurant. Her knuckles stiffened from her grip on the steering wheel as she grew more anxious. And then she'd spotted their car parked along the side of the restaurant. She'd contemplated parking near the dumpster so she could see them when they left, but who knew what time that would be? She drove to the opposite side of the lot and found a space. Just one drink at the bar, she thought. Maybe she'd meet other singles alone on this storm-delayed Valentine's Day and end up spending the night steeped in scintillating conversation.

She walked into the foyer, twisting her neck like an owl's as she inspected every face and the back of every head for Leslie's.

"Excuse me, ma'am," the maître d' said. "Are you waiting for your party?"

"Huh?" she said, startled. "Uh, no. I'm just heading into the bar."

"Very well," he said, sizing her up as if searching for an explanation as to why she was unescorted on a Saturday night before returning his nose to the reservation book.

As she shuffled toward the bar, she spotted Leslie's face partially obscured by the back of Bill's head. She froze and stared into the *dining room like a French peasant through a bakery window. Leslie positively dazzled her with her golden, feathered hair, sparkling hoop earrings, and black scoop-neck dress. She was smiling, eating what appeared to be dessert, cheesecake, maybe—her favorite. As Alice leaned against the frame of the entryway, a persistent breeze from passing wait staff and couples coming and going chilled her to her bones.*

Suddenly, as if sensing eyes on her, Leslie looked over Bill's shoulder and noticed Alice standing there. Although flight was Alice's first instinct, her shoes remained planted as her heart sank into them.

Leslie approached her and, without speaking, led her down the hall toward the restrooms. "Alice, what are you doing here?"

"I'm meeting someone in the bar," she lied.

"Oh," she said, seeming relieved. "That's nice."

Awkward silence. Alice feasted on it. Leslie was jealous.

"Anyone I know?" Leslie asked.

"No, just a guy a friend set me up with," she lied again.

"Okay. Well, I won't keep you," Leslie said but didn't budge as her eyes inventoried the crowd in the bar.

"Are you enjoying your dinner with him?" Alice said, dripping with antagonism. "Looks very romantic."

"Alice," she replied with sad eyes.

"No, no problem," Alice said, excavating phony cordiality from within. "I'm having a romantic dinner later, too, so, you know..."

They gazed into each other's eyes, their unspoken language louder and clearer than ever.

"Well, I should, you know..." Leslie said. "Bill thinks I went to the restroom."

Alice studied the bar area as the weight of her sorrow threatened to crack her façade. She'd already revealed more than she'd wanted.

"It was good seeing you again," Leslie said as she started for the dining room.

"You, too," Alice said. "Don't be a stranger."

Leslie stopped before turning the corner. "You don't either."

Was that a glimmer of allusion in Leslie's eyes or just illusion?

She wandered into the bar, imagining that she'd grabbed Leslie by the hand and whisked her out of the restaurant bound for some romantic locale like Paris or Barbados or Alice's bedroom. She positioned herself at the corner of the bar with a direct line of sight to the restaurant's entrance.

"Martini, three olives," Alice said, holding up three fingers to the bartender. Might as well start lubricating herself to make the screw job of watching Bill and Leslie walk out together go a little smoother.

As she drained the last drop of martini number one, she caught sight of Leslie walking ahead of Bill as they exited the dining room. He brushed his hand across the back of her overcoat, leading her toward the foyer. Good thing, too, or she never would've found her way out.

"Anyone ever tell you, you look just like Jaclyn Smith?" asked a man with a charming smile.

"Get the hell out of my way," Alice barked. She shoved him aside in time to see the back of their figures float out the door and out of sight. She stared at the vacant space by the entrance as though Leslie's hand had just slipped through her fingers and some dark water's surface had closed around it—permanently.

"Hey, what's the big idea?" the man said. "You spilled my whole drink."

The whine in his voice towed Alice back to shore. She felt bad for him with his wet hand and bottom lip quivering with sadness. "I'm sorry," she said. "Please, let me get you another one."

"No, no, that's okay. I'll get another one for both of us." He signaled the bartender over as he patted his martini-drenched shirt with a napkin Alice handed him.

"That's not necessary," she said politely. "I can cover my own tab, thanks."

"We have a law in Connecticut. Dynamite-lookin' ladies aren't allowed to pay for their own drinks on a Saturday night." His mustache spread across his face as he slipped a crisp five from his wallet to hand the bartender.

"I wasn't aware of that law," Alice said dryly. "Did it pass on a referendum?"

"Huh?"

"Never mind." Alice smiled meanly to herself as she lifted her fresh martini to her lips. "Thank you so much..."

"Brett," he said, his square, manly jaw accentuated by a friendly smile. His hair, a poof of brown cotton candy, seemed to stay entirely still even when he moved.

"Thank you, Brett," she said.

"By the way, what did you shove me out of the way for?"

"I thought I saw my husband walk in," she said casually and sipped her drink.

"Husband?"

"Uh-huh. He's a retired wrestler—Bill the...Bill the Big Baboon."

He raised the one brow stretching over both of his eyes. "Super," he said and checked his watch. "Looks like I gotta hit the highway. You have a good night, now."

"You have a fantastic night, too, Brett." She finished her second martini, still disgusted by the events of the evening. She ate the olives off the toothpick and instructed the bartender to keep 'em coming.

Some Time after the Martinis...

Alice rolled off the couch, lurched down the hall to the bathroom, and sprayed the toilet with martinis, olives, and something faintly resembling lo mein. When she was sufficiently purged, she rested her head on the cold porcelain and moaned softly.

"Alice."

Startled, Alice lifted her head and tried to focus on the figure producing the familiar voice.

"Alice, can you get up?" Mary Ellen shook her gently to rouse her.

"Mare, what are you doing here?"

"I live here," she said sternly. "The question I'd love an answer to is why Dave had to pick you up from that bar tonight."

"I didn't ask him to."

"No, the bartender did after he scraped you off the floor."

"Say what?"

"Come on. Let's get you back to bed." She helped Alice to her feet and led her back to the couch.

"Where's Dave?"

"In bed sleeping, where I should be."

"Aww, but you're here with me instead," Alice slurred.

"Keep your voice down. You're gonna wake the boys."

"Come and sleep with me. I miss my sissy," she said, kissing Mary Ellen's cheek repeatedly.

"Never mind. Just get back on the couch and go back to sleep."

"Where are you going?"

"Now that I know you're not going to die, I'm going to clean the bathroom and then go back to sleep. Honestly, Alice, I don't know what's come over you. You've been acting so out of character lately."

"I've got problems, Mare," she said and scrunched up in the fetal position.

"No shit," Mary Ellen said, stretching the blankets up to Alice's shoulder. *"We'll talk about this in the morning—late morning, that is."*

With a grunt, Alice finally drifted off.

Alice threw another small log on the fire and jabbed it until it flamed. "That was the worst night ever. Thanks for refreshing my memory."

Mary Ellen took the wine bottle out of the bucket and stared suspiciously at Alice. "Promise me Dave and I aren't going to have to deal with that again. He doesn't like driving at night, and I'm too old to play nursemaid to a drunk at three a.m."

Alice smirked. "Oh, please. I know how to deal with my emotions in a healthy, productive way." She glanced at the wineglass in her hand and then at Mary Ellen. "Well, nobody drinks hot cocoa around a fire on a gorgeous summer night."

Mary Ellen smiled. "You're in love with her, aren't you?"

Alice smiled too and continued poking the fire.

"Answer me, damn it. You don't need to lie or hide anything anymore. The cat's out of the bag."

"Yes, it is, but I love the look on your face when I torture you."

"I should've made Dave leave you on the floor of that bar that night."

Alice chuckled. She put her feet up on the side of the fire pit and inhaled as if she had to dive to the ocean floor for the answer. "Yes, I think I am."

"Have you told her yet?"

"No."

"Why not?" Mary Ellen shrieked.

"Now isn't the right time," Alice said, excitedly, then calmed down. "It'll only complicate things even more."

Mary Ellen scoffed. "You only waited almost forty years to be with her. Why don't you just wait another forty? Maybe by then, every single minute detail will be exactly to your liking."

"Mare, I live in Boston. Leslie is recovering from a stroke. I'm still mourning my dead wife. Can you give me a chance to get my bearings here?" She moaned in frustration. "I wish Phyllis was still here. Now that woman knew how to give her unsolicited opinion and make you think you'd begged her for it."

"She used to make me hide in the oven during hide-and-seek when she babysat us."

"Say what?" Alice said, laughing.

"True story," Mary Ellen said, then turned serious. "Ally, if you want me to keep my opinions to myself, I will. You obviously have a lot to think about. If you decide to sell that big house up in Boston, Dave and I will be glad to put you up until you find something around here."

"Yes, you've already said that, and I appreciate it. And I don't want you to keep your opinions to yourself." She reached over and pinched her cheek. "At your age it might be hazardous to break into something so new and out of character."

Mary Ellen swatted Alice's hand away and gave her a playful shove, prompting a momentary sisterly slap fight.

"Alice, listen," Mary Ellen said, regaining order by subduing Alice's hands. "I want so much for you to be happy. And I want to be part of that happiness. It still kills me that you went through such a sad, confusing period in your life on your own, even though I was here all along."

Alice tilted her head toward the stars. "Mare, it was a different time, and I was a totally different person. It's ancient history, so let it go. I have."

Mary Ellen smiled and then gazed into the fire.

"I'm going home for a few days to check on things," Alice said.

"You're coming back, though?"

"Yes, but first I need to put some space between myself and this situation. And make sure the neighbors didn't set my cats free."

"I'm behind you whatever you decide," Mary Ellen said. "But I won't deny the selfish side of me wants you to move back here."

Alice tossed a stick into the fire. "Who knew that in my seventies I'd still be trying to figure out what I want?"

"It's not that you're still figuring out what you want. You're figuring out what you want next, and that's the mark of a truly interesting life," Mary Ellen said.

Alice stood up and stretched. "I think uninteresting is underrated. Good night." She kissed her sister on the head.

"Good night," Mary Ellen said. "Tell Dave to come back outside. The coast is clear."

CHAPTER FIFTEEN

Alice was convinced Leslie's daughter, Rebecca, had some sort of special telepathic lesbian powers. She'd been home for only two days, been able to focus on something other than Leslie for only one, when Rebecca texted to let her know Leslie was being released from the rehab facility.

The news had left Alice giddy. She put an old disco album on the turntable that had been preserved on a shelf in the family room, loving the crackle of the needle on vinyl through the oversized hi-fidelity speakers. She grooved to Abba's "Take a Chance on Me" while feather-dusting lamps, shelves, and end tables dulled beneath a layer of months-old dust. The next time she'd see Leslie, it would be in a normal setting—no hospitals, rehabs, or barely palatable institution meals. Leslie's physical limitations aside, they'd be free to do anything they wanted. They could go to dinner by the shore, talk for hours, and maybe, just maybe, if the chance presented itself, share a kiss.

By Wednesday night, Alice had cleaned her house from top to bottom, bribed Jim and Patty next door to keep her two cats for another week or so, and concluded that she would accomplish no serious contemplation about life as long as the possibility of a real, live date with Leslie existed.

❖

Friday night Alice sat at the makeup table in Mary Ellen's bedroom applying mascara. She observed her sister's reflection in the mirror, her lips puckered, hands pressed together at her breast like a minister's wife. She turned around to see if the real Mary Ellen matched the reflected and somewhat bizarre version.

"Are you all right?" Alice asked cautiously.

"I haven't been this emotional since the boys' weddings," Mary Ellen said, capturing a tear with her finger before it rolled down her cheek.

"Why?"

"Alice, you're going on a date," she said dramatically. "And not with just anyone—with the one that got away." She yanked a tissue off her nightstand and blotted her eyes. "It's exactly like this Hallmark movie I watched with Tom Selleck and Roma Downey. See, they fell in love when she was in college but her father—"

"Can you go downstairs and wait?" Alice said calmly. "You're making me uncomfortable."

"But I'm your sister. It's my duty to give you my emotional support."

"You're giving me a panic attack. It's just dinner." Alice walked to the full-length mirror and threw on a sheer beige blouse over a black V-neck top.

Mary Ellen's head popped up behind Alice in the mirror. She rested her chin on Alice's shoulder as she gazed at their reflections. "Oh, it's so much more than dinner."

"Thank you for that," Alice said dryly. "Don't wait up."

She headed downstairs with Mary Ellen trailing closely behind. "And by 'don't wait up,' I mean don't stay awake past nine."

"Maybe I won't see you until tomorrow." Mary Ellen's eyebrows spiked.

"I'll see you in a few hours," Alice said and kissed her on the cheek.

❖

How strange it felt approaching the front door of Leslie's townhouse, but far less eerie than it would've been going to see

Leslie at the house where she and Bill had raised their family—and she and Alice had almost ended her marriage. Alice nudged the thought from her head. Those days were over, and this night was about appreciating the present with a woman she'd once believed she'd never see again. With a deep breath, she pressed the doorbell.

After a moment, Leslie opened the door. The bottle of wine almost slipped through Alice's fingers and smashed on the concrete porch. How could this be? How could Leslie, at sixty-nine years old, be more appealing than she was in her thirties? Yet the truth was undeniable as she stood there smiling, her age delicately beguiled by makeup and lipstick, her hair freshly coiffed, and her slender frame draped in a silky white button-down and khaki linen pants.

"Alice, you look wonderful," Leslie said, beating her to the compliment. "Please come in." She slowly stepped aside to let her in, clinging to her small, two-wheeled walker for support.

Alice greeted her with a chaste peck on the cheek. "It's hard to believe a month ago you were lying in a hospital bed, unconscious. You're a medical marvel."

"No, just stubborn," Leslie said. "But I still need this." She regarded her walker with a frown. "We can order in if it's going to be too much of a hassle going to a restaurant."

"Are you kidding?" Alice said. "After what you were forced to eat for the past month, there's no chance we're ordering take-out. Seafood by the shore, right?"

Leslie instantly perked up. "How about Dockside?"

"And Branford Point after?"

"Perfect," Leslie said.

"Forgive me for sounding corny, but that's exactly what I thought the moment you opened the door."

"Oh, Alice." Leslie batted her lashes in the most delectable shade of bashful. "I wish I could believe that even if I wasn't leaning on this walker."

"I wish you could, too."

Leslie rendered her helpless with a vulnerable smile. Alice's gaze cascaded from her mesmerizing azure eyes to her glistening pink lips. Did they still taste the same? Could they still send shivers through her body the way they had years ago? She leaned in a little, suddenly dying to find out.

"Would you like a glass of the wine you brought before we go?" Leslie asked.

With Leslie looking that elegant, even one glass of wine on an empty stomach would be dangerous. "I'm pretty hungry," Alice said. "Maybe we can save it for dessert? It's a pinot noir."

"Okay," Leslie said. "Let me get my purse."

The sun lowered over the marina, casting a golden glow across Leslie as they sat at an outdoor table. It was the last thing Alice needed—something else to make Leslie appear even more angelic. Sweat formed on her upper lip as she forced herself to stay focused on their conversation while still pondering Leslie's lips, now more enticing as they glistened from vinaigrette dressing. She absently fanned her face with a folded napkin.

"Do you want to eat inside where it's air-conditioned?" Leslie said.

"No, it's so beautiful out here."

"But you look like you're having a hot flash." Leslie seemed amused by the idea.

"Maybe I am," Alice said. "Maybe all this talking about our past has reactivated my ovaries."

Leslie giggled. "Wouldn't that be just our luck?"

"I'd rip them out with this shrimp fork," Alice said.

Leslie laughed even harder. God, why did she still have to be so stunning?

"By the way," Leslie said, "this dinner is on me tonight. I've wanted to thank you for all you've done for me, especially for being there for Rebecca those first couple of days. I still can't believe you drove all the way down here when she messaged you."

Her blush deepened. "Pffft. I didn't come down for you. I came to visit my sister."

"If you say so, but I still insist on treating."

Leslie bit her lip in her struggle to look stern—the result of which was an unexpected level of sexiness that temporarily derailed Alice's train of thought.

"Uh, well, um, you're not treating," Alice said, collecting her wits. "But okay, if you must know, I did come back to see you. Don't tell my sister."

"I don't know if I can ever express how much I appreciate it."

"I'd like to take the credit for being as altruistic as you're making me out to be, but this trip back home has been the best thing for me. I've reconnected with my sister, my old friends, and you. I feel like the fog has finally started to lift."

"Yes, but your journey started out with the most selfless of intentions." She touched the top of Alice's hand. "Thank you."

Alice smiled and picked at her broiled filet of sole. "So," she said. "What were you up to before the stroke?"

"Where do I begin? A lot's changed in twenty-eight years. I went to school and became a paralegal for almost twenty-six years before I retired two years ago."

Alice smiled like a proud mother. "Good for you."

"That career saved me in more ways than one."

"I felt the same way when I became an insurance actuary," Alice said. "But you know what's funny? It seems like I lived more in the year and a half I knew you than in all the years since."

"Boy, is that the truth," Leslie said, pausing in thought. "Do you know what I've thought about recently?"

"What?" Alice said, wishing she'd had another sauvignon blanc for Leslie's answer.

"How things would've turned out if Bill had gotten home ten minutes earlier that Friday afternoon in '78."

Alice shuddered at her suggestion. "I know how they would've turned out. I would've died young enough to leave an attractive corpse."

April 1978

Alice had slid into a stubborn depression since running into Leslie and Bill at the restaurant in late February, but she'd dismissed it to her sister as a nasty case of the winter blues. Yet even as that formidable New England winter finally lost its bite and spring's presence speckled the trees, Alice was not rebounding. She'd requested a Friday off from work to see if some fresh air and solitude at her favorite place might help snap her out of it.

She leaned back on a wooden bench overlooking the beach and let the sun warm her face, reflecting on how much her life had changed in the last year and a half. Never could she have imagined that a new hire in the steno pool at First American would revolutionize the way she viewed everything. But now that she had been awakened to a new way to love, and with a woman she could never have, where was she to go from there?

The answer to that continued to elude her as she stood on Leslie's side porch, watching her index finger float toward the doorbell, retreat, and then extend again several times until finally making contact. Like a child on mischief night, she was tempted to book down the sidewalk when she heard the doorbell chime.

"Alice." Leslie opened the screen door in a sweatshirt, her hair thrown up in a ponytail, and wearing almost no makeup. She looked exhausted, dejected, and more breathtaking than Alice thought possible.

"I'm sorry for showing up like this," she said, "but I don't know, my car just kind of drove here of its own volition."

"Are you okay?" Leslie asked, studying her with concern. "You didn't lose your job, did you?"

Alice smirked. "Do I look like I've gone that far over the edge?"

"No, I just, well, I didn't expect to see you in the middle of the day, especially after almost three months."

"Look, if this is a bad time, I'll go."

"No, no," Leslie said, her eyes darting around the neighborhood. "Please come in."

Alice followed her inside, and they positioned themselves at opposite ends of the kitchen counter. Once Alice made eye contact, she couldn't break it.

"How are things?"

Leslie shrugged. *"I've missed you terribly. Other than that, life is grand. You?"*

Alice finally looked away, down at a small clump of beach sand on Leslie's floor. "Could be better, could be worse. Mostly, I could be better."

"I fall asleep every night hoping tomorrow will be the morning you're not the first thing I think of when I open my eyes."

"We fall asleep thinking the same thing," Alice said with a sad smile. "Are you alone?"

Leslie's eyes said yes to the question and to the desire drawing them closer.

Alice slid her hand down the counter, letting it make its way toward Leslie's. When it was within reach, Leslie laced her fingers through Alice's.

"How do I stop loving you?" Leslie asked, moving closer.

"I'll let you know as soon as I figure it out," Alice said, licking her lips.

Alice grasped Leslie's ponytail and kissed her hard, inhaling the clean scent of her skin.

"I want you so much, Alice," Leslie whispered.

Tingles rushed through her, scattering any rational thoughts of moving forward and getting over Leslie. Why was she the only person with the power to do this to her?

"I can't get you out of my system," Alice said.

Leslie rested her forehead against Alice's. "Some days I feel like it's killing me. Sometimes I wish it would."

"Don't say that, love, please don't."

"Why can't I just get on with it and forget you?" Leslie asked and started to cry.

"Let's go back to crocheting together," Alice said, rubbing her back gently. "We'll keep it just friends. At least we can see each other."

Leslie wiped her tears with her sleeve. Then she threw her arms around Alice's neck and pulled her into a long, passionate kiss.

"Let's go to my house," Alice said, groping at her under her sweatshirt.

"*I can't. I won't have time to pick up the kids from school and go grocery shopping.*"

"*I want to make love to you, Les. Just one more time.*"

Leslie dragged her by the hand into the family room. Alice cascaded on the sectional sofa and pulled Leslie down on top of her. As they kissed and caressed each other, Alice's sadness lifted, a departed soul set free by the solace of Leslie's embrace. Savoring each kiss, she watched Leslie's eyes watch hers. How she'd missed that dreamy look reflecting their complete and mutual surrender.

She slipped her hands under Leslie's shirt and began lifting it.

"*No, Alice, I'm too nervous,*" Leslie said, pulling it down.

But after several moments of hungry kissing, Leslie had Alice's pants below her knees. As they made love, Alice had never felt more connected with Leslie or more consumed.

After Alice made love to her, the thump of a car door shutting floated in through the family room window from the driveway.

"*What was that?*" Leslie sprang up, fixing her clothes as she scurried to the window. "*Oh my God, it's Bill,*" she said, her face a mosaic of panic and confusion.

"*Shit.*" Alice leapt up, smoothed down her shirt and attempted to straighten out her wild hair. "*What do we do?*"

"*Get back in the kitchen.*"

They scrambled to the kitchen and into some sort of casual arrangement, Alice plopping into a chair at the kitchen table, Leslie sticking her face in the refrigerator.

When Bill walked in he seemed surprised. "*Hey, hon,*" he said.

Leslie popped up from the refrigerator. As Bill pecked her lips, his eyes were trained on Alice.

"*What are you doing home?*" Leslie asked as she dragged out a bowl of grapes from the refrigerator.

"*It was a slow afternoon. Freddie and I flipped a coin, and I got to head out early.*" He turned to Alice. "*Slow day for you, too?*"

Was that a note of suspicion in his voice, or was Alice just being paranoid?

"*Uh, no, I actually had the day off and went to lunch with my sister here in Branford. So I thought I'd stop in and say hi to Leslie.*"

She forced a smile while scolding herself for that long, unnecessary explanation that reeked of guilt.

"I was just about to put on a pot of coffee," Leslie said, her face looking like it was ready to crack and shatter from her phony smile. "Want to join us?"

Bill shook his head. "It's so nice out, I thought we could pick up the kids a little early from school and take them to the aquarium in Mystic."

"Oh, well, uh, Alice just got here," Leslie said, glancing helplessly at Alice.

"Hey, that's okay," Alice said, secretly crushed. "We'll have coffee another time."

"Are you sure?" Leslie's eyes pleaded with her not to be angry. "You can join us if you want."

Alice and Bill launched looks at her from both sides of the room.

Bill threw his arm around Leslie's shoulder as if Alice weren't already keenly aware she belonged to him. "Come on, Les," he said with a heavy glare. "I'm sure Alice has more exciting things to do on a Friday night than being a third wheel with us and our crazy kids."

"Of course she does," Leslie said softly, taking Bill's lunchbox from him and placing it on the counter.

Alice stood up, as the room seemed to be getting smaller. "Thanks for the invite, but yes, I have big plans tonight," she lied.

"Call me this week, okay?" Leslie said as Alice breezed past her.

Alice stopped at the door. "Next Friday we're crocheting, if you'd like to come."

"Yes, I'd love to," Leslie said.

"Decent," Alice said, unable to stop her smug eyes from drifting over to Bill.

After Alice got into her car, the amusement of her perceived last word over Bill faded as reality set in. What the hell had gotten into her? She was on a collision course to utter disgrace being that reckless. Making love to someone's wife in his own home? She shivered with disgust. It was only the fortune of an unseasonably warm April day that had spared them from Bill walking in and discovering the whole sordid scene. What if they'd been caught? She'd be humiliated, but Leslie would be destroyed. Alice could never live with herself. Things were going to have to be different.

❖

"I don't think anything ever startled me more than the sound of that car door closing," Alice said. She stared through the windshield at the moonlight dancing over the calm waters of Branford Point.

"The risks we took," Leslie said, shaking her head. "Only true love could've brought out that kind of madness in us."

"I was truly mad about you."

Leslie took her hand. "I'm sorry for what I put you through. I should've ended it as soon as it began. I was just so in love with you."

Leslie kept using past tense. Did that mean she no longer had feelings for Alice? That her feelings hadn't come rushing back the way Alice's had? She cupped Leslie's hand in both of hers over the car's console, fighting that familiar feeling of inexorable motion, something akin to being swept up in a landslide.

"Are you all right?" Leslie asked.

Alice nodded. "Rebecca tried to worm the truth about us out of me before you were conscious."

"Really? What did you tell her?"

"Everything but the truth. I was more evasive than an indicted politician."

"She's asked me a few times if I'm a lesbian."

"Why do you deny it?"

"Because of her repeated threats to introduce me to her single lesbian friends," Leslie said facetiously.

"Are you?"

"Going to meet her single lesbian friends?"

"No. Are you a lesbian?"

"If anybody knows the answer to that, it's you," Leslie said.

"But you still hide it."

"I'm hiding from my daughter's attempts to turn me into a cougar."

Alice couldn't help her guffaw at that one. "You could definitely land yourself someone Rebecca's age."

"I wouldn't want someone my daughter's age. I'd have to go out and buy a kayak, become a vegan, and stream *Orange is the New Black*. I don't even know what that last one means. Rebecca says it all the time."

Alice gave in to the silliness. "I don't think anyone's ever seamlessly crammed so many lesbian stereotypes into one sentence before."

It took a moment for their laughter to die down. "If she pesters me about it again, I probably should be honest with her."

"I know she'd love it if you were. She misses the closeness you two had when she was younger."

Leslie smiled. "I do, too. And in light of recent events, this seems like the perfect time to become close again."

Why was Leslie smiling at Alice when she said that?

"So, if girls your daughter's age don't interest you, what type does?"

"Why, Alice Burton, the least you could do is ply me with pinot noir before you ask me questions like that."

"As it turns out, I know where there's a delicious bottle waiting to be opened."

Alice started the ignition with a grin and backed out of the parking space.

❖

Leslie pushed her walker to the side and shuffled on her own toward the utensil drawer, keeping her hand close to the counter. She opened the cabinet and reached, shakily, for two wineglasses.

"Les, let me help you with that," Alice said, sliding up behind her. It would've made for a stellar romantic overture had Alice not been so worried the wineglasses might slip from Leslie's unsteady hand.

"I've got it," Leslie said. "It's good therapy. But I will need you to open the bottle."

"That's my specialty," Alice said. "Are we headed out to the deck?"

Leslie nodded and indicated her walker. "I'll keep this here if that's okay with you." She looped her arm through Alice's.

Alice's heart fluttered as Leslie leaned into her for support. And she was worried about Leslie dropping the glassware?

They settled into cushioned chairs on Leslie's deck overlooking a small lake, wine in hand and citronella candles for ambiance. When would it stop feeling like some magnificent illusion whenever she glanced up and saw Leslie glancing back at her? She swished a mouthful of wine over her tongue, trying to slow the fluttering.

"Getting back to this closet question," Alice said.

"Yes?" Leslie said, dragging out the word.

"If you're not in the closet, but you haven't told your own daughter, who exactly are you out to?"

Leslie stalled with a slow sip of wine. "Alice, you're the only woman I've ever been with. In case it's slipped your mind, I was married at the time. How would I work that into a conversation with anyone?"

"Let me get this straight," Alice said. "You're a lesbian who doesn't date women, and you're not in the closet, but no one knows you're gay."

"Well, sure, it sounds ridiculous when you put it that way."

They looked at each other and burst into laughter.

"I have never understood what makes you tick, Leslie O'Mara."

"Actually, it's pretty simple when you think about it."

"Is that right?" Alice was still grinning from Leslie's earlier remark.

"How could I have loved another woman when I never got over you?" In the candlelight Leslie's eyes sparkled with a timeless longing.

The exquisiteness of the revelation caressed Alice like an evening breeze. Her mind buzzed with reckless thoughts and tempting possibilities. Was she on the precipice of realizing the dream she'd let go decades earlier? And then Maureen's memory came crashing in. She'd passed only thirteen months ago, and here was Alice having a grand old time with Leslie, reliving and reviving all those old feelings. How could she betray Maureen like that?

"Alice?"

She snapped out of her trance and turned toward Leslie.

"Have I said something to make you uncomfortable?"

"No, I'm fine." Alice placed her empty wineglass on the table. "I just thought of Maureen for a moment. Bad timing, I know."

"I'm sorry. How insensitive of me. You're still grieving."

"No, please don't apologize. I've come to terms with her death, honestly."

"What was she like?" Leslie said after a brief silence.

"Amazing. Everything I wished I could be—compassionate, driven, selfless. Maureen was my savior. When I moved to Boston, I'd given up all hope of finding love. I was bewildered and self-destructive. And then she walked into the insurance company I worked for and slowly changed the trajectory of my life."

"I'm so glad she found you," Leslie said. "She sounds absolutely amazing."

"She was," Alice said, staring at the stillness of the lake. She then turned to Leslie. "But she wasn't you."

Another awkward pause.

"I hate myself for saying it," Alice said, "but…"

"I know what that feels like—too well."

They both gazed out at the lake as crickets and a boisterous bullfrog filled the long, heavily laden silence. Alice could no longer bear the tension.

"It's getting late. I better get going." She offered a supportive hand under Leslie's armpit as she rose from her chair.

"Thank you for coming tonight," Leslie said. "I had a wonderful time."

"So did I," Alice said with a hint of a smile. "Sorry it kind of went south toward the end."

"Don't be silly, Alice." She held Alice's arm as they walked to the front door. "I'm here if you ever need to talk about Maureen."

"Thank you. That's kind of you to offer."

Suddenly, Leslie threw her arms around Alice's rib cage and hugged her as tight as her meager strength would allow. After a moment, Alice relaxed into the embrace and held Leslie, treasuring the completeness of being in her arms.

"How I've missed your friendship," Leslie said, her voice muffled against Alice's shoulder.

"We don't have to miss it anymore," Alice said.

Still in each other's arms they smiled as their eyes played all their old dirty, sexy tricks. Leslie licked her lips, setting Alice's heart racing. One kiss. What harm could one kiss do?

Foul everything up. Completely.

Summoning a towering effort of will, Alice let go of her. "Uh-oh," she said. "How are you supposed to get back to your walker in the kitchen?"

Leslie chuckled. "Actually, I can manage on my own."

"You what? This whole night you had me thinking you needed to hold on to me?"

Leslie confessed with a mischievous smile.

"Good night, you little con artist." Alice favored her with a kiss on the cheek, shaking her head at Leslie's endearing scam.

CHAPTER SIXTEEN

Alice's eyelid twitched as she sat across from Rebecca on the deck of the brewery overlooking the marina. Had Rebecca's spur-of-the-moment invitation for an afternoon craft beer-tasting been a ruse for another inquisition about Leslie? At this point Alice had neither the energy nor the inclination to fabricate the lies necessary for such a conversation.

After sipping each sample in her flight while watching Rebecca thumb the screen of her cell phone, she could no longer stand the suspense.

"Rebecca?"

"Hmm?" Rebecca looked up from her phone and then slid it away from her.

"Are you going to tell me why you invited me here on a picturesque Sunday afternoon and didn't bring your mother along?"

She smiled. "I was hoping you wouldn't notice."

Alice chuckled. "No such luck."

"I wanted to talk to you about me and Sage. If I tell my mother too much, she has a tendency to lose her shit. God forbid one of her kids has to deal with an ugly, real-life issue."

Alice relaxed into her chair. "What's going on?"

"Well, after Sage came home and settled in, we had a long talk. It was honest, a little harsh, but it felt good that we were so open with each other."

"That's wonderful. Have you worked it out?"

"That's why she came back. She wants to, but I'm not sure if we can."

"Why not?"

Rebecca stalled, analyzing the color of her beer in the sunlight. "She had kind of an affair."

Alice licked a bit of beer foam from her lip. "How do you have kind of an affair?"

"It was with a woman in the Chicago division of her company. They met when the woman came here for training. They stayed in contact through work email after she went back, and then pretty soon it turned into Facebook messaging."

"An emotional affair?"

"Sage admitted it but swears there was nothing physical."

"That's good, isn't it?"

"I think I'd prefer they just had sex once and got it over with rather than carried on an emotional attachment for five months. And how do I know it didn't get physical? Sage was out in the San Diego division for a couple of weeks. How do I know that woman wasn't out there with her?"

"Did you ask her?"

"She said she, Bianca is her name, was never out in San Diego. She said I could call Chicago to verify it."

Alice finished off the hoppy beer sample as she contemplated. "It seems Sage is sincere about wanting to work it out. She could've kept the affair a secret from you, right?"

"I want to believe her," Rebecca said. "I want to work it out. We've been together fifteen years. We have Jake and dogs and a vacation cottage in P-town. Aside from the last couple of years we've been drifting apart, we've had a pretty strong relationship."

Alice patted Rebecca's shoulder. "You can't have a long-term relationship without hitting some bumps along the way. The ones that are solid and meant to be will endure."

"She said she'd go to couples' therapy if we need to work on trust."

"I have no doubt you'll do what's best for everyone."

Rebecca sipped her beer as she observed a boater docking his small boat. "Speaking of my mom," she said. "I had dinner with her last night."

"Did you?"

"We had an interesting chat. Very interesting."

"Really? About?"

"For starters," Rebecca said, spitting out canary feathers, "you'll be happy to know you can stop all this bad acting. She told me everything."

Alice gulped salty air. "Everything?"

"Well, yeah—that she thinks she's a lesbian."

She *thinks* she's a lesbian. Alice smirked. Oh, that Leslie and her semantics. Her confession seemed to conveniently overlook their torrid love affair. Suppose Leslie was to try to give a normal romance a shot. How long would they have to hide their past in the closet before everyone around them could digest the truth?

"Alice, it's serendipity," Rebecca said excitedly. "You're single, she's single. You could go out on a date. It'll surprise the shit out of my dad, but I think it'll be awesome."

He'd be the least surprised of all.

"Let's not get carried away, Rebecca. Your mom and I are friends, and that's fine." Something in Alice made her believe it. It was hard enough having a relationship with Leslie back then, but now at her age, she needed those same old complications like she needed a broken hip.

"Well, you don't have to rule it out," Rebecca said.

Alice smiled patiently. "How about we talk more about you and Sage?"

❖

Alice's Bluetooth dialed Leslie's phone number the minute she drove out of the brewery's parking lot.

"So, you *think* you're a lesbian, huh?" Alice said when Leslie answered.

"Hi, Alice."

"I just had quite an enlightening conversation with your daughter."

"I did, too. I came out to her yesterday," Leslie said, sounding proud.

"You didn't come out," Alice said, trying to control her agitation. "You cracked open the closet and waved at her from behind the door."

"I kept it simple, so she wouldn't start asking a lot of questions."

"You certainly wouldn't want to have to answer a lot of questions—truthfully anyway."

"Alice, what are you so upset about?"

She waited at a red light. What was she so upset about? It's not like they were dating. Or were they? What was Friday night? Maybe less than she'd thought. She exhaled. "Nothing. I'm just not a fan of revisionist history."

"I'm sorry, Alice. I don't know why Rebecca called you and got you involved in our conversation."

"I know why. She wants us to go out on a date."

Leslie chuckled into the phone. "Wait till I get my hands on her."

Alice mocked her chuckling. "Sorry, but I don't see the humor in any of this."

"Alice, I said I was sorry." Leslie finally sounded appropriately wounded. "I'll talk to her about minding her own business."

"It's not her fault that she didn't have all the information. Please don't say anything to her. It's really no big deal."

"Alice…"

"What?" In the long pause Alice thought she'd lost the call.

"I'm sorry," Leslie finally said.

"You should have that monogrammed on your shirts."

"I don't know what else to—"

Alice sighed in frustration. "Take care, Les."

"Yeah," Leslie said softly. "You, too."

Alice ended the call and drove on. Why was she even entertaining the idea of reuniting with Leslie? She recalled the night of their love affair's grand finale and the pain of it, as sharp as if it occurred only moments ago.

April 1978

A week after Bill came narrowly close to discovering her and Leslie in the act, Alice wandered around her living room, adjusting picture frames on the wall and picking lint off her carpet. Leslie was never that late for their Friday-night get-togethers. In fact, she had been early to most of them ever since they became involved, but now that everything was so uncertain, there didn't seem to be the same urgency to steal moments alone.

Was she going to show up at all? What if Leslie had finally tired of the double life she'd been living and wanted nothing more to do with her? She swallowed hard at the thought. How would she stand it if it were true? The last few months without Leslie, Alice had barely functioned. Leslie could simply return to her busy, fulfilling family life as though Alice had been nothing more than an extended daydream. Leslie had said several times she was never unhappy in her marriage. But what would become of Alice? Her entire essence had been irretrievably changed since meeting Leslie. What had she to go back to?

Leslie finally arrived thirty minutes late. She breezed past Alice at the door and paced in the foyer.

"What's wrong?" Alice attempted to settle her by holding her hands.

"It's Bill."

Lips slightly parted, her jaw locked in momentary panic. "What about him?"

"He asked me if I was having an affair."

"What? With me?"

"Not in so many words, but he's suspicious of something. I'm scared, Alice. What if he hires a private detective to follow me?"

"Look, calm down. It would never come to that." She wanted to reassure herself as much as Leslie. The last thing she needed was some dime-store Columbo skulking around, asking her friends

and co-workers intrusive questions about her. "What made him suspicious enough to assume you're having an affair? Did he say?"

"He said I've been acting different for a while, like I've been preoccupied with other things."

"That's a pretty big leap from preoccupied to having an affair. Like the distance across the Grand Canyon."

"He also said you and I seemed like we were hiding something last week when he came home."

"What the hell?" Alice joined in the pacing, rubbing her forehead in thought. "What is he, paranoid?"

"Alice, he doesn't need to be paranoid to sense something's different with me. I mean, my God, something is different with me. I'm totally distracted by you."

Alice's bones quivered beneath her skin. The fear in Leslie's eyes unraveled her as her own fear of what was next spread inside like a salacious rumor. "Did you come here to end this?"

"Alice," she whispered and touched her arm. "No, but I think—"

"I know what you think, so just tell me straight out and get it over with." Alice's voice betrayed her with the vibrato of a defeated heart. She turned away to hide the visual confirmation pooling in her eyes.

Leslie hesitated.

"We've been going back and forth with this for months," Alice said. "Now you're finally ready, aren't you?"

"Alice, we have to end this. It's torture keeping it going."

"So is not being together. Or was it only torture for me?"

Finally a reassuring lip quiver. "Alice, I'm an absolute mess over you. But I'm a married woman, and we're doing things that two women shouldn't be doing, let alone a married one. I'm not very religious, but I'm pretty sure what we've done is going to land us both in hell."

"Fantastic. Then we can finally be together," Alice said.

"This isn't a joke."

"I've never taken it as one." Alice walked toward her cocktail cart at the end of the living room, preferring a display of stoic

indignation to utter despair. "So tell me," she said, pouring a shot of Jack Daniels, "is this religious awakening of yours real, or did you suddenly receive Jesus when Bill came home early last week while my face was between your legs?"

Leslie covered her face with her hands and sobbed.

Alice faced the wall, sipping the Jack as Leslie's soft whimpers bit into her. She'd never felt anguish like this before, not even the day Tony came home and informed her he'd met someone else, an affectionate woman who made him feel like a man in a way that Alice never had.

When Leslie cried, it was Alice who drowned in the tears. She wanted to abandon her there weeping as punishment for hurting her, for saying their love was going to land them in hell. Mostly, she wanted to punish her for being so kind, so beautiful, and so intoxicating that she'd rendered Alice helpless or reluctant to stop the plunge into her and into such turmoil. Instead, she walked over to her, wrapped her arms around her from behind, and kissed her hair.

"I understand if this has to be good-bye," she whispered.

Leslie spun around and stretched her arms over Alice's shoulders, clutching her as though Alice were the only thing stopping her from plummeting off a cliff. "I don't want it to be," she sobbed. "God, I love you so much."

"I love you, too, baby," Alice whispered into her ear as she stroked the back of Leslie's hair.

"The thought of losing you makes me unspeakably sad." She buried her face in Alice's neck.

"You know what makes me unspeakably sad?"

Leslie wiped her eyes and looked at her. "What?"

"Watching you walk away from me at the end of the night." Alice gently pushed strands of hair wet from tears out of Leslie's face. "You take a little piece of me with you each time you go. If we stay together, soon I'm going to be small enough to fit in your purse."

"I'm sorry, Alice, so sorry." She held her tighter, digging her fingers into Alice's flesh.

They spent the rest of that night making love, Alice melancholy with the notion that it truly was for the last time. Leslie was her usual paradox—making love to her as though Alice were the air she needed to breathe, the water she needed to survive. And then when it was over, she would get up and go home to the man she'd promised her life to.

As she watched Leslie dress, Alice lay in bed hugging bunched-up covers to her chest. She couldn't move, couldn't think of a single thing to say. Leslie faced the mirror over the dresser and raked her fingers through her messy hair. A wife couldn't go home to her husband with the back of her head looking like she'd been swept up in a tornado.

Leslie turned and leaned against the dresser, staring back with a gaze that mirrored Alice's misery. "Aren't you going to walk me out?" she finally asked.

Alice closed her eyes, releasing the tears she'd been storing. "If I don't, will you stay?"

"Don't you know that's all I want to do?"

"But you can't. I know." Alice threw on a terry-cloth robe and hugged Leslie, trying to imbibe every last particle of her being.

"Do you know the only thing good about driving home?"

"What?" Alice said, her head still resting on Leslie's shoulder.

"The smell of you on me."

Alice chuckled softly. "That's the only saving grace in going to sleep alone. When I turn over, I smell your perfume on my sheets."

Leslie cupped Alice's face in her hands and kissed her delicately, sending Alice into a world from which she didn't want to return.

"I have to go."

Alice shrugged. "So go."

Leslie laced her fingers through Alice's, and they headed down the hall to the kitchen.

Suddenly, Alice jerked her hand away and shouted, "How could you walk away from me like this?"

Leslie was startled silent.

"How can you say you love me, make love to me, and then just go home?"

"Alice, you know why," she said softly, clearly unnerved by Alice's mood swing. "I'll lose my kids if I don't."

"You should get that branded on your fucking forehead." Alice rested her weight against the door, staring at Leslie.

"Alice, please. I have to go home now."

"Not until you admit it."

"Admit what?"

"That your kids are a convenient excuse not to abandon your cushy life with Bill to slug it out in the mud with me."

"Alice, where is this coming from? I've told you the truth all along. I know it's hard for you to understand—"

"Just come off it, Leslie." Alice's indignation was not to be dissuaded. "It's different nowadays. Women with children can leave their husbands when it's not working anymore and not lose their kids."

"They can't if they leave them for another woman. Do you really think Bill would be okay with having his kids exposed to this? He'll fight for custody and most likely win."

"Exposed? Is our love a goddamn disease or something?"

"It's not to me, but it is to society."

"Who gives a shit about society? All that matters is our happiness."

"If I didn't have kids, I could afford to agree with you. Alice, this isn't some philosophical feminist issue we're discussing with the girls while getting high. It's my life."

"It's my life, too," Alice shouted. "I'd make any sacrifice to be with you."

"You can't compare our lives and our levels of sacrifice. That's not fair. Now please stop trying to make me feel worse about this than I already do."

"You don't feel so bad when we're making love. Your conscience only seems to flare up when I need something more from you."

"I can't give you more. You've known that from the start."

"I didn't know anything from the start except that I woke up one morning head over heels in love with you and you telling me you felt exactly the same way."

"I do feel the same, Alice, but I'm not going to lose custody of my children. I couldn't live with myself if I did." Leslie began to pace, her voice quavering. "Look, I don't know why this happened. I didn't set out to have an affair on Bill. I didn't intend to crash into you like this. I didn't even know it was possible to love you so much, but I do, and now my heart aches for you, Alice. Desperately. I'm all torn up over it."

Leslie collapsed into a chair and sobbed.

Alice rushed to Leslie and dropped to her knees. Resting her head in her lap, she cried with her.

They had to stop before it was too late.

CHAPTER SEVENTEEN

When Alice got back to Mary Ellen's from the brewery, she was still annoyed. The most annoying part of her annoyance was that she was mostly annoyed with herself. For all the proselytizing she'd done to anyone who would've listened about age equaling wisdom, she hadn't felt too wise at the moment. She stormed into the house, up the stairs, and into the closet of the guest room. After tossing her suitcase onto the bed, she started plucking clothing items from dresser drawers and flinging them into it.

Mary Ellen appeared in the doorway. "Was it something I said?"

"No," Alice said dourly. "I need to put rubber to asphalt."

"Mind if I ask why?"

"It's just time, Mare. Staying here any longer will put me in a position I do not want to be in."

"Seems to me like you're already there."

"Yes, but like colon cancer, it was detected early enough, so there's an excellent chance for a complete recovery."

Mary Ellen grimaced. "Ugh, that's morbid, even for you." She positioned herself against the dresser to prevent further marauding by Alice. "Why don't you talk to me about it?"

Alice threw a pair of shorts into the suitcase and dropped on the bed. "Do you know what she told her daughter? That she *thinks* she's a lesbian. Thinks. Can you imagine?"

"Was that a wrong answer?"

"If she were interested in pursuing anything with me, don't you think she should've said she is a lesbian and maybe told her daughter that I mean much more to her than a friend? God knows, I paid my dues long enough to have earned that much."

"I think I've missed something. Friday night you said it was just dinner with a friend. Did something else happen?" Mary Ellen sat on the bed across from the suitcase. "Did you go to bed with her?"

"No, no, nothing like that."

"Did you talk about rekindling your romance?"

"No."

"A kiss good-night?"

"All right, Mare." Alice leapt from the bed and glared at her sister. "I see what you're trying to do here, and I don't appreciate it. I'm not overreacting. I'm being practical. There's nothing wrong with self-preservation, especially after what I already went through with her. And what about Maureen? I'm behaving like she never existed."

"Alice, calm down. Don't start pacing. Sit down."

Alice sat, chewing the inside of her cheek to keep her composure.

"Nobody's forgotten Maureen," Mary Ellen said. "She'll never be forgotten, by any of us. But she's gone—for over a year now. You don't have to prove your devotion to her by being sad and alone the rest of your life."

"But I am sad and alone without her." Alice covered her eyes with her hand as she cried.

Mary Ellen put her arm around her, resting her head against Alice's. "I'm sure that feeling will always be with you to some degree, but I've also seen happiness and excitement in you with Leslie—whatever's going on between you two. I'd hate to see you run off again before you have a chance to—"

"Get my heart broken again?"

"No, that's not what—"

"Do you know what it was like saying good-bye to Leslie back then?"

Mary Ellen shook her head, chastised into silence.

"Let me tell you about it, and then you can let me know if you'd be as blasé about giving it another try as you're advising me to be."

July 1978

One afternoon, Alice appeared at the local ballpark where Billy played his youth-league baseball games. After spotting Leslie's family car and then homing in on her on the bleachers, she lingered by the concession stand, believing she was safely out of sight. Leslie was arresting in white sunglasses and straw sunhat, her tan legs peeking out of denim shorts.

When Billy got what looked like an ordinary hit, Leslie leapt up and yelled and clapped like a woman possessed. Bill, appareled in a coach's uniform, waved his arms at his son to come home. Billy slid in, beating the throw home, winning the game. Leslie bounded down the bleachers and joined everyone patting and hugging Billy at home plate.

At one point, Leslie, Bill, and the kids stood in their own family huddle celebrating Billy's in-the-park homerun. If shame could stop a heart, Alice would've dropped in the dirt right then and there. Leslie had once told her she couldn't live with herself if she were to break up her family just so she could have something she wanted. Watching them, Alice asked herself how could she?

As she crept back toward her car, Leslie called out her name. She stopped and turned around, averting her eyes as though Leslie's face was the sun.

"I thought that was you," Leslie said. "You weren't even going to say hello?"

"I don't know, Leslie. I don't even know what I'm doing here."

"I'm glad you are."

"Are you really?"

"In spite of everything, yes. I still miss you, Alice."

"As weird as it sounds, so do I."

"Do you want to try crocheting again?"

Alice cocked her head. "You know what will happen if we do."

Leslie glanced over to where her family was still celebrating and seemed to choke back emotion. "I'm thinking of going to see a shrink," she whispered.

"That's probably a good idea. I should give that a try myself."

"Want to make appointments together? A two-for-one special," Leslie said, but neither of them was in a joking mood.

Alice struggled to make eye contact. She'd only missed Leslie more as the days went on. To Alice, she was her lover and confidante, even though that woman had always been an illusion.

"I don't know what to do with this, Les," she said, making swirls in the dirt with the ball of her tennis sneaker. "What keeps us holding on to something we know we can never have? I can't figure it out."

"Sometimes I call your office just to hear your voice and then hang up."

Alice smirked. "I always pretended, hoped it was you."

"And drive by your house on the off chance I'll catch you coming or going." Leslie smiled mirthlessly. "Wow, I guess I really do need a shrink."

Alice smiled, feeling Leslie's anticipation as she searched for words. Finally, she looked up, closing an eye against the sun. "I put in for a transfer at work."

"To where?" Leslie asked, almost demanded.

"The main office in Hartford. I got an apartment in West Hartford."

"Why?"

"So I can stop doing things like this. Leslie, I'm completely lost in you, and I have to do something to find myself again."

"You think you're the only one," Leslie said. "I am too, but I don't get to pack up and run off like you."

Alice's eyes rolled before she could stop them. "You don't need to. You're doing a killer job staying away from me now."

"You asked me to. What was I supposed to do, keep calling you? Honestly, Alice, you have no idea what I've been going through."

"Really? My heart's been slit open and is bleeding all over everything, and I have no idea?"

"So is mine, except unlike you, I have to act like everything's A-Okay in front of my family every single day. Do you know what my new routine is?"

Alice folded her arms in defiance.

"I take a longer shower each morning so I can cry like I need to. I know I don't deserve any sympathy. You didn't force me into this situation. I was an all-too-willing participant, but I didn't know I would fall so hard for you."

Alice swallowed against her tears. "Leslie, we keep saying the same things over and over. I need to get away. This past year has been insane. I don't know who I am anymore, and it scares the hell out of me. I mean, I never in a million years believed I was the kind of woman who could have an affair with a married person."

"I can't talk about this now," Leslie said, fidgeting. "Can we meet for coffee?"

"No. I'm leaving tomorrow."

"Tomorrow?" Leslie's eyes flamed. "Why did you come here and tell me this in front of my family?"

"I'm sorry. I didn't intend to tell you at all. I didn't even want you to see me. I just wanted one last look at you before I left."

"You were going to up and move away without even telling me?"

"Leslie, it's the only way I can move on. We need to get on with our lives."

"You're a coward," Leslie spat.

"Leslie, please try to…" She reached out, but Leslie jerked her body back.

"Go to Hartford, Alice. Go and have yourself a nice life."

Leslie stormed off to her family without looking back.

Mary Ellen hung on Alice's words even after she'd finished talking. "This story gets more tragic with every new installment."

"It got worse from there," Alice said. "I had a stretch of promiscuity, abused alcohol, and for my encore, was arrested for drunk driving after I took out part of the guardrail on the Merritt Parkway."

"Jesus, Alice. Who the hell were you?"

Alice smirked at the bitter precision of the question. "I was only beginning to find out."

August 1978

After her tumultuous time with Leslie, Alice knew what she was. She imagined that Leslie did, too, but circumstance had her firmly implanted in a life she was not going to alter for Alice or her own individual happiness. Alice, on the other hand, was unfettered by any responsibility other than to herself. Even if she had been so inclined for convenience sake, she couldn't have gone back to relationships with men. She was no longer for sale for membership in the exclusive world of block parties, PTA meetings, and picket fences.

After she'd skipped numerous crochet meetings, Kathy tracked her down and asked to meet her for a drink at a lounge in Hartford. After about five minutes, Alice realized that the lounge catered to a specific type of clientele.

"This is certainly an interesting choice of venue." Alice eyed the young, slicked-haired waitress wearing a white tank top and black Dickie workpants with suspenders who delivered their first round of beers.

"You have some sort of objection?" Kathy asked.

"No. It's eclectic," she said, still taking in the scenery. "And there isn't one man in the whole place."

"That's sort of the point."

"I see."

Kathy grew antsy. "Look, I'm not gonna beat around the bush anymore. I have a pretty good idea why you and Leslie don't come crocheting anymore."

"What are you insinuating?" Alice said, riled up. "I'm coming back. I've just needed some time to get settled up here."

Kathy placed a hand on Alice's. "Alice, you don't have to defend yourself against anything. I just wanted to introduce you to this place since you're living so near to it now. Whether you come back on your own is your business."

Alice took a long sip of her beer and avoided Kathy's eyes. Why was she embarrassed to confide in Kathy? She'd moved away to live the life she felt would bring her happiness, and now she was shying away from the first chance she had to explore it.

"I think I just might drop by again," she said, finally looking at Kathy. "If I can work up the nerve."

Kathy smiled. "I don't mind taking a ride to come here with you sometime. There's also a place in New Haven, but I'm more comfortable up here."

"Thanks. I'm sorry I got so testy with you the last time you tried to talk to me about it."

"It's okay. I understand how that goes. So what about Leslie?"

"What about her?"

"I was just wondering if she was in a situation similar to yours."

"No, no," Alice said. "She's happily married. There was nothing between us, if that's what you're suggesting." No matter how compassionate Kathy was being, Alice would protect Leslie to the end.

"I gotcha." Kathy lit up a cigarette and perused the burgeoning crowd. "But I'm right about you having a thing for her."

Alice pursed her lips, a reluctant confession, as her knee bobbed on the barstool.

"I remember what that was like. I don't think any lesbian's ever dodged the dreaded curse of the straight girl. Mine was in college."

"I'm thirty-three years old, a little old for schoolgirl crushes."

"Age has no bearing on it. It's all relative to when you realize you're a lesbian. A woman can be sixty and have her first schoolgirl crush if that's when she finally has a sexual epiphany."

Alice observed a group of women in softball uniforms doing shots and cheering each other on. "I don't get it. How did I just wake up one day and realize I was in love with Leslie?"

Kathy exhaled a stream of smoke. "It's not like we're given the option of liking girls when we're kids. A lot of us grew up doing what's expected of us until that one woman came along and said, 'Tag! You're it.'"

"Is that why you knew in college?"

"No. I knew long before that, but I went to Sarah Lawrence. There was no way I was getting out of there without an encounter."

"Guess I should've gone to college."

"So what's next for you?"

"I have no idea," Alice said, scanning the crowded pub. "I just can't see myself as part of all this. I'd rather sit home and read or watch television."

"You need time to get over Leslie."

"How do you get over someone who made you feel like no one else ever has?"

"I don't mean to sound insensitive, but you can start by finding someone you can actually have. A married woman with kids is kind of like the Mount Everest of love interests for someone who's barely climbed a hill."

"I agree, but it's not like I can go pick one off the lesbian tree. Anyway, Lynda Carter's taken right now."

"Hmm, Lynda Carter," Kathy said with a lascivious gleam. "That's one hell of a fox. Now I understand why you'd want to stay home and watch TV."

Alice raised her beer mug in a toast and then took a sip.

"So then can I tell the girls you'll be coming Friday night?" Kathy asked.

"Yes, I'll be there. But let's keep this conversation between us, okay?"

"Of course."

❖

"Okay, so now I know why acknowledgement is so important," Mary Ellen said. "But if you're just friends, is it really your concern how much she tells her daughter? I couldn't imagine having to drop a bombshell like that on my boys."

Alice shot her a nasty look as she resumed rummaging through drawers. "Christ, I hope I live to see the day when people will stop acting like being gay is a disease or a declaration of war."

"Ally, it's not even the gay thing anymore. It's the shock of thinking you knew someone so well when all along there was this whole side they kept hidden from you. When you finally came out to me years ago, I swear, it wasn't the fact that you're a lesbian. It was that you're my sister, and I thought I knew you better than anyone. Then I find out you had this whole other life you concealed from me."

Alice plunked down on the bed in defeat. Damn Mary Ellen and her gift of reason.

"You know that whatever your fight is," Mary Ellen said, rubbing her back, "I'm on your side."

"I know you are. Right now, I just need to disappear for a while to figure things out. Alone."

"You're driving me crazy, you know that?" Mary Ellen stared at her with no trace of her usual easy-going nature.

"Well, that unconditional sisterly support didn't last very long."

"Stop running off, Alice," she shouted. "Every time you run away from Leslie, you run away from me. Just go to her and tell her exactly what's on your mind, for better or worse, and then put it behind you."

"What the hell do you mean that I'm running off? I live in Boston. I've lived there almost half my life. I'm just going home."

"It's a move you never would've made if you hadn't become involved with a woman you couldn't have."

"And I also never would've met Maureen. Sometimes people move away, Mare, without it meaning they're running away from something. I'm sorry I left you, all right? I'm sorry we couldn't remain as Siamese-twin close as we were for the first half of our lives, but I had to do what was right for me. And to be honest, I have no regrets."

"I'm glad you don't," Mary Ellen said. "But before you rush home, talk to Leslie so you can keep it that way."

After Mary Ellen went downstairs, Alice crawled up the bed and rested her head on the pillow to consider her sister's advice.

CHAPTER EIGHTEEN

The next morning, after a refreshing night of sleep, Alice showered and then cowered as she crept into the kitchen. The house was mortuary quiet, Dave at work and Mary Ellen MIA, as she waited for her cup of dark roast to finish gurgling. Her little sister was not pleased with her last night, and in the golden morning sun glaring off stainless-steel appliances, Alice couldn't blame her. Patience wasn't her most notable trait.

When the garage door opened, Alice plastered on an enchanting smile waiting for the side door into the kitchen to open. Mary Ellen came in with a bag of fresh bagels.

"Good morning," Alice sang, perky as Debbie Reynolds in *Singin' in the Rain.*

"I thought you'd be on the road by now," Mary Ellen said. "Don't let me keep you."

"Even though I deserve your unnecessary passive-aggression, I'll only forgive you if you got me an 'everything' bagel."

"Of course I did." Mary Ellen reached into the bag.

"Thank you, love," Alice said and threw a pod of coffee on for her sister.

They started eating in silence. When Mary Ellen opened the newspaper, Alice sighed extra loudly for attention, but she clearly intended to make Alice work for it.

"So I had my first good night's sleep in a while," Alice said.

"Is that right?" Mary Ellen hadn't even looked up.

Alice took her time chewing a large bite of bagel and cream cheese, and then said, "What the hell, Mare," sucking a poppy seed out of her front tooth.

That got her to look up. "I'm sure you'll be sleeping like a baby all the time once you're back in your own bed."

"Especially when my own bed is back here in Connecticut."

Mary Ellen looked up again, this time beaming. "Really?"

Alice smiled as the decision seemed to make itself.

"Wow, I had no idea mother guilt worked on sisters, too."

"I was leaning toward it anyway," Alice said. "But you weren't exactly wrong when you accused me of running from Leslie. Old habits." She shrugged. "Anyway, I'm going to make an appointment with a realtor friend in Boston this week."

Mary Ellen got up and sat in Alice's lap, nearly choking her with a hug around the neck. "I'm so happy."

"Me, too," Alice said, secretly enjoying her sister's excitement. "But I don't want to talk about Leslie anymore, okay? That's not what this is about."

Mary Ellen sat back in her own chair and pulled an imaginary zipper across her lips.

Alice's cell phone chirped with a text. "Leslie."

"I'm not saying a word," Mary Ellen said. "What does it say?"

"She wants me to call her when I have a chance."

"Call her now. I'll take my coffee on the patio." Mary Ellen stood and headed for the sliders.

"No, not right now."

"Why not? What if it's important?"

"If it was important, she would've called."

"So call her and find out."

"I will in a minute." Alice's flip-flops slapped across the kitchen floor. "I just have to…I mean I need to…"

"This is pathetic," Mary Ellen said. "You have such a crush on her."

"I know what I'll do," Alice said, relishing the small victories. "I'll text her back instead of calling. That'll keep the playing field level."

"Let me know when you do something," Mary Ellen said and headed outside. Alice padded into the living room as she texted and watched for the three undulating dots indicating Leslie was writing back. Finally, they appeared.

Are you still here?

Yes, but leaving tomorrow.

Can you come by before you go? Tonight maybe?

Alice huffed, familiar with the old routine. She would visit Leslie that night, and the next day, she'd feel about as cheerful as she would being shipped off to war. But if Leslie wanted to see her, it must be important. What if she just wanted to clear her conscience once and for all? Alice knew not to get her hopes up. Leslie and surprise requests to get together hadn't been such a successful combination in the past.

May 1987

Alice daydreamed as she packed her dishware and kitchen utensils into moving boxes. Her lease was up in a week, and she was about to embark on a new, balanced life with Maureen in her Beacon Hill cape. Now forty-three, Alice had survived a long journey full of unexpected twists and turns to arrive at a place in life where she'd finally felt at home. Maureen wasn't Leslie, but she was devoted, loving, and passionate about the same values. Luckily, Alice had realized those were the qualities she needed in someone.

When the phone rang, she said hello with a smile in her voice, assuming it was her partner asking how the packing was going.
"Alice?"
The caller's familiar voice smudged out her smile. "Leslie?"
"Yes, how are you?"

"Uh, I'm fine," she stammered as she attempted to wrap her head around the call. "How are you?"

"I'm doing fine. I'm calling because I'm coming up to Boston Thursday and Friday with Rebecca to look at colleges."

"Wow, college already?"

"Yes. It's amazing how time flies."

Leslie's tone was so chummy, she had to question for a moment whether they'd actually had a passionate love affair, or it had only been a fantasy. "It sure is," Alice finally said.

"And also how slowly it can seem to pass at other times."

Leslie's softer, somber tone cleared up Alice's momentary confusion.

"Mmm." Alice rested her elbows on a box on the kitchen table, too rattled by the interruption to continue packing.

"So, since I'm coming up to your neck of the woods," Leslie said, "I was wondering if you might like to have lunch on Friday."

"With you and your daughter?" Alice winced at the resentment in her voice. She'd thought those feelings were dead and buried after so many years, but like frogs in winter, they'd only lain frozen in hibernation awaiting the thaw.

"Well, no, just me. Rebecca has an information session and then some activities at BC for prospective students on Friday."

Alice was silent as she processed the scenario as it developed. For the first couple of years, every ringing telephone was a psychological battering she'd had to recover from every time it wasn't Leslie. And it never was.

"If you can't, I understand," Leslie said. "I figured it might be a long shot that you'd be available anyway."

"Actually, I am available Friday," Alice said without thinking.

"Oh," Leslie said with a note of surprise. "That's great. Okay. Why don't you call me with the address of a restaurant near your work, and I'll meet you there."

"I have a vacation day Friday, so we can meet anywhere."

"Okay, fantastic. How about a little bistro around Quincy Market?"

"I'll come up with a place and let you know," Alice said. "It's good to hear from you," she added softly.

"I almost didn't call. I wasn't sure if you'd want to hear from me."

"You'll always be a friend, Leslie, despite the past. I'll always be glad to hear from you."

"That's nice, Alice. I hope you know I feel the same."

Alice swallowed hard. A silence heavy with innuendo hung on the line. It was time to hang up. *"Listen, I have to run, but I'll call you the end of the week. Has your phone number changed?"*

"No, it's still the same. Do you remember it?"

Alice's knees were knocking. *"Yes, yes, I believe I do."*

"You can always call Information if you don't."

Alice hung up the phone and reminded herself it was only lunch with an old friend—an old friend around whom her sun once rose and set. But it was long over, and she was in love with Maureen. So why were her knees still knocking?

She picked up the telephone again and dialed Maureen's office. *"Hi, Colette. Is Maureen in?"*

"Yes, she's just come back from a meeting. I'll put you through."

"Hi, honey," Alice said when Maureen answered. Was it Alice's imagination, or was there a twinge of guilt in her voice?

"Hi, sweetheart," Maureen said. *"How's the packing going?"*

"Fine. I took a little break when an old friend called. How's your day going?"

"Busy. Your call is a perfect excuse to take a breather. Who's the old friend?"

"Leslie O'Mara from Connecticut. She's bringing her daughter up to look at colleges on Friday and wanted to meet for lunch."

"That sounds lovely. You should take her to Ronaldo's in Quincy Market. The reviews are fabulous."

Alice closed her eyes and breathed. The conversation was getting weird. All she was doing was planning to meet Leslie for lunch, and already she felt like Reverend Dimmesdale hiding the flaming scarlet "A" branded into the flesh of his chest.

"That's definitely an option," she said coolly. *"Or that fantastic deli place in Faneuil Hall."*

"Your friend is driving all the way up from Connecticut," Maureen said. *"You can't take her for a bowl of chowder."*

"Hey, they make a mean chowda over there."

"You're a pip, honey," Maureen said. "You take her anywhere you want. I trust you."

"What do you mean? Why wouldn't you be able to trust me?"

"I meant with your restaurant choice. You have impeccable taste when it comes to food."

Alice smiled into the receiver. "And women."

"A trait we have in common. I can't wait to see you tonight."

"Me, too. I'll bring the pizza?"

"Not a chance. I'm cooking you dinner."

"How do you have the energy to run an ad agency and then come home and whip me up a culinary feast? Never mind. I'm just glad you do."

"It's easy when you finally meet a woman you want to please as much as I do you."

"Call me when you're ready to leave," Alice said through a smile.

She replaced the receiver in its wall cradle and resumed packing. Before meeting Maureen a year ago, she'd spent more nights than she cared to remember cursing the universe for conjuring someone like Leslie into her life. Why would the fates expose her to the most intoxicating passion and soul-crushing love she'd ever known and then make the woman responsible for it completely unattainable? It seemed like some eternal punishment Zeus would mete out to hapless mortals in Greek mythology.

For a long time, she'd believed she would never recover or feel whole again without Leslie. But slowly, almost without awareness of it, she had. And then along came Maureen, who could be everything to her that Leslie couldn't. If she'd thought long enough about Friday, she'd probably cancel. Or maybe Leslie would. What good could possibly come from opening old wounds and digging around inside? Still, the curiosity to see Leslie again after so many years was too strong to ignore. What harm could a little lunch do?

❖

Mary Ellen walked into the living room, jolting Alice from her flashback. "Did you talk to her?"

"We texted. She wants me to stop over tonight."

"That's good," Mary Ellen said, casually. "What harm could that do?"

"I've decided to stop asking that question."

CHAPTER NINETEEN

As they sat at Leslie's kitchen table having a light summer dinner, Alice was vigilant in reminding herself she was leaving in the morning and to pay no attention to how stunning Leslie looked, or to how inexplicable it was to feel so comfortable and thrilled in her presence. Their conversation flowed too easily, felt too natural for it to have been decades since they were intimately involved. Yet the fine lines on their faces proved it was true. She also braced herself for the possibility that Leslie wanted to see her merely as a "farewell, it's been swell, but this dream's over" kind of deal—that illusive quest for closure even as the heart fights to the death not to let go.

"This is an interesting choice of a drink." Leslie smiled as she sipped the organic pomegranate-blueberry acai juice Alice had brought for dinner in lieu of wine.

"I hope you don't mind," Alice said. "When I checked my credit card and got a load of how many stops I've made at liquor stores since I came back to Connecticut, I figured I was due for a cleanse."

"Not at all. It's delicious and complements my teriyaki grilled chicken so well."

"So how is therapy going?"

"Good. I'm down to twice a week now, but I'm still doing my exercises at home every day."

"You look like you're getting around much better."

"I am," Leslie said. "I take the walker if I have to be out for any length of time because I still tire easily, but I'm really good at not using it around the house."

Alice smiled as she enjoyed Leslie's satisfaction with her progress and the meal Leslie had made.

"And my doctor says I should be able to drive again soon."

"That's fantastic. You must've been so relieved to hear that news."

Leslie beamed. "I don't know if I'll ever be able to drive to Boston on my own, but maybe we could meet halfway once in a while—if you wanted."

"If my plan to sell my house goes through, you wouldn't have to drive farther than across a town or two."

"You're moving back to Connecticut?"

"After giving it serious thought, I realized I have a lot of good friends up in Boston, but Maureen was my family. Now that she's gone, my family's here."

"You have a lot of good friends here, too."

She was right. Alice's recent lunch date with Cynthia and Kathy was all the evidence she'd needed. But what about Leslie? Was she including herself in that mix, or did she feel she belonged in a category all her own? Alice could no longer bear the tension.

"Why didn't you ever fight for me?" she asked.

"What? What do you mean?" Poor Leslie. Blindsided yet again when she'd thought she and Alice were having a perfectly friendly conversation. "Do you know the risks I took to be with you that year we were together?"

"Yes, you took risks then, but when you came to Boston in '87 claiming you were ready to divorce Bill, why didn't you fight for me then?"

"Don't you get it, Alice? By that point I felt like I'd already asked too much of you. You were moving in with Maureen and seemed happy. I didn't have the audacity to interfere."

Alice looked away, trying to keep her emotions in check.

"What would you have done if I had?" Leslie asked.

"I don't know."

"Gee, I thought you were going to say you would've told me to go to hell and moved in with Maureen anyway."

"I thought I would have said that, too." Alice smirked. "Damn it if your effect on me still isn't as unpredictable as…"

"The path of a tornado?" Leslie offered.

"Yes, exactly."

Leslie smiled. "That's not much of a compliment, is it?"

"On the contrary. Only you've ever had the power to sweep me up and carry me away like that."

"What if I told you it was the same for me—that you've always been my tornado?"

Alice smiled. "I'd say a devastating natural disaster is the ideal analogy for our love story. Just enough to bring us to our begging knees without killing us."

"And after it's gone," Leslie said dreamily, "you spend so much time rebuilding the leveled parts of your life. But even when you think the job is done, you find that things will never be the same as they were before it struck."

"Hey, you're pretty good at this metaphor stuff."

Leslie smiled. "In addition to the anti-depressants my therapist prescribed back then, she also suggested I try journaling about my feelings to come to terms with them. I said to her, how do you expect me to write down my thoughts about my extramarital affair when I still live with my husband?"

"Good point," Alice said, fascinated.

"She gave me a collection of poetry and said I could learn to use extended metaphors to express what I'm feeling, like a storm or a war or even death."

"Was it helpful?"

"Very. It gave me an outlet and a sense of purpose beyond my limitations, something to fill the hole left by your absence."

"I'd love to read them sometime, if you wouldn't mind."

Leslie examined her nail polish for a moment, suddenly bashful. "I have a collection of twenty-four now, on all sorts of subjects, not just my shattered heart."

"How do you manage it?"

"Poetry?"

"How do you always manage to amaze me with a new side of yourself?"

"It's just poems."

"Tell that to Maya Angelou."

"Didn't she die?"

"Yes, she did, and that's not the point."

Leslie giggled at Alice's mock sternness. Alice wasn't buttering her up when she said she was amazing. They'd both suffered the same heartache back then, but while Alice was careening her car into guardrails and neighbors' garbage cans after closing time, Leslie was cultivating herself into a poet.

"How is your heart now?" Alice asked.

"It's been experiencing a renaissance."

"One of those 'snatched from the jaws of death' type deals that give you a brand-new outlook on life?"

Leslie's eyebrow arch was provocative. "Do you mind if we go into the living room? I can't sit too long on these kitchen chairs. I've worked too hard at rehab to lose feeling in my side again."

"Of course," Alice said. She helped her up, placed a hand around her waist, and guided her to the sofa in the living room.

"I told you I didn't need help walking across the room anymore." Leslie gazed at her, reclaiming her heart with those soulful blue eyes.

"Really? Gee, I don't recall." Alice winked and sat next to her on the sofa.

When Leslie lifted her leg onto the coffee table, Alice slipped a throw pillow under Leslie's foot, then began gently massaging it.

"You'd make an excellent therapist," Leslie said.

Closing her eyes, she rested her head against the back of the sofa. Alice continued massaging with both hands to work deep into the tissue in her foot and lower leg.

"This feels so good," Leslie whispered, and then a groan, sexy as hell, escaped through her parted lips.

Alice withdrew her hands as though Leslie's feet were a toaster tumbling into a bathtub. "Is your air conditioning on?"

"Yes," Leslie said innocently. "I thought it was a little chilly in here, but I can turn it down a bit more if you're uncomfortable."

"No, that's fine," Alice said, flapping her arms to dispel the moisture under her shirt. "I think I just need a cool drink." She stood, fearing that if she hadn't, the foot massage would've devolved into the kind that prompted massage-parlor raids.

"Get some water from the fridge," Leslie said.

Alice plucked out two bottled waters and pressed one of them against her forehead. Even libidos long-thought dead and buried could be revived under the right set of circumstances.

She returned from the kitchen and allowed an appropriate amount of interpersonal space between them when she sat. "So tell me more about these poems. When can I read them?"

"I've got one more to finish, and then I'll think about it."

"Think about it? That's not fair." Alice feigned a pout. "If I inspired one or two of them, shouldn't I be allowed to read them?"

"You've inspired more than one or two." Leslie swiveled her position on the sofa to face Alice. "How about the next time you come for a visit, I'll let you read a few?"

"If you're going to keep me in suspense all that time, how about you read them to me?"

"That could get interesting," Leslie said with a grin.

"So could foot massages," Alice replied, seeing Leslie's flirtation and raising it a notch or three.

"It almost did." Leslie took a drink of her water and folded her legs Indian style. "I mean before your hot flash."

Alice blushed. "Hey, in my defense, it's been an unusually hot summer."

"It's been a ridiculously unusual summer, and the heat has had nothing to do with it."

"Right-on, sister," Alice said, raising her water bottle in a toast. "What's the poem you're working on about?"

"Unfinished business. It's been my most challenging and the one I've worked on the longest."

"Why do you think that is?" Alice asked.

"I think I'm still hoping to finish the business."

Leslie's sparkling eyes were weapons of Alice's destruction. Staring into them, she no longer cared about consequences. She leaned over to Leslie, lured by those moist lips that seemed to be already anticipating hers. As her mouth brushed across the delicate sweetness, the doorbell rang and the door opened simultaneously.

Alice seemed spring-loaded as she launched herself toward the arm of the sofa.

"Hey, Mom," Rebecca said, helping Jake carry in his overnight bag and several *Star Wars* action figures.

Propped at opposite ends of the sofa, Leslie and Alice were as pale as a pair of pickpockets on the "T" apprehended mid-pick.

"Hey, Alice," Rebecca said, still oblivious. "Hope we're not intruding."

"Well, uh, no, uh. What are you guys doing here?" Leslie said.

"What do you mean? You said to let Jake sleep over so he won't have to get up early to come over tomorrow. Remember?" She lowered her voice and spoke through the side of her mouth. "Sage and I have our appointment at eight a.m."

"Oh," Leslie said, dragging out the vowel sound. "I, uh, yes, it would appear that I did forget." She glanced at Alice, appearing mortified and contrite.

"It's okay," Alice said. "I was just leaving." Suddenly, Alice was queasy from the haunting familiarity of the situation.

"Really?" Leslie said. "It's only eight thirty."

"Please don't feel like you have to entertain Jake," Rebecca said.

"It's not that. It's um, well, I'm getting an early start home tomorrow to beat the traffic." She gave Leslie wistful eyes and a two-finger salute off her forehead. "Les, it's been a hoot."

Leslie stood and watched Alice walk out the door.

"Alice, wait."

Barely at the driveway, Alice stopped and whirled around to Rebecca. "Yes?"

"I interrupted something, didn't I?"

"And not a moment too soon." Alice moved toward her car.

"Alice."

"What?" she said tersely.

"Whatever it was, please give my mother a rain check."

"I'm really not a gambling woman, Rebecca. I learned a long time ago, the house always wins."

"If you learned that from her, it's not the same game anymore. The rules have changed."

"Have they?" Alice was skeptical.

"Yes," she said excitedly. "I mean I really think so. Talk about it with her, at a time and place where you won't be interrupted."

Alice jangled her car keys as she stared pensively into the fire-orange sky. "Rebecca, I don't know. When you messaged me to tell me your mom was in ICU, I got in my car and flew down here out of instinct with no plan, no expectations other than I wanted her to wake up and be okay. That's it. I mean I was still grieving for Maureen—at least I thought I was.

"And then by the grace of God, she woke up okay. We started talking, laughing, reminiscing, and it was the most uplifting surprise. But I don't know if I can go through th..." She stopped short of fully incriminating herself by finishing the sentence with *that again*.

The dejection contorting Rebecca's face only made Alice's attempt to extricate herself from the conversation more agonizing. She walked over to her and hugged her tight. "Take care, Rebecca, and good luck with Sage."

"Don't be a stranger, Alice," she said as they separated. "I know how to find you."

Alice drove away wearing a smile, wondering if the ancient river of tears that had always flowed for Leslie had finally run dry. Once at a safe distance from Leslie's house, she relaxed enough to recall the last time she'd had the chance to give Leslie a rain check and what it would've cost her if she had.

May 1987

Alice grabbed the handle of the entrance to Ronaldo's and stopped suddenly. This was the dumbest idea she'd ever consented to. What made her think she could approach this reunion like it was simply lunch with an old friend? Every other time she'd given in to her compulsion to be in Leslie's presence, she'd left feeling like a mouse that survived a trap. Sure, she'd gotten a taste of the cheese before the wire snapped, but who could be satisfied with just a taste of something that good?

She walked inside and spotted Leslie right away, sitting at a table for two by a window in a sunny corner. Her hair was different— shorter, blond-frosted highlights, but there was no mistaking that radiance. Maybe they were right about life beginning at forty.

"Betty," Leslie said as she rose from her chair and embraced Alice.

"Hi, Bella. I can't believe you remember that," Alice said, still clinging to her.

"Some things you don't forget."

"Truer words..." Alice muttered as she sat. "You look lovely, as always. I love your hair."

"Thanks," Leslie said, touching it. "I've worn it like this for a while. I'm thinking of going shorter."

"I'm sure that'll look terrific on you, too."

"Thank you." Leslie broke a moment of intense eye contact with the menu. "Everything here sounds delicious. I hope you can recommend something."

"Actually, I've never been here, but from what I've heard and read, you can't make a wrong choice." Alice shifted in her seat from the small talk. "So how are the kids?" That one was particularly painful.

"Growing up too fast. Billy is a junior at the University of Rhode Island, and Rebecca's graduating high school next year."

"Ah, the proverbial empty-nest syndrome."

"I didn't know I was raising them so they could fly so far away."

"It's a great experience for them, and I'm sure they'll both be back when they graduate."

"Not Rebecca," Leslie said. "Once the flash of the city gets hold of her, she'll stay right in the thick of it. She's interested in computer programming. That's becoming a big thing now, I understand. I think all the job opportunities are in big cities, anyway."

"Speaking of jobs, did you ever go back to work?"

"Are you kidding?" Leslie said like the classic harried housewife. "As soon as Rebecca started junior high, I said to Bill, 'That's it. I can't stand staying home any longer. I'm getting a job.'"

"How did that go over?"

"He didn't mind at all. Billy had just gotten his learner's permit, so there wasn't such a dire need for me to be around every minute. And not a moment too soon, either," Leslie added. "I really think I was starting to lose my mind. I'd been on anti-depressants long enough."

"Why did you need anti-depressants?"

Leslie's sunny disposition was suddenly overshadowed. She sipped her water and gazed out the window.

"I didn't mean to upset you," Alice said. "I had a period of medicating, too—three years of self-medicating. With Jack Daniels."

"Oh, dear. Did you have to go to rehab?"

"Luckily, no," Alice said. "My DUI arrest was the only rehab I needed. I stopped haunting the bars and moved up to Boston to start business school. I became an actuary and got a job with Metropolitan Insurance."

"I always wondered why you left Connecticut. After I heard, I felt pretty bad for a while thinking it was because of me."

Alice was tempted to shout, It was because of you, fool, *but such bluntness clashed with the restaurant's elegant decor. "If it makes you feel any better, I'd probably still be Engle's lackey at First American if it weren't for you. So thank you for driving me over the edge and into a career I love."*

Leslie scowled.

"I'm kidding, Les. Just trying to keep it light while we play this little game."

"What game?"

"That we're old pals catching up over lunch portions of fettuccini Alfredo and white-wine spritzers. Are we really pulling it off?"

Leslie stared like a toddler not understanding why she'd been scolded.

"I'm sorry." Alice reached out and then retracted her hand. "I didn't mean to sound so harsh. I must be more anxious than I realized."

"No, you're right, Alice. I've had to repress my feelings for the past nine years. When I'm with you, I shouldn't have to."

Alice relaxed into a smile. "Listen, before this gets too heavy, let's put in a food and drink order."

"Sure. White-wine spritzers?"

"Definitely," Alice said as the waiter appeared at their table.

They did their best to keep the conversation as light as possible, nursing two spritzers each as they picked on their meals. A mild tension lingered throughout lunch, though, and the length of each round of eye contact lasted proportionately longer with each sip of their drinks.

Her face flush, Leslie polished off the last drop of her second spritzer and waved her hand in front of her like a Southern belle with a case of the vapors. "Whew. I should've suggested we meet for dinner. Then I'd feel better about being this buzzed."

"You were always a lightweight," Alice said.

"No one knew me better than you," Leslie said, dead serious. "I've missed that connection."

Alice poured Leslie a fresh glass of water and motioned the waiter over. "I'll have one more spritzer. She's all set." She turned back to Leslie. "What? I'm half Irish. I need three to feel what you feel on two."

Leslie took a deep breath and then several gulps of water. "I'm glad we could do this, Alice." She looked down and played with the unused spoon left after the lunch dishes were cleared.

"I am, too." Alice was sincerely glad. Leslie was her first true love and would always be special to her, no matter what.

"I have something to tell you, but I wanted it to be in person, not over the phone."

"What's wrong?" Alice asked in a near panic. "Are you sick?"

"No, I'm not sick. I'm going to divorce Bill."

Alice's stomach plummeted like a run-away elevator.

"Close your mouth," Leslie joked. "You're going to catch flies."

"I don't know what to say." It wasn't a platitude. She truly was speechless.

"I understand. It's all you wanted to hear nine years ago, and now, what feels like a lifetime later, I'm finally saying it."

"What happened?"

"You know what happened, Alice. Things were never the same with Bill and me after I met you. I tried my best to be a better wife to him after you, but I couldn't be the person I was before. I didn't know how to be. When you moved to Hartford, I sank into a depression. Thankfully, my kids kept me from losing it altogether."

"I'm sorry, Leslie." Alice reached across the table and folded Leslie's fingers in hers.

"You don't have to be sorry."

"How could I not? To be honest, I'll never regret our love affair because of what I've learned and how I felt in those brief moments of paradise I spent in your arms. But I'm genuinely sorry you suffered."

"You suffered, too."

"At least I was able to get through it on my terms," Alice said. "I took off and changed my scenery, my whole way of life."

She glanced around the restaurant. The thought of causing Leslie such pain was still a fresh wound. "Strange as it seems, even though my own marriage ended, and I practically caused the end of yours, I still believe in it. I still believe in love."

"I do, too," Leslie said. "You might think I've regretted our love affair, but I haven't. I tried for a very long time not to love you, to forget that you made me feel the way nobody ever has, and then I realized how silly that was. It's part of me. You're part of me."

Maureen swooped into Alice's mind like a chaperone separating pubescent kids at a junior-high-school dance. She sucked in a breath, suddenly smothered by the thought of moving her belongings into Maureen's place the next day.

"Are you still living at your house?" That was all she could think to say.

Leslie paused, as though derailed by the truth. "I haven't actually filed yet."

"Bill's still living there, too?"

"Well, yes. I haven't told him yet."

"You're not even separated?" Alice shouted, furious for allowing even the smallest bud of hope to flower in her.

"I want Rebecca settled in college before I break the news. Something like this could devastate her and send her whole life off track."

"I'm familiar with that feeling." Alice stood, collecting her purse and light jacket from the back of her chair. "I have to be running along now. Great seeing you."

Leslie jumped up, startled. "Alice, what's wrong?"

"What's always been wrong. Except this time I'm not waiting for you." Alice marched to the door and shoved it open.

Leslie trailed closely behind as Alice headed out of Quincy Market.

❖

After a peaceful month home with her two cats in Boston, Alice felt better equipped to handle the major decision she'd been grappling with since her extended visit in Connecticut earlier in the summer. Pressure from Mary Ellen over her alleged desertion decades ago, from Rebecca about Leslie, and her own complex feelings for Leslie had become too intense and had set her mind reeling.

Despite semi-regular texts from her sister and Rebecca that revealed their thinly veiled ulterior motives—Mary Ellen claiming she wanted to make sure Alice was okay home alone in her big, barren house, and Rebecca wanting to keep her apprised of the auspicious progress she and Sage were making in couples' therapy—she'd done a fair job of keeping the distractions to a minimum as she attempted to sort out what she wanted.

Cynthia and Kathy had also contacted her, saying that after their lunch date in July had reaffirmed the importance of their friendship, they wanted a pledge that they would never again allow so many years between get-togethers. Alice was in total agreement.

But even as the for-sale sign stood on her front lawn, and all logical signs pointed to relocation back to Connecticut, she still questioned if being in such close proximity to Leslie was the best thing for her. Leslie still electrified her like no other. After all that time, all those tears, amazingly, she still had a lock on Alice's heart. Even on the eve of her lifetime commitment to Maureen back in '87, she had still been vulnerable to Leslie's lure. Although she'd loved Maureen, and Maureen loved her with a safety and contentedness Alice had never felt before, Leslie had possessed the power to drive her to recklessness far-reaching enough to toss all that away for the shadow of a promise.

May 1987

"Why are you running off?" Leslie said, still trailing Alice through Quincy Market. "We were in the middle of an important conversation."

"I've heard quite enough," Alice said, taking longer strides.

"I don't understand," Leslie said, then shouted, "Jesus Christ, Alice, will you stop and talk to me?"

Alice halted under the Samuel Adams statue and whirled around to face her. "I'm with someone, Leslie," she said, trying to catch her breath. "In fact, I'm moving in with her tomorrow."

Leslie's mouth hung open for a moment as she processed Alice's news. Alice squinted against the afternoon sun, trying to compose herself.

"Why didn't you tell me this on Monday when I called?"

"What difference would it have made?" Alice said. "I thought this was just supposed to be lunch with an old friend."

"I wouldn't have opened up to you like I did," Leslie said. "I feel like such a fool. I practically admitted I'm still in love with you, and you wait until now to inform me you're with someone?"

"I'm sorry, Leslie. Your phone call really threw me for a loop, and if I'm honest, it made me immensely curious. I'll say one thing for you—you have impeccable timing."

"Who is she?" Leslie said, her eyes dilating with jealousy.

"She's an advertising exec."

"What's her name?"

"Maureen Cavanaugh."

"Where did you meet her?"

"She did some work for the insurance company I work for."

"Is it real? Are you happy with her?"

"I'm moving in with her, aren't I?"

"That's not what I asked you." Leslie's eyes practically pinned Alice to the base of the statue.

"I know what you asked me. The questions made me feel uncomfortable."

"The questions or your answers?"

"Why are you doing this?"

"The woman I love is moving in with someone else," Leslie said. "Don't I have a right to know a little about her?"

Alice scratched at her chin in frustration. "I'm not sure you have a right to anything where it concerns me and my attempts to heal and get over you. You made your choice."

"Yes, I did, and there isn't a day that goes by that I'm not reminded of it."

"Aren't you being a little dramatic? It's been almost ten years."

"You know what, Alice? Some wounds can't be healed by time. Just when I think I'm really over you, a goddamn song comes on the radio, and the lyrics paint a picture of you, of us, and I feel it all over again."

Impatient with the conversation, and Leslie, Alice glanced around the market at the assortment of people, wondering if any of them could possibly relate to the mess she'd found herself in at the moment. Leslie's martyr routine seemed to have lost its mystical power to elicit Alice's sympathies.

"Why did you come here?"

Leslie looked at once surprised and hurt by the question. "To tell you I'm getting divorced."

"You're not getting divorced. You're thinking about it. The poles of difference couldn't be any farther apart."

They stared at each other for a moment—a moment that could've changed everything.

"I'm sorry I bothered you, Alice. I wish you the best with Marlene." She turned to walk away.

Alice stopped her with a yank on her purse strap on her shoulder. "It's Maureen, and you're not gonna do this to me again."

Leslie looked frightened as she tried to pull away. "I have to get Rebecca. Her seminar is almost over."

"I don't care," she spat as she flung Leslie's arm free. "How dare you rip open my heart again and leave me bleeding while you run off and hide behind your kids? Why did you come here? To get me hooked on you again, so I can agonize in withdrawals wishing for something I'll never have? Again."

"Alice, no," Leslie said softly, her face contorting as she obviously tried to stave off tears. "That was never my intention. Honestly, I didn't think after all this time it would still feel like this, for either of us. I didn't know you were still so angry."

Alice hadn't known either. Now she was the one choking back tears. Why had she grabbed Leslie's arm when she was about to walk out of her life for good?

"I'm sorry, Alice. Obviously, I was wrong when I thought maybe we could be friends."

That would be wonderful if it was even remotely possible. As it was, Alice was having difficulty remembering Maureen was expecting her and the moving truck early the next morning, an occasion she was supposed to be excited about.

Alice sighed. "Remember how all our previous attempts at 'just friends' worked out?"

"I know, and I won't bother you anymore." Leslie had given up trying to stem the tide of her tears. "Please, just tell me you don't hate me."

Alice covered her eyes with her hand for a moment and then pulled herself together with a deep breath. "'We women love longest even when all hope is gone,'" she finally said, staring absently at the mountainous staircase leading out of Quincy Market.

"Huh?"

She looked Leslie in the eyes. "It's a Jane Austen quote."

"Oh." Leslie crossed her arms over her chest as she digested its meaning. "Well, it's certainly fitting."

"I could never hate you, Les. Never." She offered a wry smile. *"It would sure make things a lot easier if I could."*

Leslie snaked her arms around Alice and squeezed like a boa constrictor with something to prove. Alice didn't want to enjoy it, but despite the guilt, she held on to Leslie and absorbed her with all her senses.

"Good luck with your move," Leslie said into her ear.

Alice's skin tingled long after Leslie finally let go. *"Tell Rebecca I hope she gets her first choice."*

"Thanks. I will."

"You're welcome." Alice smiled. She wanted to walk away—she really did. But as usual, she waited for Leslie to make the first move.

Leslie turned to walk away, then stopped. *"Alice?"*

Alice's heart hammered her chest as she anticipated the rest of the question. Ask me to come away with you. Ask me right now, and I swear I'll go.

"If you ever make it back to the New Haven area, don't be a stranger, huh?"

Alice released breath it seemed she'd been holding forever. *"You bet."*

Again, Leslie turned away, but that time, she ran back to Alice and embraced her, whimpers escaping into Alice's ear.

"I do, too, Les," Alice whispered.

"Always?"

"Forever."

Alice pushed Leslie away and walked off without looking back. If she hadn't right then, a phone call to the movers canceling her appointment the next morning would've followed.

CHAPTER TWENTY

Alice was quiet as she followed Mary Ellen back to the car, a fusion of sentimental farewells and tempered enthusiasm for things to come. After touring her fourth and final condo unit of the day, she was grateful for a late-September breeze that ruffled her hair. It was hard to believe that less than three months earlier her life had been stagnant, her home an empty warehouse with only memories and mourning to keep her company. What a contrast to the whirlwind of change she'd experienced since that chance message from Rebecca in early July. Although she'd lived almost an entire lifetime away in Boston, returning to Connecticut and the people she loved was indeed a homecoming.

"What do you think of that one?" Mary Ellen asked.

"It was nice," Alice said with a noncommittal gesture.

"You'll never beat that view of the water."

Alice arched an eyebrow. "You sound like you're getting the closing commission. If it's any consolation, I'm just as tired of looking as you are."

"I'm not tired of it at all." Mary Ellen cranked up the air-conditioning in her SUV. "I just want you to sign on the dotted line before you change your mind and go back to Boston."

Alice smiled. "Mare, my house is sold. I'm here to stay."

"I'm so excited." Mary Ellen air-clapped her hands and then remembered her manners. "How are you doing with that?"

"I'm doing okay, you know? The magic of that house died when Maureen did. I could never get used to the echoes of only one set of shoes on the hardwood floors. It was time."

After a moment of silence, Mary Ellen squeezed her hand. "Think you'll make an offer on one of them?"

Alice's mouth relaxed into a tentative smile.

"Yes!" Mary Ellen said and hugged her.

Alice's cell phone chimed with a text from Kathy. She smiled as she read that Kathy and Cynthia were arranging an authentic crochet-klatch gathering that Friday night and that her attendance was not optional.

"We're going to have so much fun shopping for your new place," Mary Ellen went on, but Alice was otherwise engaged.

She typed back, still smiling.

You got it.

"Pier One is having a huge sale. We should stop there now." Mary Ellen glanced over as she drove. "What the hell are you grinning at?"

"A text from one of my friends."

Kathy replied immediately.

Bring Leslie. Kidnap her if you have to!

Alice's smile shriveled. "Bring Leslie. Sure. Just like that."

"Are you going to let me in on any of this?" Mary Ellen asked.

"You'll be hearing all about it soon enough."

❖

The drive to Cynthia's house in Middletown seemed longer than Alice had remembered. As comfortable as she'd felt in Leslie's presence, when those awkward silences drifted in, they blanketed the atmosphere like a stalled weather front.

"How does it feel living in Connecticut again?" Leslie said.

Thank God somebody said something.

"Some days it feels like a different world, and others, like I never left."

"Which kind of day are you having so far?"

Alice smiled and gave her a quick glance. "It's definitely leaning toward like I never left."

"I'm glad you came back."

"I am, too."

"Maybe we can go to lunch sometime. I'm planning to return to my pre-stroke routine of volunteering and babysitting Jake, but I'll still have plenty of free time."

Alice smiled at Leslie's eternal gift for optimism and diplomacy. Friendship at this stage would be a wonderful thing. She'd had time to reflect since the last occasion she'd stormed out on Leslie in frustration and had come to realize that if she would stop expecting more from Leslie than she was able to give, they would have a real shot at an authentic friendship.

"I'd like that," Alice said. "I've signed up for Literacy Volunteers of New Haven, but I'll still have plenty of free time, too."

"I can't wait to see the girls again," Leslie said, staring out the passenger window. "Too bad poor Dolores can't be with us."

"She'll be there with us in spirit, I'm sure."

"I think I'm going to keep this in the car." Leslie indicated the quad cane resting against her leg.

"Sure, if you don't think you'll need it."

"I don't think I will, but I'd feel self-conscious hobbling in with a cane—like such an old lady."

Poor Leslie. Would she ever learn that she didn't have to live her life according to the expectations of others?

"What are you talking about? We're not old ladies," Alice said. "Cynthia's seventy-five now, with rheumatoid arthritis, and Kathy's got sciatica. Everybody has something."

"You don't."

"Yes, I do. Sky-high cholesterol and a sketchy-looking mole on the back of my leg. I should make an appointment to get that looked at."

Leslie pursed her lips. "You better."

"We may not be pot-smoking disco queens with pencil-thin eyebrows anymore, but we're certainly not old ladies. I say if you need that cane, you strut into Cynthia's house with it like you're starting a new fashion trend."

"Oh, Alice." Leslie laughed. "You always know the right thing to say to make me feel better."

They exchanged smiles.

"But I hate to remind you that we were never disco queens."

"Speak for yourself," Alice said. "I came in second in a 'Do the Hustle' contest at Studio 54 in seventy-nine."

"Impressive," Leslie said. "I stand corrected."

"Here we are." Alice pulled into Cynthia's driveway, then turned off the ignition and glanced around. Everything was different—the house was sided gray, bushes plucked from the front of the house, a small garden of marigolds in the center of the front lawn. "Thirty-eight years," she said.

"Amazing, isn't it?"

They exchanged smiles, and as was becoming the custom, Alice looped her arm through Leslie's and escorted her up the sidewalk.

❖

Alice, Leslie, and Kathy sat around Cynthia's round glass coffee table snacking on dip, flax-seed crackers, and chardonnay.

"Cynthia, this spinach dip is fantastic," Kathy said.

"So is the wine," Alice said. "Does anyone remember how to crochet?"

"I do," Leslie said. "Once I learned it, I never gave it up." She took the hook and yarn from Alice. "I'm slower at it now, thanks to you-know-what."

"Les, they know you had a stroke," Alice said. "I'd like to think we've all outgrown our secrets."

Kathy raised her wineglass. "It's nice to be able to talk about Gretchen now the way everyone else talks about their significant others."

"Sure, now that all ours are dead, rub it in our faces," Cynthia said.

Alice snorted into her wineglass. "It's sad but true. However, I completely get it, Kath. I could enjoy boring all of you for hours about how wonderful Maureen was."

Leslie's head sprang up from her crochet square with a curious expression. Was it sincere interest or a nip of jealousy?

"I'll listen to anyone's stories," Kathy said. "It's just wonderful that we can all share them now. That's true liberation."

Everyone nodded, and someone threw in a "right-on."

"Every woman has an important story to tell," Cynthia said. "Thanks, Kathy. I think you've just given us our discussion topic." She stared into space pensively. "Women finally finding their voices," she said as though announcing the title of a documentary.

"I've heard of that," Alice said seriously. "Isn't the subtitle, 'Women who become old and bitchy enough to finally speak up for themselves'?"

Kathy and Leslie laughed.

"Leave it to you, Alice," Cynthia said. "You're cracking jokes, but older women are devalued by our society—a culture that rewards women for their looks and obedience and scorns them when they no longer care about being sexy for men or competitive with other women."

Leslie returned to her careful work of hooking yarn. "If you told me back in the seventies we'd be complaining about the same issues into the next century, I never would've believed you. Why haven't things changed?"

"This is getting really heavy, sisters," Kathy said. "Don't we have anything stronger than wine?"

Every head jerked toward Alice.

"What are you looking at me for? I gave it up over twenty years ago."

"Say what?" Kathy said.

"When I turned fifty, I adopted a cleaner way of living," Alice said.

"I'll be right back," Cynthia said.

"Weed is organic," Kathy said. "You can't get any cleaner or more natural than that."

Alice pulled a face. "Then why didn't you bring any?"

"Gretchen won't let me keep it in the house," Kathy said, defeated. "She's a retired army sergeant and informed me long ago she wasn't going to cohabitate with any kind of radical hippie pothead."

Alice and Leslie laughed with her.

"You're a kept woman," Alice said.

Kathy smirked, seemingly unmoved by their teasing. "I'm a woman who waited until I was in my early fifties to meet the woman of my dreams. You better believe I'll do anything to make her happy."

"Aww," Leslie gushed.

"Now where were we?" Cynthia said, sitting down slowly, clutching a silver cigarette case. "C'mon, kiddies, gather 'round."

"What's that?"

"Medical marijuana," Cynthia said, clearly excited and proud to display a fatty. "I got a card, and I gotta say the government grows some grade-A stuff."

The others cheered and shrieked with laughter. After everyone took a hit, they got back to business.

"Leslie made a powerful observation before," Cynthia said, exhaling.

"I did?" Leslie said.

"This must be primo," Alice said, nudging Leslie in the arm.

"Yes," Cynthia said. "You said forty years ago, you never would've imagined we'd still be facing the same issues women faced when we were young. Why do you think that is?"

"The Amazon women's secret plot to wipe out all men was unsuccessful?" Alice said, passing the joint to her left.

"We need more lesbians?" Kathy said. "No offense, girls," she added, regarding Cynthia and Leslie.

Cynthia threw up her hands. "Okay, so we're just going to sit here getting high and making jokes."

"We could be doing worse things," Alice said.

"As in pushing up daisies like Dolores."

They all bowed their heads for a moment.

"To our fallen sister." Cynthia raised her wineglass in Dolores' memory and observed a moment of silence.

"I'm a lesbian," Leslie said out of nowhere.

Alice choked and rubbed out a stream of smoke burning her eyes as Cynthia and Kathy glanced at each other.

"Well, right-on," Kathy finally said, clinking her wineglass against Leslie's.

"Thank you for sharing, Les," Cynthia said with a reassuring smile. "That must've felt so freeing to say."

Leslie smiled. "It did."

"And I'm assuming by the beet-red blush on Alice's face," Cynthia said, "that she had something to do with you figuring it out."

"Um, getting back to Cynthia's relevant topic," Alice said, "aren't you all sick of movies that pair up craggy old men with beautiful young girls? Why isn't it ever the other way around?"

Cynthia and Kathy were perched on the edge of their throw pillows, clearly anticipating further elaboration from Leslie.

Against all hope, Alice persevered. "And why are respected female news anchors replaced at the first sign of a wrinkle, but the men practically have to die of old age right there at the news desk before they get the boot?"

"Alice, who cares?" Kathy said. "You were saying, Leslie?"

Leslie put down the hook and yarn, and sipped her wine. "Okay, um, yes, I discovered I was a lesbian after I realized I was in love with Alice."

"I knew it," Kathy shouted, leaping to her knees off her pillow. "I knew it." She quickly sat down again, rubbing her backside. "For the love of Christ, there goes my sciatica."

Alice passed Kathy the second joint after a puff.

"This certainly explains a lot," Cynthia said. She leaned on her side as if settling in for a campfire story. "Were you two actually involved?"

"Of course they were," Kathy said. "It was so obvious."

"When? You were still married to Bill, right?" Cynthia asked.

"Cynthia, let's not make Leslie uncomfortable, okay?" Alice said. "You know now, so let's just let it go."

"No, it's okay, Alice," Leslie said with a reassuring touch of her hand. "Yes, I was with Bill at the time. I'm not at all proud to admit that I was unfaithful to him, but I was. Alice made me feel like nobody else ever has, and in my ignorance of such things, I handled the situation poorly, hurting both her and my husband. I still don't know how to make things right by either of them."

"I can't speak for your ex," Kathy said, "but judging by Alice's expression, I'd say it's happening for her right now."

When Leslie turned to look at her, Alice swept her up in a hug so tight, she nearly pulled her off her pillow.

Cynthia wiped the tears under her eyes. "You broads just killed my friggin' buzz."

Kathy wiped her eyes, too. "No problem, Cynth. You got a prescription for it." She ambled to her feet and over to the stereo.

"Is that why you moved back to Connecticut?" Cynthia asked. "To be with Leslie?"

"Uh, we're not together," Alice said. "Just good friends."

"Yes, best friends," Leslie added.

"*Frampton Comes Alive*," Kathy said. She loaded up the CD, and "Baby, I Love Your Way" filled the room. "Come on, let's dance." She gave Cynthia her hand, and they began slow-dancing— smiling and hooting.

Alice looked at Leslie, her eyes asking the question.

"I'm sure it's excellent therapy," Leslie said.

Alice helped Leslie to her feet. At first they danced like eighth-graders keeping enough distance so the fabric of their shirts didn't touch. Soon Frampton's voice had them holding each other close, swaying in a slow, sexy rhythm.

When the song ended, they all sat down and enjoyed the rest of the evening—sharing, debating, eating, drinking, smoking, and strategizing to take over the world.

"I could stay all night," Kathy said, "but the missus expects me home at a decent hour."

"I had the best time, ladies," Cynthia said. "Too bad we couldn't solve the world's problems, too."

"It's a lucky thing we're all back together," Leslie said, "so we can keep working on them."

Alice surveyed their smiling faces. "I've got the time."

❖

The ride home to Leslie's was more like a journey to the surreal. They'd been alone many times in recent days, but that night, the mood was at last like the full-moon sky, light and uncomplicated. After touching briefly on Leslie's impromptu coming-out party, they reflected on other profound revelations of the evening.

"Tonight reminded me how important friendship is," Leslie said, "especially at our age."

"Nothing compares to good old-fashioned conversation with like-minded women," Alice said. "That was one of the best aspects of the movement. We truly understood about being on each other's side."

"Sometimes it seems like women don't care much about solidarity anymore."

"Unfortunately, it seems like that a lot."

"Then it looks like our clique reunited at exactly the right time," Leslie said with a smile.

Alice secretly swooned at Leslie's timeless allure. When she pulled into the driveway, she found herself mesmerized by Leslie's profile.

"Would you like to come in for coffee or tea?" Leslie asked when Alice hadn't turned off her ignition. "If it's too late, I understand."

"What? No," Alice stammered. "It's not too late for me. I'm retired."

"Me, too." Leslie grinned. "Hashtag: senior-citizen life."

Alice laughed as they walked into Leslie's townhouse. "How do you know about hashtags?"

"I have three grandkids. Billy's twins force me to make an account on every social-media site that comes out."

"That's adorable," Alice said, then added with a flirty drawl, "I should look you up on Facebook."

"Yes, you should," Leslie replied in kind.

As Leslie washed her hands at the kitchen sink, Alice stealthily checked out her rear end, still respectably round and firm for a woman on the cusp of seventy. God bless Leslie's yoga teacher.

"What would you like to drink? Tea or coffee?"

"Actually, just a glass of cold water," Alice said. "I forgot about the cotton mouth."

"Awful, isn't it? But the weed was so good. I should ask my doctor for a prescription."

Leslie's mischievous grin put Alice away. How the hell was she supposed to pull off this just-friends business with that dimpled cheek mesmerizing her like a siren luring ancient mariners to their rocky demise?

Alice took the water bottles from Leslie, and they walked arm in arm to the couch. Leslie turned on her television to the seventies cable music station.

"This is nice." Alice slipped off her shoes and stretched her legs on the coffee table. "You mind?"

"Not at all. Make yourself comfortable."

"Say, curious thing—you took your cane into Cynthia's house but didn't use it all night."

"I told you I'm not relying on it anymore. My balance is almost back to normal."

Alice narrowed her eyes at her. "Then why are you still holding onto my arm whenever we walk somewhere together?"

"Oops," Leslie said, feigning contrition. "You always could see right through me." She surprised Alice further by resting her head on Alice's shoulder.

If there was ever a more clear-cut moment to get up and flee in panic of falling irretrievably back in love with Leslie, that was it.

"You and Rebecca," Leslie added.

"What about her? Did she catch you cheating on your rehab exercises or something?"

Leslie shook her head. "I'd never cheat on my exercises. They're making me stronger."

Alice gestured expectantly. "What are we, playing Twenty Questions?"

"Boy, are you impatient in your old age," Leslie said, teasing her.

"And you're terrible at being just friends."

"What are you talking about?" She batted her lashes innocently.

"You're flirting with me. You can't flirt with your friends."

Leslie was failing badly at her attempt not to smile. "I'm not flirting. I'm just trying to get you to guess about Rebecca."

"What, that she guessed you're a lesbian?"

Leslie nodded proudly.

Alice rolled her eyes. "That's not news. The first day I met her, she told me she suspected you might be."

"Well, now she knows for sure."

"How the heck did that come up in conversation?"

"She was telling me a little about her and Sage's sessions with the therapist. I told her I was glad they were trying to work it out, but I advised her to think twice before she stayed in a marriage for the sake of the kids."

"Why would you say that?"

"I love Jake with all my heart and want the best for him, but if I think of my daughter experiencing the kind of heartache I went through, I might as well lie down and die right now."

Alice gushed, awed by Leslie's capacity to love.

"Thankfully, Rebecca truly loves Sage, and they both seem fully committed to fixing what went wrong."

"I'm happy to hear that," Alice said. "Your daughter's an amazing woman—but knowing her mother as I do, that's not at all surprising."

Leslie's expression turned grave. "Alice, I can't be your friend."

"Wait," Alice said, broadsided. "After all that talk in the car, you don't want to be friends anymore?"

"No, I want to, but Rebecca also said that unless I wanted to lose you again, I better tell you how I really feel—that I'm hopelessly in love with you."

Alice's water bottle slid out of her hands and bounced off the floor.

"I can't lose you again, baby." Leslie leaned toward her.

Their sensual kiss was a potion, a mystical balm that erased time and fear, cured sickness and aging.

They sat quietly for a moment, their fingers entwined, heads resting together.

"By the way," Leslie said. "Thanks for the ending to my poem."

"The one about unfinished business?"

Leslie nodded.

"Seems like it's finished now," Alice said as she caressed Leslie's arm.

"As far as I'm concerned, it is."

They exchanged another kiss, a sweet gift they promised they'd give to each other from that moment on.

About the Author

Jean Copeland is an English teacher and author from Connecticut. Taking a chance on a second career in her thirties, she graduated summa cum laude from Southern Connecticut State University with a BS in English education and an MS in English/creative writing.

Jean's debut novel, *The Revelation of Beatrice Darby*, won a 2016 Alice B Readers Lavender Certificate and a 2016 Golden Crown Literary Society award for debut author. She's also had numerous personal essays and short fiction published in print and online.

After a fulfilling year watching her students discover their talents in creative writing and poetry, Jean enjoys summer decompression through writing in coffee shops, beach bumming, and winery hopping with her lady. Organ donation and shelter animal adoption are causes dear to her heart. Visit Jean at www .jeancopeland.wordpress.com

Books Available from Bold Strokes Books

Camp Rewind by Meghan O'Brien. A summer camp for grown-ups becomes the site of an unlikely romance between a shy, introverted divorcee and one of the Internet's most infamous cultural critics—who attends undercover. (978-1-62639-793-4)

Cross Purposes by Gina L. Dartt. In pursuit of a lost Acadian treasure, three women must not only work out the clues, but also the complicated tangle of emotion and attraction developing between them. (978-1-62639-713-2)

Imperfect Truth by C.A. Popovich. Can an imperfect truth stand in the way of love? (978-1-62639-787-3)

Life in Death by M. Ullrich. Sometimes the devastating end is your only chance for a new beginning. (978-1-62639-773-6)

Love on Liberty by MJ Williamz. Hearts collide when politics clash. (978-1-62639-639-5)

Serious Potential by Maggie Cummings. Pro golfer Tracy Allen plans to forget her ex during a visit to Bay West, a lesbian condo community in NYC, but when she meets Dr. Jennifer Betsy, she gets more than she bargained for. (978-1-62639-633-3)

Taste by Kris Bryant. Accomplished chef Taryn has walked away from her promising career in the city's top restaurant to devote her life to her five-year-old daughter and is content until Ki Blake comes along. (978-1-62639-718-7)

The Second Wave by Jean Copeland. Can star-crossed lovers have a second chance after decades apart, or does the love of a lifetime only happen once? (978-1-62639-830-6)

Valley of Fire by Missouri Vaun. Taken captive in a desert outpost after their small aircraft is hijacked, Ava and her captivating passenger discover things about each other and themselves that will change them both forever. (978-1-62639-496-4)

Basic Training of the Heart by Jaycie Morrison. In 1944, socialite Elizabeth Carlton joins the Women's Army Corps to escape family expectations and love's disappointments. Can Sergeant Gale Rains get her through Basic Training with their hearts intact? (978-1-62639-818-4)

Before by KE Payne. When Tally falls in love with her band's new recruit, she has a tough decision to make. What does she want more—Alex or the band? (978-1-62639-677-7)

Believing in Blue by Maggie Morton. Growing up gay in a small town has been hard, but it can't compare to the next challenge Wren—with her new, sky-blue wings—faces: saving two entire worlds. (978-1-62639-691-3)

Coils by Barbara Ann Wright. A modern young woman follows her aunt into the Greek Underworld and makes a pact with Medusa to win her freedom by killing a hero of legend. (978-1-62639-598-5)

Courting the Countess by Jenny Frame. When relationship-phobic Lady Henrietta Knight starts to care about housekeeper Annie Brannigan and her daughter, can she overcome her fears and promise Annie the forever that she demands? (978-1-62639-785-9)

Dapper by Jenny Frame. Amelia Honey meets the mysterious Byron De Brek and is faced with her darkest fantasies, but will her strict moral upbringing stop her from exploring what she truly wants? (978-1-62639-898-6E)

Delayed Gratification: The Honeymoon by Meghan O'Brien. A dream European honeymoon turns into a winter storm nightmare involving a delayed flight, a ditched rental car, and eventually, a surprisingly happy ending. (978-1-62639-766-8E)

For Money or Love by Heather Blackmore. Jessica Spaulding must choose between ignoring the truth to keep everything she has, and doing the right thing only to lose it all—including the woman she loves. (978-1-62639-756-9)

Hooked by Jaime Maddox. With the help of sexy Detective Mac Calabrese, Dr. Jessica Benson is working hard to overcome her past, but it may not be enough to stop a murderer. (978-1-62639-689-0)

Lands End by Jackie D. Public relations superstar Amy Kline is dealing with a media nightmare, and the last thing she expects is for restaurateur Lena Michaels to change everything, but she will. (978-1-62639-739-2)

Lysistrata Cove by Dena Hankins. Jack and Eve navigate the maelstrom of their darkest desires and find love by transgressing gender, dominance, submission, and the law on the crystal blue Caribbean Sea. (978-1-62639-821-4)

Twisted Screams by Sheri Lewis Wohl. Reluctant psychic Lorna Dutton doesn't want to forgive, but if she doesn't do just that an innocent woman will die. (978-1-62639-647-0)

A Class Act by Tammy Hayes. Buttoned-up college professor Dr. Margaret Parks doesn't know what she's getting herself into when she agrees to one date with her student, Rory Morgan, who is 15 years her junior. (978-1-62639-701-9)

Bitter Root by Laydin Michaels. Small town chef Adi Bergeron is hiding something, and Griffith McNaulty is going to find out what it is even if it gets her killed. (978-1-62639-656-2)

Capturing Forever by Erin Dutton. When family pulls Jacqueline and Casey back together, will the lessons learned in eight years apart be enough to mend the mistakes of the past? (978-1-62639-631-9)

Deception by VK Powell. DEA Agent Colby Vincent and Attorney Adena Weber are embroiled in a drug investigation involving homeless veterans and an attraction that could destroy them both. (978-1-62639-596-1)

Dyre: A Knight of Spirit and Shadows by Rachel E. Bailey. With the abduction of her queen, werewolf-bodyguard Des must follow the kidnappers' trail to Europe, where her queen—and a battle unlike any Des has ever waged—awaits her. (978-1-62639-664-7)

First Position by Melissa Brayden. Love and rivalry take center stage for Anastasia Mikhelson and Natalie Frederico in one of the most prestigious ballet companies in the nation. (978-1-62639-602-9)

Best Laid Plans by Jan Gayle. Nicky and Lauren are meant for each other, but Nicky's haunting past and Lauren's societal fears threaten to derail all possibilities of a relationship. (987-1-62639-658-6)

Exchange by CF Frizzell. When Shay Maguire rode into rural Montana, she never expected to meet the woman of her dreams—or to learn Mel Baker was held hostage by legal agreement to her right-wing father. (987-1-62639-679-1)

Just Enough Light by AJ Quinn. Will a serial killer's return to Colorado destroy Kellen Ryan and Dana Kingston's chance at love, or can the search-and-rescue team save themselves? (987-1-62639-685-2)

Rise of the Rain Queen by Fiona Zedde. Nyandoro is nobody's princess. She fights, curses, fornicates, and gets into as much trouble as her brothers. But the path to a throne is not always the one we expect. (987-1-62639-592-3)

Tales from Sea Glass Inn by Karis Walsh. Over the course of a year at Cannon Beach, tourists and locals alike find solace and passion at the Sea Glass Inn. (987-1-62639-643-2)

The Color of Love by Radclyffe. Black sheep Derian Winfield needs to convince literary agent Emily May to marry her to save the Winfield Agency and solve Emily's green card problem, but Derian didn't count on falling in love. (987-1-62639-716-3)

A Reluctant Enterprise by Gun Brooke. When two women grow up learning nothing but distrust, unworthiness, and abandonment, it's no wonder they are apprehensive and fearful when an overwhelming love just won't be denied. (978-1-62639-500-8)

Above the Law by Carsen Taite. Love is the last thing on Agent Dale Nelson's mind, but reporter Lindsey Ryan's investigation could change the way she sees everything—her career, her past, and her future. (978-1-62639-558-9)

Jane's World: The Case of the Mail Order Bride by Paige Braddock. Jane's PayBuddy account gets hacked and she inadvertently purchases a mail order bride from the Eastern Bloc. (978-1-62639-494-0)

Love's Redemption by Donna K. Ford. For ex-convict Rhea Daniels and ex-priest Morgan Scott, redemption lies in the thin line between right and wrong. (978-1-62639-673-9)

The Shewstone by Jane Fletcher. The prophetic Shewstone is in Eawynn's care, but unfortunately for her, Matt is coming to steal it. (978-1-62639-554-1)